a comfortable madness

a novel

by Francine LaSala

Author of:

Rita Hayworth's Shoes
and
The Girl, the Gold Tooth & Everything

Publisher's Note: This is a work of fiction. Names, characters, places, and incidents are a product of the author's imagination. Locales and public names are sometimes used for atmospheric purposes. Any resemblance to actual people, living or dead, or to businesses, companies, events, institutions, or locales is completely coincidental.

A Comfortable Madness/ Francine LaSala. -- 1st ed.
ISBN-10: 0-9903580-2-X
ISBN-13: 978-0-9903580-2-2

"I turned over on my face when I came to that and got a good grasp on the hair on each side of my head, and wrenched it well. All the while knowing the madness of my heart to be so very mad and misplaced, that I was quite conscious it would have served my face right if I had lifted it up by my hair, and knocked it against the pebbles for being such an idiot."

—*Great Expectations*

prologue

---

the past.

A woman sat on the bed in the room that had once belonged to her parents. Now it was like a tomb. The lonely quarters of a soul broken by love.

The air was filled with the acrid stench of stale vodka. The sheets were rumpled and musty and burned in countless places from cigarettes neglected during far too many boozy hazes. The once crisp-white curtains were dingy and yellowed, and the windows were never opened to let in sunlight or fresh air. A small statue of the Blessed Mother situated on the night table presided sadly over the whole mess.

In her small hands, the woman held a revolver. She ran her tiny fingers across the barrel, glided them over the shaft. As she sat there, she looked at the picture of her love and she thought about them, together. She thought about love. About the rush that came from the first wave, the utter thrill and electric jolt that seized the senses and filled the heart with a sense of bliss and infinite hope. And she thought about the absolute and bottomless torment, the despair that fermented when love was lost or ripped away.

She knew, watching this unraveling these past years, that there was no pain more severe than suffering the loss of a lover. Cringing at the image, she tucked herself into a small ball, protecting herself from what she was sure would become her fate.

No. There was no way *her* love was going to leave her, no matter what he thought. The power to stop that desertion, that rejection, lay in the cold metal pistol she weighed between her hands.

She looked down at his picture again. Her love. Her one and only. She looked into his eyes and the sparkle of a thousand stars that shone from them. Into the face that gazed back at her after countless nights of endless passion. The silky, baby-fine hair that framed that face in golden-brown wisps. The strong, chiseled chin that rested on her shoulder after she gave herself to him.

"I won't let you leave me. I just won't," she sobbed, and a tear dropped onto the photograph. She gently wiped it away with her thumb.

Not for a minute did she think this plan of hers was a sane one. Oh no. It was definitely the last-resort scheme of a woman teetering on the brink of her own sanity. But for some reason, that was okay. For as crazy as this act she was considering was, it gave her a feeling of peace, and that was all that mattered.

She had the power to protect herself from a pain so severe she might never recover.

And she was going to use it.

chapter one

the present.

It was much too cold for April—especially considering that April was nearly over. This is what Annie Collins thought to herself as she made her way through the cemetery, searching for the grave of Jason Scott. Shivering in a too-short skirt and light sweater, she tried hard not to think of anything else but the weather. But the other thoughts came. They always did.

Her love. Her loss. Her life. All still too much to handle, even after all this time.

Nestled in the crook of her left arm was a single long-stemmed yellow rose, the flower of friendship. She wasn't quite feeling the warm pangs of friendship right now. She wasn't exactly sure what she was feeling. Except that maybe this had been a mistake. One of many she'd made in her thirty-two years, to be sure, but a mistake all the same.

As she walked she thought about the past. About her wedding day at the family's church—the church in Queens where her mother, the oppressive and highly sanctimonious Bridget, had been baptized and raised. A church that wasn't all that far away from where Annie lived now.

Her mother had not wanted her to get married—and especially not to Jason. She had been adamant about it.

Annie's father, Mark, was a different story. A head injury had made his judgment, as well as his overall disposition, somewhat soft. Something her mother seemed to loathe about him especially in recent years, but something Annie tolerated. It was less like living with a father and more like living with a little brother sometimes. So Mark was thrilled about Annie getting married, even at eighteen. A joyful grin plastered on his face, he whispered to his daughter through his gleefully clenched teeth. "I'm so glad you've found him, Annie!" he told her with his childlike charm as he walked her to the altar. "Your true love! This is the most magical day!"

For Annie, it had been the most glorious day of her life. Gliding up the aisle in a gown she had purchased for herself with saved-up babysitting money from a second-hand store in the same quiet neighborhood as the church, her father's arm looped around hers, all she could feel was happy.

But as she proudly made her way to her waiting groom and the ancient monsignor, a close friend of her mother who had agreed to perform the ceremony even against her mother's wishes, Annie made the regrettable mistake of glancing over her right shoulder. There was Bridget, a rosary clenched tightly in her fists, the strands strangling her fingers from the intensity with which she held it. She was sitting with Rebecca, Annie's best friend—then and still. Rebecca wasn't even looking at Annie, but Bridget was. And as she passed, her mother's mouth formed those two harsh, unforgivably painful words: "Big mistake."

Her mother, alas, had been right.

Falling for a man who, pushing thirty at the time, was much older than she was. Diverting her plans to attend the college of her dreams by staying with him. Moving in with him and marrying him before she was legally old enough to drink.

Growing, in spite of him. And "shrinking" at times so maybe he could catch up. And, well, ending him… The biggest of all the mistakes? She still could not be sure.

As she circled through the stones, squinting at the writing on them, she tried to figure out what she thought she'd be getting from this. From being here. What had compelled her to get out of her bed on a Saturday morning, get into her car, and drive out to her Long Island hometown? To a place she never came anymore. Because there wasn't any reason to come here anymore.

What was she seeking? Forgiveness? Absolution? What was done was done. There was no changing it now.

Another big mistake: She hadn't stopped in the grounds' office to find out where Jason's grave even was. She hadn't attended the funeral. She wasn't welcome. But she figured she'd just be able to find where her husband had been buried. That she would somehow just be able to *feel* where he was.

Husband.

That was a funny thing to call him. While they had been apart now for almost as many years as they had been married, the divorce had only become final fairly recently. Still, calling him "husband" was a bad habit of hers. There were some habits that couldn't be broken, no matter how much you wanted to break them. Annie was hoping this ritual of closure would help her to shake at least that one.

After about half an hour of wandering, she finally found what she sought. No, she hadn't attended his funeral, but she had covered the expenses, including paying for the standing granite headstone. A splurge, but guilt and spending money went hand-in-hand. Guilt and a lot of things went hand-in-and, actually. Something she'd learned all too well these past years.

Francine LaSala

She looked down at the stone and read it carefully. Still finding it difficult to separate her own ideas from generations of her family's oppressive Catholicism and, as she generally tried to believe, mythological notions about the afterlife, she couldn't help but wonder whether Jason was right now looking down on her from Heaven—or peering up her skirt from what her mother had always dramatized as "the fiery pits of Hell."

He would have liked this skirt, she mused, then caught herself.

Religion. Another habit that seemed so hard to break. Though in Annie's mind, if Jason was in Hell, he was there because Annie had put him there. One of the many reasons she was here this day, trying, at last, to make her peace with him.

She knelt down and traced the letters of his name with her index finger. She wanted to make this experience as real for herself as possible so that maybe she could finally move on.

Annie placed the flower she'd been carrying in front of the stone. "Goodbye, love," she whispered.

She pulled herself up to a standing position and backed away without turning around. In this trance-like state, she was aware of nothing but the inner workings of her mind. So it came as quite a shock to Annie when she was hit on the back of the head with a camera.

chapter two

the present.

Hugh Jeffries felt like he had struck gold. As he navigated through the stones on a gorgeously brisk April afternoon, he found himself getting evermore excited about this cemetery. It was rich with possibilities.

If he seemed too giddy to be in a cemetery, well, it wasn't that he was a ghoul or anything like that. Hugh had long ago stopped going to cemeteries to visit *his* dead. He used to do it entirely too often. Hugh's parents had been killed in a car accident when he was twenty-four. For years after they were gone, he, an only child, would sit for hours at their gravesite—several times a week.

It took years after his parents were gone for him to come to terms with the fact that they weren't actually there at all, but that they lived with him in his memories. Eventually, Hugh weaned himself away from visiting them. He couldn't pull himself away entirely, though, which was how he came to be intrigued by the dead of others.

As an aspiring photographer, an *artist,* he liked to think, Hugh preferred the weather-worn angels and majestic mausoleums that rivaled some churches in size to the modern slabs of granite in newer cemeteries. He never missed a detail.

Hugh stopped at an in-ground gravestone that was nearly obscured by overgrown grass and caked-on dirt. He came prepared for these kinds of things. He didn't like mess. He liked to fix mess. He reached into his camera bag and took out a small brush and dustpan, and went to work clearing away what he surmised was probably years of neglect, until a name appeared: Alice Hayes.

As Hugh cleared away more and more of the dirt, he saw that the marker had actually been intended for two people. After Alice's name was a heart icon wrapped in the words "Together Forever." On the other side of the heart was a blank plate waiting for an engraving. Mrs. Hayes had died in 1962 at the age of sixty-seven; it was unlikely that her husband would be joining her now. He'd probably been dead for years, possibly remarried and buried next to his new wife. Hugh let out a sigh and shook his head. What could be a worse fate than to have put eternal hope into something as huge as everlasting romance, and to be let down? And in stone, no less, for everyone to see?

"Sorry Alice, but I don't think he's coming," he said sweetly, bending over the stone.

Hugh was well aware it was nuts that these cemetery jaunts brought out his romantic side. He liked to make up stories about the dead. It made him happy when couples ended up together, and he scrupulously read the stones and did the math, calculating how long a surviving spouse may have lasted after the death of his or her true love. For Hugh, true love was everything, and he firmly believed that in the case of true love, and unless the deceased had passed at a very young age, not a lot of time would pass before the other would follow. That was how he rated the success of the marriages. He'd never told anyone about this before, and, judging from his tragically unsuccessful past track record with women, he imagined he'd never get close enough to a woman to share this with her.

He snapped the stone with his camera. He didn't want to forget Mrs. Hayes like her husband had. If he was religious, he might have said a prayer or something. But he wasn't religious. He hadn't been raised that way, and he hadn't even turned to God to find comfort, as he had been encouraged to do by so many after his parents died. Like his only close friend, Charlotte O'Reilly, who had incessantly tried to talk him into going to church with her after their deaths because she was also not religious, but had read numerous books on grief. Oh Charlotte. Dear, weird Charlotte. She had latched on to Hugh when they were sophomores in high school and never let go.

Hugh felt a deep affection for Charlotte because she had always been so nice to him. He never quite fit in in Michigan, except with her really. He was an odd duck. Quirky. Awkward. Imaginative. Artsy. They didn't really make them like that in the Midwest. Sometimes he dreamed of getting away from Michigan—that maybe somewhere out in the world there was a match for him. A girl who would really get him. A true love of his own.

Though he also wasn't much for change. Even if things didn't quite seem right, he was still wary of changing things up. But a few years after his parents were gone, he finally started to feel ready.

Initially it was what was in the local cemetery blocks from his home that had kept him in Lansing; however, it was the promise of a world full of cemeteries that finally gave him the push he needed to leave.

"I'm going," he told Charlotte one day while she followed him on one of his cemetery photo shoots. "I've decided it's time I moved away."

"What? You *are* not!" she chided.

"I am. Why wouldn't I?" he asked, annoyed.

"You?" She laughed. She flipped back her curly chestnut hair and then shook her head at him.

"Me," he persisted.

"You." She stopped laughing. "Oh, honey, now don't get me wrong," she breathed, "but we both know that you don't like change."

"That's not true!"

"That is true. You like things to stay just as they are."

It was irritating him that she was right and he had a vicious urge to challenge her. "I'm going to have to disagree here…"

"Look at the way you handle breakups. You get dumped and you can't break away. I mean, you get humiliated, and still you follow your exes around like a lost puppy."

"I get used to them…"

"And what about the furniture in your house? I mean, you were married once and you never changed it." He wished she would stop bringing up his exes like this. Especially Alicia. The woman who had begged him to marry her when he was twenty-three, after only about two months of dating, and who had taken off with another man about six weeks later. It had taken him the better part of a year to recover from that.

"Look, you know I love you. And you have lots of great qualities, you do. But you're just not the sort of person who's going to decide one day to pack up his life and move away. You like it here," she said, indicating the cemetery with her sweeping arm gestures.

"No. There's nothing left for me here," he said, mimicking her arm movements and making a special point to dramatically end on his parents' grave. "They're gone," he said. "It's time to go."

She pursed her lips at him. "Okay, well where to then?" she asked.

"New York, I think."

"New York? New *freakin'* York! I am *so* there!"

Her words filled him with dread and he hated himself instantly because of it. "Well, I thought I would go alone, you know—"

"Alone? You'll be eaten alive! Oh no, my dear. I'm going with you."

He reflexively cocked an eyebrow at her.

"You know I hate when you do that," she said.

"Do what?" he asked.

"That thing," she nodded, "with your eyebrow."

"Oh, sorry," he said.

"It seems so... I don't know... Condescending...? I hate it and all women hate it. Stop doing it."

"I don't mean it that way. I'm sorr—"

She'd moved on. "So? Are we going together or not?"

Now he felt guilty. The last thing he'd ever want to do is to make Charlotte feel bad. "Um... Okay?"

She tossed two fists in the air in a victory salute. "FAN-tas-TIC! This is going to be just fabulous!"

"I guess...?" It wasn't at all what he had had in mind, but maybe it was best she come with him. He was always stronger when she was with him.

"No! This is great! We can get an apartment together and go to great parties and I can finally get a *real* job!" She was downright manic now. "And I'll find us a place to live and I'll make arrangements with movers and we'll get a fresh start.

And my parents, oh, they'll be so scandalized, and it will be so wonderful and—"

"Yeah. You're right." Hugh half-smiled. "It'll be great." Hugh was aware, sometimes, of Charlotte's tendency to railroad him. Mostly he brushed it off. He was a lonely soul after all; she really was all he had.

Charlotte may have orchestrated many of the aspects of their new life together, but it was Hugh who decided exactly where they were going to live. He had heard of this section of New York before called Queens. After emailing back and forth for a few weeks with a realtor whom he had found on the Internet, he'd decided on a two-bedroom apartment in a section called Woodside, which was, as the realtor sold it, "Just a few minutes' commute to Manhattan."

That was nice, but Hugh's main reason for moving to Woodside had little to do with its proximity to the Big Apple. It was because Woodside boasted the big daddy of all the Queens cemeteries.

Calvary would be worth the move. The cemetery covered 365 acres in two locations—an acre for each day of the year, he rationalized. And "residents," as he liked to consider them, numbered in the thousands. Yes, that would give Hugh enough to keep himself good and occupied for a while.

Hugh paced himself, though. He only visited Calvary about once a month. He didn't want to treat it like a tourist visiting a large country over the course of a couple of days. He wanted to savor it. He knew that when he was done with it, it would be time to move on. Hugh was not a fan of moving on. He never understood why he was like this, but there was something about letting go that terrified him.

So, to ensure he didn't get through it too quickly, Hugh had opted to fill up some of his weekends visiting other cemeteries, which is how he'd landed here in this obscure Long Island cemetery this Saturday morning.

Just beyond Mrs. Hayes's grave, Hugh caught the figure of a tiny blond woman bent over a tombstone in his lens. He usually wasn't interested in the living and generally tried to avoid them. But this one, and, if he was to be honest, her too-short skirt, piqued his curiosity. He figured he could easily sneak up behind her and see who she was there to see. But then he couldn't help himself. He had to have a picture as well for his portfolio.

Hugh carefully, stealthily bent over the small woman in a way he could capture both her and the gravestone in his frame. He hadn't anticipated she was going to get up so soon.

"What the fuck is that," she said in a jarringly calm voice, which made Hugh more nervous than he usually was. "And what the fuck is that?"

The woman scowled at his face and her eyes ran down the front of him. She glared at his T-shirt and he looked down, regretting now wearing his "Stop or I'll Shoot!" shirt with the antique-looking camera under the antique-looking font. It felt more on the nose right now than ironic, and he could feel the heat of hot embarrassment rising in his cheeks.

"This..." he stammered. "This... um... I guess it's just a camera."

"I know *what* it is, ninny. But what are you doing with it here?"

"Oh, you mean like in the cemetery? Right. Well, you see, I kind of like to walk around and read the stones. You know, like a hobby?"

"Sounds like a pretty sick hobby to me," she said, quietly seething. "And harassing mourners? This is part of the thrill?"

Hugh backed away slightly and looked down at his shoes. "Uh, actually, no. I try to leave the living alone."

He didn't have to look at the woman to feel her eyes on him, but he kind of wanted to look up because he thought she was sort of pretty. When he finally did, he felt bad because she was rubbing the back of her head where his camera had hit her.

"So why bother me?" she asked, coolly.

Because you're so, so pretty...

No, idiot! He couldn't tell her the truth. He'd just violated her private moment to take a picture of her in her grief. What a stupid, stupid thing to do. So he just smiled dumbly at her.

Then inspiration struck: *Why not just change the subject!*

"So who is this guy anyway?" he asked, leaning past her. "Let's see...Jason Scott. Nineteen-seventy—"

"Are you kidding me? Why is this any of your business?"

Hugh felt instantly stupid. Of course the only thing worse than his being nosy and ruining her moment was being more nosy, and yet, he couldn't stop himself. "Uh, sorry. I was just trying to figure out what he is... *was*... to you. And what's that... I mean...." He continued to stammer, now nodding at a rose she had placed down. "Why yellow?"

She stared coldly at him. She tilted her head and squinted at him. "Why. *Yellow*?"

He felt like such an ass now. He was only making it worse and he just couldn't stop himself. "Oh God. Oh no, I'm sorry. Man, I'm such a dork," he said.

The pretty, angry woman stared at him a moment before bending down to pick it up. She waved it in his face while she ranted. "What this *is* is a yellow rose. It's supposed to mean friendship. Who he is... was... is none of your concern. And who you are is kind of a dick."

He had not been expecting that. "Whoa now. Hey...is that nice? Well, I guess I deserve that. I mean, here you are...and here I am... Oh, man, I'm really sorry... I mean... Just oh..."

"Sorry? You're fucking *sorry*? You bet you're sorry. You're the sorriest fuck ever. Traipsing around here with a camera!"

"Hey, not that it's any of your business, but cemeteries interest me because my parents are dead and..."

She peered up at him, leaning in. She smelled like peppermint soap and maybe a little like wine, though not in an unpleasant way. Her electric blue eyes seemed to pierce right through him as she snapped. "My father's dead. So what? What difference does that make?"

Hugh craned his neck to take another look. "Father?" he mused, somewhat confused as the math didn't seem to make sense as he tapped it out on his fingers. She seemed older than him, at least a little older, so it was impossible that her father could have been born in the 1970s.

At that she grabbed his arm, which shook him back to reality. "Do you really think I give a fuck-damn about your stupid sorry life? Do you?"

Hugh was terrified now, but even as fierce as she was, she was tiny. And somewhat vulnerable. He could almost feel that about her. But as she stood there, raging at him, all he could see was how blue her eyes were. The way her dark blond hair perfectly framed her face. How her crooked, cute mouth scrunched into a scowl. He inadvertently cocked an eyebrow at her.

Oh jeez, why did you do that eyebrow thing? You know women don't like that!

He wanted to kick himself. Instead he shifted from one foot to the other and hoped she hadn't noticed his stupid eyebrow raise.

She seemed to calm for a moment. *The calm before the storm?* And then words tumbled out of his mouth before he could stop them. "You know, you're kind of pretty. I mean, for an angry person."

At that, she unleashed a fresh tirade of profanities on him. No one in real life had ever spoken like this to him before. Did people really speak like this in real life? In New York? In *Scarface*, maybe? He hated himself a little that he was enjoying it, and he couldn't squash the urge to irritate her more. There was something about the way her eyes sparkled when she was annoyed. Something sort of delightful. He couldn't help himself.

"I bet *Mr. Scott* wouldn't like to hear you talk like that," he quipped.

The woman was clearly on the verge of flipping out, and Hugh was quickly going from charmed to nervous. When Hugh was nervous, when he was terrifiedly nervous, he laughed. It just happened like that. So now, on top of everything else, he couldn't keep a straight face. But he tried hard, really he did. However, suppressing the giggles had contorted his face into a series of sarcastic grins, one more offensive than the next, which naturally seemed to aggravate her more.

She threw up her hands, shrugged, and took off in a huff. He could only smile as he watched her leave, her arms flailing around like a tiny, angry octopus. He had to admit it was kind of cute.

Just then his cell phone rang. He looked away for a moment from the pretty, angry girl to answer it.

"Hey... yeah I should be home by then—no problem. See you later," he said and hung up. When he looked up again, the woman was gone.

Hugh was not going to let the maniacal ravings of a cute blonde ruin his jaunt, so he continued to explore the cemetery. Before he set out, he leaned over the grave of Jason Scott, still puzzled about who this might be to a woman he'd probably never see again. But he couldn't get her out of his mind. Those eyes. Those legs. She had intrigued him.

Looking down at his camera, Hugh noticed a smudge on the lens where it had hit her. Quickly, he slipped a clean tissue from the pocket of his freshly pressed jeans and wiped the lens clean—over and over again, until not a spot remained. Then he took a photo of Mr. Scott's grave. He zoomed in closely on the writing and snapped another one.

A mausoleum caught his eye and he wandered over to it. He stopped in front of it and read the name over the doorway out loud: "Histerman." Noticing a crack in the stained-glass window, he couldn't help but be curious; he peeked inside. There he spotted an extra-wide crypt, which he surmised housed both Histermans. Pulling away, he read the plaque posted on the left side of the front doors. *"Here is the final resting place of Bill and Shelly Histerman. They had no children, but they had each other."*

Hugh photographed the message. Satisfied now that lovers did sometimes end up together, he walked away, pleased with himself for not losing the faith that true love was indeed eternal. No matter how many broken hearts he'd already had to endure. He knew someday he would meet the right woman and live the "happily ever after" that his parents had.

Which is why, as he headed out through the front gates of the cemetery, he considered it a very good thing that he hadn't hit it off with the pretty little fireball.

chapter three

---

circa 1943.

The sun shone brightly as Maggie Ellis, blond, petite, and carefree, sauntered down the sidewalk on a warm April day. She was dressed in a smart, sky-blue, button-down dress that matched her eyes, the hem playfully swishing at her knees with every step she took. Around her neck a diamond cross hung from a thin, white gold chain and sparkled in the sunlight.

Maggie was feeling particularly pleased with her appearance even if her dress was several seasons old. Part of the reason she was so happy was that she had just splurged on a new hat from Smitty's Fine Apparel & Home. Dark blue satin with a black ribbon and a couple of jaunty peacock feathers jutting up in the back, the hat also featured a short veil in front. It wasn't just because the hat was so pretty that she was so tickled to wear it. It was because for the first time in months, she had treated herself to something special, something she had wanted for so long, and for that reason, the hat seemed to have a magical property that lifted her chin and spirits. Of course the hat was only part of it.

The other reason Maggie was feeling more lovely, more tall, more confident this afternoon was a man. A very special man, actually. It had been his idea for her to splurge on this hat that she had admired for so long, and she couldn't wait to show it off to him.

About three weeks earlier, Maggie had walked this sidewalk on her way back from work at the H&L Factory. Like most unmarried women her age, Maggie was doing her part in keeping the economy going while most of the eligible men were fighting overseas. Not all of them, though.

"Hello there, Maggie," a priest who was a few years younger than Maggie greeted her as he approached her. Members of the clergy were exempt from the draft although many enlisted voluntarily to lend spiritual support to the boys fighting overseas. She was glad this particular clergyman, with his smoldering gray eyes and jet-black hair, was one of them.

"Hello, Father Phillip," she returned, warmly, her heart beating fast in her chest. She fought to hide her attraction. "I really did like your sermon last week. You know, about the, you know, gratitude thing." The words never came out the way she wanted when she spoke to him. She always felt so stupid when she opened her mouth around him.

He raised one eyebrow at her. There was something so sexy about that—that thing he did with his eyebrow. It melted her. Until he chided her. "Last week was about passion and keeping passion for Christ alive." Her heart jumped each time he said the word "passion." The emphasis he was putting on it—he was flirting with her, she was sure. She bit her lip. "Now, two weeks ago…"

She reddened. "Oh gosh. Sorry. I guess I missed last week," she confessed, annoyed, remembering the family distraction that had made her miss his mass. One of so many. She absently thumbed her cross. Maggie actually enjoyed going to mass, and not just for the handsome preacher. There was something about church that grounded her. That gave her a sense of peace—the kind she couldn't get at home. And when something at home made her miss attending mass, she resented her situation at home even more.

"That's okay, child," he said, which immediately cooled her. Talk about something she resented. He was younger than her, for heaven's sake, and while it didn't bother her to call him "Father," oh, how it irked her when he called her "child" like that. "I'm taking confessions later this afternoon, if you'd like to come by?"

"Sure, I'd love to," she returned, almost giddy, as if he'd asked her on a date. *Nuts.* She quickly caught herself. "See you later," she said.

"See you later, child," he replied, and then seemed to saunter away from her. She hadn't realized she was watching him walk off until he turned after several steps to shoot her a smile. He then looked her up-and-down approvingly before turning back around and heading in the direction of the church.

Maggie let out a long, steadying breath. She knew she had to find a way to get over the priest, but she hadn't really planned how she was going to accomplish this. Lucky for her, minutes later, fate intervened.

Something had compelled her to stop and peer into the window of a barber shop. And there he was. Walter.

Boy-next-door good looks. Eyelashes so long they were wasted on a man. A smile that gleamed. No wedding band on his finger... As she took him in, he looked up. Noticing her noticing him, he smiled and waved. Embarrassed, she looked away but quickly looked back. He mouthed a soft "hello" to her, and she tried to wave back, but as she did, she accidentally spilled the contents of her purse. He began to laugh, and she, now feeling like a fool, quickly packed up her things and ran off.

Despite the humiliation, Maggie was compelled two days later to walk by the shop again, squaring her shoulders and trying to keep her cool. This time, it was as if he had been waiting for her. Not wanting to seem a fool again, she tried to appear bored and unimpressed, and quickly walked off.

Maggie didn't notice that the young man had walked to the window to watch her leave, so she didn't know he was watching her as she did a quick, little dance and practically skipped away.

It would be several more days before Maggie walked by the shop again. This time, though, the nice-looking man was not at his chair. Instead, cutting hair at his station was an oversized man with creased skin and silver hair. Her heart sank. It wasn't the first time in the past years that a young, eligible man was here one day, gone the next.

The War.

No, it couldn't be that. She refused to believe it would be that. She shielded her eyes from the sun to try and get a better view inside the shop.

"You looking for something?"

Maggie turned to see him standing there. Instantly her face felt like it was on fire. "Oh no, I..."

"I'm Walter," he said, and the half-grin through which he spoke made the hair on the back of her neck and arms stand on end. Fear, but not a bad fear. She parted her lips to speak but could not force any words out. She smiled awkwardly instead.

"I work here," he said.

"I know," she said, wanting to punch herself for answering so quickly, so eagerly. Like a yappy little puppy desperate for approval. He didn't seem to mind. He moved closer to her.

"So, you're *not* looking for me?" he asked, that half-grin returning, causing tingles to shoot to life beneath her skin. Currents crackled through her, pulling her closer to him. She had never felt anything like this before, this connection, this electricity.

"Of course not," she breathed, and stepped back. Then he too stepped back, creating a more comfortable distance.

"Ah, that's too bad," he said. "Because I thought maybe you'd like to have dinner with me or something tonight."

A calm now came over her. "Sure," she said, and breathed in the incredible sense of joy standing even this close to him made her feel.

Three weeks later, the intensity of that joy hadn't waned—though her fixation on Father Phillip had. To a point. She still attended mass every Sunday, whenever possible, but for now, at least for now, it had lost that other dimension for her.

chapter four

---

fourteen years ago.

Annie had wavered on bringing Jason home to meet her parents for quite some time. While it had been love at first sight for Annie, she already knew, even in that electric moment of meeting him, all the reasons he wouldn't live up to her mother's standards. His age was only one of those reasons. But one otherwise quiet Sunday afternoon, Jason had apparently decided it was time he met them, and without discussing it first with her.

Annie had been preparing dinner when the doorbell rang. She rushed to the foyer to answer it but her father had beaten her to it. And as he ushered her boyfriend into the house, she groaned. "Oh no..." Not only was she *not* happy to see Jason here, against her wishes, but now he'd encountered her father before she'd had a chance to explain why her dad was the way he was.

On top of that, she'd also neglected to mention to Jason some of the other, well, peculiar, things about her family and home life. As Annie looked at her home through Jason's eyes, a hot panic rose in her.

Their living room seemed typical enough if one didn't look too closely. Though if one did, one might notice a corner shrine to Jesus—a melodramatic portrait about as tasteful as a paint-by-numbers piece, with votive candles burning in holders on a shelf underneath. One might also take note of a crucifix that hung between two large, curtained windows, as well as a small statue of Mary perched on an end table next to a lamp and a candy dish. Oh, and the row of Palm Sunday fronds tied into crosses that hung over the inner entryway, which was pretty hard to miss.

When she looked at Jason again, it seemed like he hadn't noticed anything out of the ordinary. He seemed friendly and poised, and she began feeling bad that she hadn't wanted him here. Annoyed at herself that she may have been slightly embarrassed of him. Because here he was. Her Jason, her wonderful Jason, trying to impress everyone. Her love, dressed in a suit, perfectly manicured from head to toe, and holding a bouquet of flowers. Annie's mother blushed when Jason handed the flowers not to Annie but to her.

"A pleasure to meet you, ma'am," he said, his eyes sparkling like glass. She loved that his eyes sparkled the way they did. She had no idea at the time exactly why they'd sparkled like that. The revelation years later of why would cleave an irreparable chasm in their marriage...

"Well, no one's ever given me flowers but my husband," her mother said, then gave Annie a look she couldn't quite decipher. It was partly charmed and partly confused. "Uh, thank you, young man..."

"You can't possibly be Annie's mother." He smiled, taking her hand in his.

"I don't know what to say," her mother said, still a bit confused. "Please, won't you come in?"

"Jason," Annie said.

"Jason... Yes..."

"May I call you Bridget?" he asked, not letting go of her hand, his eyes still improbably shiny.

Annie wanted to die right then and there. Bridget Collins was proper and old-fashioned. None of her friends were ever allowed to call her mother by her Christian name. "You may call me Mrs. Collins," her mother replied coldly.

"Until I can call you Mom," Jason said, in that same tone that had just turned her mother off. *Didn't he know how to read a room?* Winking at Annie, he released Bridget's hand and showed himself to the couch. *He must know what he's doing*, she thought. *Of course he knows what he's doing.*

Her father followed Jason into the living room like a puppy, while her mother shot Annie a quick disapproving glance before taking in a deep breath. "Let's go put those in water and get us all something to drink? Come on."

"Sure, Mom."

Bridget turned her attention back to Jason. "Lemonade okay?" she asked.

"Mike's Hard Lemonade?" Jason said, and smiled at Mark, who smiled dumbly back at him.

"We don't have liquor in this house," Bridget snapped. Annie glared at Jason. She was frustrated. Didn't he notice all the religious paraphernalia in the room? She knew he wasn't educated, but couldn't he piece it together? That highly religious people usually weren't big drinkers? That alcohol was generally viewed as a device of the devil? Unless it was communion wine? She sighed. Surely he knew some of these things?

He shrugged his shoulders. "Oh sorry," he said, oozing charm with every word. "Just lemonade is perfect, Mrs. Collins. Please."

In the kitchen, Annie searched for a vase big enough to hold her mother's bouquet while her mother pulled a can of lemonade concentrate out of the freezer. "Bit of a charmer, isn't he?" she said without looking at Annie. Instead she pulled a glass pitcher from a high cabinet and proceeded to fill it with water.

Annie let out an annoyed sigh. "I knew it! I knew that would get you. God, Mom, most normal people *do* drink."

"Annie!" Bridget gasped.

"Sorry. I meant gosh."

"I wasn't referring to that," Bridget said as she added the concentrate to the pitcher of water and stirred. She then set four glasses on a tray and placed the pitcher in the middle.

"Then what do you mean?" Annie rolled her eyes. She approached her mother. "Please just give him a chance," she said, her hands now on Bridget's shoulders. "You're going to love him, Mom. I know I do," she said, and she grabbed the tray from Bridget and headed back to join the men.

"That's what I'm afraid of," she heard her mother say but decided not to confront her about it just then. What good would it have done?

Annie's mother sat down in a chair next to her father just as Jason scooped a hand into the candy bowl presided over by Mary. He nearly knocked over the statue as he helped himself to a handful of Bridget's M&M's. "Whoops!" he sang.

You could cut the fear and the tension in the room with a knife. Not even Annie's father, who usually had no self-control when something seemed funny—inappropriate or not—dared to react with anything but somber reverence. Annie could feel her throat start to close with dread as she watched her mother watch Jason, desperate to know what she was thinking, but already having a pretty good sense of it.

"So what is it that you do for a living, Jason?" she asked.

"I—" Jason began, but Annie quickly took over.

"He's a painter, Mother. He makes everything so beautiful," Annie cooed as she snuggled into Jason's shoulder.

"A painter?" Her mother rubbed her chin. "Oil or watercolor?" she asked.

"Oh, I *do* like paintings," her father said with his usual childlike enthusiasm. She reached out and stroked his hand. Sometimes he was annoying. Other times, like now, he was endearing.

Jason scrunched up his face and then burst out laughing. "Ha! I get it. Good one, Mrs. C."

The dread now spread to Annie's chest.

"I don't understand," her mother said.

"Painter? Yeah, you thought like the *faggot* kind?"

Annie spit out the lemonade she had taken into her mouth and it sprayed all over her shirt.

"Oh," said Bridget, and Annie watched any hope her mother may have had that Jason would be an okay match for her slowly begin to peel away from her in strips.

"I paint houses," Jason said.

Mark giggled. "I *like* houses!" he said.

Both Annie and her mother looked away as Jason leaned in closer to Mark but addressed the women. "Is he okay?"

"He's fine," Annie said sternly, to her mother, not to Jason.

Bridget stared into her glass. "So this is why you're not going to Brown," she said more than asked.

Annie was incensed now. This was all a huge mess. She jumped to her feet. "I already told you it had nothing to do with him!" she shouted, and then turned to Jason. "Sorry," she told him, softly. "Do you want to go?"

31

Jason looked like he was taking it all in his stride. Of course he did. Wasn't this one of the things she loved about him? His easy charm? He caught her mother's glance and actually gave her mother a "can you believe her?" look. About Annie!

Now it was Bridget's turn to dive into the M&M's. Although in her state, it was she who ended up knocking The Blessed Mother to the ground.

"Oh dear," she gasped, and dove to the floor to retrieve the statue. The M&M's still clutched in her fist were promptly shoved into her mouth. She chewed completely and swallowed before speaking again.

"Look, Annie," she began, cautiously, "I know you think you have it all figured out but—"

"But what? We're in love, okay. We don't want to live in different states. We want to be together."

Jason now stood and pulled Annie close. She closed her eyes and buried her face in his chest. God he smelled so, so good.

He pulled away from her and gestured sternly toward the couch. She bent to his will and sat down again.

"What are your plans?" Bridget asked, looking at Annie's father, who was staring down at his shoes. She sighed.

"What do you mean?" Annie asked.

"What I mean is, what are your *real* plans?" Bridget glared at them. Her eyes revealed that she already knew the answer.

"Well," Annie began, "if you must know, we're talking about getting married."

Her mother glared at Jason. "She's not ready to get married yet. She's barely eighteen years old. You know that, don't you?"

"Yes, of course," said Jason.

"And how old are you, if you don't mind me asking?"

"Twenty-nine next month."

"Hmmm," Bridget said, then paused. "Isn't she a bit young for you?"

"Mother!"

He shrugged. "She's always seemed much older to me. More mature," Jason assured. "Maybe too old for me," he joked. No one, not even Mark, laughed.

Annie's mother cleared her throat to get her husband's attention. He grinned for a while, before taking the cue that he was supposed to say something. "You're thinking about getting married!" her dad gushed. "Well, isn't that nice!" He smiled at his wife, who glared back at him.

"She's going to have a big career one day. She's going to be a success." Bridget said and she glowered at Jason.

"I have no doubt about that," Jason smiled, squeezing Annie's leg just above the knee, making Annie slightly uncomfortable that he was touching her so intimately in front of her parents.

"Please don't get in her way."

"Mom!"

"It's okay, Annie," Jason assured her. "Mrs. C, I'd never dream of holding this one back, believe me. She's a fireball."

"Jason!" Annie giggled and he planted a sweet soft kiss on her nose.

"I only want my sugar pop to be happy," he said.

"Yes, I imagine you do," said her mother.

Jason then kissed Annie, a little too long and a little too deep for the living room.

"Married! Why, this sure is wonderful!" her dad said as her mom grabbed up another fist of M&M's and shoved them into her mouth. Annie watched as Bridget closed her eyes tight, seeming as though she was trying to suck solace out of the candy.

"Just wonderful," Mark repeated as he jumped up and embraced the young couple. Without pulling away, Mark said: "Welcome to the family, Jason."

"Thank you, Mr. Collins," Jason said, his eyes now fixed on Bridget. "I mean... Dad."

———————————

Shortly before their wedding, and well against Bridget's wishes, Annie moved in with Jason. His studio apartment had been too small for them to share, so they soon found a small one-bedroom apartment they could sort of afford. The space was plainly decorated with hand-me-downs and Ikea furniture. Plastic horizontal blinds covered all the windows. It wasn't a palace by any stretch, but in that apartment she felt a deeper sense of home than she ever had before. And there wasn't a single religious artifact to be found in the space.

Annie had pretended to be sleeping when Jason entered the bedroom. When he turned to pull open the blinds, she noticed he'd placed a tray down on her night table. She could feel him standing over her a few minutes, watching her sleep. When she finally opened her eyes, he swooped down and kissed her. "Morning, my love," he whispered into her ear.

"What time is it?" she asked, groggy. Annie and Jason shared a full-sized bed, which had been hers from her childhood room. The bedding didn't match, just like the night tables that flanked the bed, but everything was comfortable and homey and clean. Annie liked it that way, and worked hard to keep it that way.

"Time for my bride-to-be to get up and pick up her wedding dress."

Annie groaned and buried her head back under the blankets. "Nooooo. That's not today. So tired…"

"Come on, kitten," he said, so sweetly. "I made you some coffee and food."

Annie opened her eyes again. She sat up and examined the tray: A small pot of coffee and mug; scrambled eggs, toast and fruit salad; a bud vase with a single pink peony in it. She was always amazed at how considerate he was. How he always made just that little extra touch. Her heart warmed. "How long have you been up?"

"Maybe an hour or so?"

Annie couldn't help but be excited that he was up so early. It was usually her up, trying to get him to budge. There was only one thing that ever got him up earlier than her. "You have work today?" she asked, trying not to sound as anxious as she felt.

His face fell. "No," he replied, sounding somewhat annoyed. "Just couldn't sleep. I guess I'm just excited is all, you know? Your dress and everything. Kind of makes it more *real*. I thought you'd be more…"

"Excited. I am." Annie felt guilty. "I am so excited. You know I am," she assured him, and she took a bite of toast. "How come you didn't wake me sooner?"

He smiled now. "I guess I was just too caught up in watching you sleep," he said.

Annie stroked his face and Jason picked up her coffee mug and held it to her mouth. "With two and a half sugars and cream—just like you like it," he said.

She waved it away but he gently insisted that she take a sip of coffee that she didn't want, thinking nothing of the way it had been imposed on her. Had she been told early on to look for "signs," this surely would have been one of them. But she wasn't thinking that way. Not back then. Then, Annie dutifully sipped the coffee and once she had complied, he placed the mug down.

She threw her arms around his neck. "I can't wait till we're married!" she said, and noticed Jason was hiding something behind his back. "What is that?" she asked.

"What's what?" he replied, pulling away.

Annie couldn't help but get her hopes up. Jason hadn't been able to buy her an engagement ring because of his shaky finances, but she was always hopeful that he would come through one day. That he would find a way. She was giddy that day had finally arrived. "Behind your back? What do you have there?"

"Oh, you mean this?" he said, and he produced a stuffed chick toy, dressed in a bridal gown. It was the stupidest-looking stuffed animal she had ever seen, especially as she had wanted so badly for it to have been something else.

"Oh..." she said, trying to hide her disappointment.

"Now I feel stupid."

"No, it's okay. I—"

"It kind of reminded me of you..." he said.

Annie felt his frustration as if it were her own. She took the chick away from him and held it against her heart. "Oh Jason. It's so cute. So thoughtful!"

"You're not mad it's not a ring? I mean, I'm trying, but Manny..."

Annie pressed the tip of her finger against Jason's lips. "I love it," she said. "And I will *always* love it." Annie played with the veil as she spoke. "What should we call it?"

Jason got a devilish look on his face. "How about Chicky Licky?"

"Chicky Licky? Why..."

Jason dove under the covers. She gasped with delight when she felt his hot tongue on her. He knew so well how her body worked.

"Oh... wow... Jesus... I see.... that's why..." she breathed. "Oh Jason. You're so good to me."

Jason poked his head from under the blankets. "I'm all for you, Annie," he said with a sincerity so deep, it unhinged her. "What I am, I am for you."

chapter five

_____

the present.

Hugh made it back to the station just as his train was scheduled to depart. He slid into a three-seater bench, all the way to the window, and placed his camera bag down on the seat next to him, looping the strap around his arm.

Then he leaned his face on his hand and stared outside as the train pulled out of the station. His thoughts drifted to Michigan and his life before, and to moving to New York. How, right from the get-go, Charlotte seemed to know everything there was to know about moving. She had purchased and read several books on the topic and took copious notes. "Pack light" was a tenet she'd followed religiously—at least when it had come to Hugh's stuff.

By the time the movers had arrived at Hugh's house, they seemed broken by life. Hugh could see why when Charlotte, armed with a clipboard and whistle, emerged from the cab of the truck. She had pretty much dismantled their masculinity, and now seemed intent to start working on his, such as it was. When he motioned to a couple of the guys to grab his parents' Victorian-style living room couches to put in the truck, she screeched on her whistle, causing the movers to cringe and shake as they folded their arms over their ears.

"Not those," she had scoffed. "In fact," she now turned her attention to Hugh, "nothing in this house—except your bedroom furniture. That I can deal with as I'll never have to see it."

"But..." he said.

"Fresh start! Fresh start!" she snapped. "Besides, this stuff is just so grotesque. It's garish."

"It's not garish," he told her. "It's English."

"Garish, English, whatever. It gives me the creeps," she responded.

"Why can't we just take these maroon couches? We can leave everything else."

"Are you kidding me? The couches are the worst of everything here. That color! Just awful. Trust me, sweetie. We have to throw away the past to make a new start. It's in the book."

"What book?"

"All of the books."

"Okay, then how come that truck's more than two-thirds full of your stuff?"

"Because all of my stuff is from this century and the last. And it's cool," she tried to convince him. "We do need some furniture."

Hugh rolled his eyes.

"Listen, I'm not saying don't take anything. Take your clothes. Your camera equipment, that's fine. Just leave what isn't specifically *yours* for the Salvation Army."

Charlotte noticed one of the movers sneaking away towards the kitchen and she clutched her clipboard and followed. Hugh was starting to get tired of Charlotte pushing him around and he got an idea. He ran outside to suss out the contents of the truck. He took a quick tally of what was there, made a few guesses on size and pliability, and estimated that one of her dressers, a beanbag chair, and three boxes took up all the space he'd need for his couches. He ran back into the house.

"Hey Charl," he called. "Can you do me a favor?"

She came out of the kitchen and rolled her eyes. "Busy," she said, impatient.

"Yeah..." he stalled. "The thing is, I forget to pick up my inhaler prescription again and..."

"Oh come on. Why do you always—"

"I know, I forgot again." Of course, he could have picked it up on his own on their way to the airport, but he wasn't going to volunteer that.

"Why can't you—"

"Still packing," he said, with a smile that generally annoyed her but usually defused her. "Can you help me out?"

Charlotte sighed loudly and then handed him her clipboard. She slipped her whistle into her mouth and blew a shrill shriek, startling the movers. One nearly dropped a box he was carrying from Hugh's room.

"Listen up!" she barked. "This guy's in charge of the operation for the next half hour or so," she instructed, pointing at Hugh with her thumb. "Anything he says goes." Even though Hugh was now officially "in charge," she gave him a play-by-play itinerary on what she expected to be accomplished upon her return.

After she left, he jumped up on the open trailer of the truck, and, using it as a kind of stage, he cupped his mouth with his hands and shouted out to the movers.

"Hey? Guys?" he yelled to them, but no one acknowledged him. "Hey! Yoo-hoo!" Then Hugh had an inspiration. "Hey, guys!" he tried again. "If you help me out now, I can make it worth your while."

"Really?" a man with the name "Bob" stitched onto his shirt snarkishly replied.

"Really. Fifty bucks each?" He cocked an eyebrow at them. Unlike how it generally affected women, this gesture of his seemed to propel men to action.

The movers pulled themselves into a huddle and whispered for a while. "Bob" nodded at Hugh. "Hundred," he said.

Hugh peered into his wallet. He had been carrying more cash than he usually did, for the move, and decided this was as good a time as any to tap into the reserve his parents had left him. "Okay, a hundred then. Each."

The three men exchanged glances and nodded. "You got yourself a deal."

They headed to the truck where Hugh pointed out the items he wanted removed. "We'll hide them behind the garage," said Bob. "She'll never look there."

Once the couches were securely planted in the back of the truck along with some boxes he'd packed from the kitchen, Hugh paid the movers and then helped them carry the rest of his things out of the house. They closed and locked the back of the truck just as Charlotte returned.

"You're all done?"

"What can I say? I guess I'm just a good manager or something," he said, causing the men to erupt with laughter. Charlotte looked at him, a challenge in her eyes. Hugh shrugged.

When the truck finally arrived in New York, Charlotte was annoyed to see that some of her stuff had not made the trip— but was horrified to learn that the couches had. "I must have screwed up somewhere," offered Hugh, following her around their new living room.

Bob came to his defense. "No ma'am. It was us," he told her as he and Hugh walked behind her. Without Charlotte noticing, Bob held out his hand to Hugh. Hugh pulled his last fifty out of his wallet.

"It doesn't matter," Charlotte said. "I'm too tired to argue about it."

It was hard to believe that was already two years ago. In that time, Hugh had gone through three jobs and about thirty girlfriends since. All disasters. The most recent of these debacles had been Sheila Simon, Charlotte's coworker, whom he'd met at a company bowling outing Charlotte had dragged him to that winter. Just when he started to really get into her, to feel really comfortable with her, she dumped him. Par for the course when it came to Hugh and his interactions with women, it seemed.

He had just started to nod off, thinking about how much he had liked Sheila's smile when the conductor called out his stop, startling him. He grabbed his bag and headed down the stairs and to the street.

Now only a few minutes' walk from his apartment, Hugh pulled his jacket closed and flipped his collar up to protect his neck from the icy wind that had picked up since he'd left Long Island. Out of nowhere, the sky opened up and it began to rain. Hugh quickened his pace, happy to have his jacket.

Then, for reasons he couldn't explain, he started thinking about the underdressed, pretty, small woman in the cemetery and wondered if she'd been able to get home before it got too cold. He didn't know why he was thinking of her, but he couldn't stop thinking about her. Who was the man she was visiting? Her older brother who'd died in an accident? A professor with whom she'd had an illicit affair? Her favorite uncle, who had died from a drug overdose?

Why did he care?

By the time he arrived at his building, the rain stopped and the sky cleared. As he entered his apartment, he caught a glimpse of his parents' couches out of the corner of his eye. And just like every time he entered and saw them, a huge grin formed on his face.

"What are you so happy about?"

Charlotte O'Reilly sat on one of Hugh's parents' couches, dressed in a bathrobe.

"Nothing really. Interesting day," he said, taking off his wet jacket and hanging it on a coat tree in the entryway. Charlotte's hair was wrapped in a towel. She was reading a book and at the same time messily eating a chunk of cake with her hands. Hugh winced as pieces of the cake fell off the slab and all over the couch and the floor. He made a mental note to grab the Dustbuster once she left the room. He ran a hand through his soaked hair.

Charlotte looked up from her book. She giggled.

"Wet much?"

"Ha, ha," he said sarcastically, though the dumb look he wore must have told a different story that she immediately picked up on. She sized him up, squinting. Then a look of fear fell over her face. "Wait a minute, I know that look. Don't tell me you met someone because I know that look..."

"Nah," he replied. "Well, actually yes. But I won't see her again."

"Good. Because remember, you are still working on yourself. Repeat after me: I am still—"

Hugh sat down next to Charlotte and gave her a friendly squeeze. He craned his neck to see the title of the book she was reading. "What is that?"

Charlotte held up the book before placing it down on the coffee table with much more drama than was warranted. "This..." she began, tapping the cover. "This is the book that's going to change my life. And when I'm done with it, you're going to read it and it's going to change yours too."

Hugh slid slightly away from Charlotte and was annoyed to see some of her cake crumbs now clung to his pants. He picked up the book. "*Executive Fang Shoe-aye?*" he asked.

Charlotte snatched the book back. "*Executive Feng Shui,*" she corrected. "It shows you how to realign your professional life to welcome success."

"Here we go again," Hugh said playfully. "My job is fine, but thanks. Let me guess though—you're taking a new class?"

Charlotte rolled her eyes. "East for Zest—Ancient Secrets to Modern Advancement."

"Nice." Hugh smirked.

"Mock me if you want. But at least I'm doing something with my life. Trying to get somewhere. Look at you."

"What's the matter with me?"

"All I'm saying is that you need to open your mind, Hugh. All of these ideas in here... You can apply them to everything you do, not just work. You can really make something of yourself."

"I'm okay with who I am," he said. He understood Charlotte meant well, but sometimes it rubbed him wrong when she pushed him.

She shook her head. "Yes, of course you are," she said. "You're just *dripping* with success," she joked. "So tell me—how was your day? What did you do?"

Hugh held up his camera bag and smiled.

"Ah yes. Gallivanting with the dead again," she said.

"I'll have you know I got some great shots for my portfolio today. That's how I'm going to get ahead."

"Sure you are," said Charlotte.

"What's that supposed to mean?" There she was, pushing him again. Why couldn't she just leave well enough alone?

"When will you show it to me?"

"When it's ready."

"You've been telling me that for years," she said. Hugh tried to speak, but she cut him off. "You know, The Annex has a class..."

"You can't learn art in a class."

"Whatever," she said, and she rose from the couch. As she stood, she distractedly brushed crumbs off her lap. For a split second Hugh had an image of himself armed only with a vacuum as a pack of oversized cockroaches feasted on Charlotte.

Oh, the cockroaches! Not something the realtor or any apartment ads would have mentioned, but about as notable in this neighborhood as the view.

There were many risks you took if you wanted to live in New York, Hugh had learned shortly after moving into their apartment. This was definitely one of the biggies. And talk about big? Hugh had heard the legend of the New York cockroach before, but nothing could ever have prepared him for what welcomed him in the shower his second week in the apartment. It could have been a cigar. It could have been a half-eaten chocolate cruller. Hugh remembered having a hamster as a kid that was smaller than this thing. And the most horrifying thing about it: It actually flew.

Francine LaSala

Not the bravest being, when Hugh went to "remove" the thing, he did so by hurling an aluminum tissue-box holder at it. Big mistake. First of all, he missed. But then, he seemed to incite it. He could swear that the thing cocked its head, looked over at him, sneered, and then hissed. It spread out its enormous wings and charged right at him. It wasn't a bug; it was more like a bat. Hugh darted out of the bathroom and into his room, burying himself under the covers with his inhaler. He didn't go back into the bathroom again until Charlotte came home and took care of the problem.

Knowing he couldn't rely always on Charlotte for protection, Hugh thought it was about time they got a cat, so he lured in one of the friendlier neighborhood strays that hung out on the front stoop. The next day, the cat's friend was there—lonely and despondent at first, and then mewing and whining like a fiend. So he brought that one upstairs as well. Everything in pairs. That was how Hugh liked things. He named them Harold and Maude. When he'd taken them to the vet and learned Harold was actually female, he'd decided to keep the name anyway.

Charlotte hadn't really cared too much for the cats, and they didn't seem to care for her either. In fact, they pretty much never came out from hiding unless Hugh was home, or so Charlotte had said. But they seemed to be doing their jobs. It had been several weeks since a waterbug had been spotted. Though just the thought of them unnerved Hugh, so he asked her, as he did every day: "Any sightings today?"

"I'm pretty sure the last extermination got it under control."

"And the cats..." Hugh said, and as if on cue Maude came out of hiding and rubbed up against his legs, purring. He knelt down to pet her, and Harold also appeared and brushed

46

against her human buddy. When Charlotte took a step in Hugh's direction, Maude jumped and hissed at her.

"No, the exterminator," she said.

"Well, it's good we've been more careful about leaving food out. Making an effort to be cleaner about things," he said, sarcastically.

"I'm not the slob around here," said Charlotte, unwrapping her hair from the turban and thoughtlessly tossing the wet towel onto the couch. "So what are you doing tonight?"

"Nothing really," he replied, squinching his face as he watched her hands get trapped in her wet hair, causing strands to snap loose and fall to the floor. He knew what he'd be doing tonight: He'd be going over that area a hundred times with the vacuum to pick up that hair. He spent most of his time at home hunting those strands with a Dustbuster as red hair, unlike blond or brown, showed up on both darks and lights. Their cats didn't shed as much as Charlotte did. He loved her, sure, but sometimes she was a real pain in the ass to live with.

"Why don't you come out with us?" Charlotte asked.

Like now. "I don't think so. Not tonight. Thanks, though," he said, and Charlotte darted into her room. Hugh took the opportunity to grab the Dustbuster from the kitchen and suck up the mess Charlotte left behind. Just as he turned off the vacuum, Charlotte materialized in the living room, fully dressed and made up. "Come on, it will be fun. Do you remember Phyllis?" she asked, tossing lipstick and keys into her bag.

Phyllis… Phyllis? Short girl with the black hair, nearly shaved off?

"She's tall? Long blond hair?"

He drew a blank.

"Oh yeah," he lied. "What about her?"

47

"Well, she and her husband—the banker? They just bought a huge apartment in the West Village and they're having a party tonight. Why don't you come along?"

He had no interest. He hated parties. But he knew if he didn't at least pretend to be intrigued, she would ride him incessantly on the life expectancy of hermits.

"Do I have to?"

"You do," she said, and walked into the kitchen. She came out carrying a bottle of white wine. Hugh hadn't budged. "Come on," she insisted. "Just go put on some dry clothes and let's go."

"Fine," he said. He complied. He always did. The truth was, if it weren't for Charlotte, he'd probably never leave the house. So it was probably best she did push him once in a while. It's not like he was ever going to get laid watching TV on his couches with his cats. And, more importantly for him, it wasn't like he was ever going to fall in love again if he never left his apartment.

chapter six

---

the present.

After the cemetery, Annie headed to meet one of her favorite people, her best friend, Rebecca, at one of her least favorite places, the mall.

Annie and Rebecca had been friends since they were children, but the two could not have been more different. Rebecca was calm, introspective, and confident; Annie had always tended to be chaotic, flighty, and insecure. Her friend was sort of like an office building—solid and stable on the outside, with warmth and humanity and life bustling within. Annie had no structure. Not really. She felt she was more like a carnival—transient and exciting for a while, but then exhausting. Something you anticipated and enjoyed while it was around, but were relieved when the trucks were finally packed up and left town. Her divorce, Jason's death, and all the drama surrounding these events had definitely added to the "circus" of her mental state—but hadn't necessarily sparked it.

After her split with Jason and everything that had transpired around it, she had dated, quite a lot. But it wasn't long before the "crazy" surfaced and her antics drove men away. She was avoiding that kind of drama now. As much as she could. Rebecca was definitely helping to keep her grounded.

As Annie waited for Rebecca, a booming, screeching, and incongruously tiny voice cut through the crowd, parting it like Moses had the Red Sea. Not only had Rebecca not come alone, but that she'd brought the worst of her three kids with her.

"Annie! Over here!" yelled Rebecca.

Annie hid under her hand, hoping no one would know she was with them, but Rebecca marched right up to her, giving her a warm hug and blowing her cover.

"You bad monny. I hate you!" the child said with a sneer.

"Yes, sweetie," said Rebecca, tenderly. "And Monny hates you, too."

"Stufid bick!" cursed the three-year-old, just as a properly dressed older woman passed them. The matron shook her head and clicked her tongue at Rebecca, who flashed the intruder a quick smirk.

She took a deep breath and politely addressed the woman. "It's important to raise kids to speak their minds..."

Meg manically scream-laughed at the woman. "Stufid bick!"

Rebecca continued in the same even tone. "...because otherwise nosy assholes will just get all in their business. And why should my kid ever have to put up with that?" She patted Meg on the head. "That's a good girl, sweetie," she cooed.

"Well, I never," the woman scoffed and walked off in a huff.

"And I hope I never again," Rebecca called after her.

Annie laughed. "You told her."

Rebecca sighed. "I'm so tired. But I just get really tired of people judging me and judging my kids, you know?"

A darkness fell over Annie any time she thought about children. Over the child she might have had with Jason. If things had been different with Jason... She hoped Rebecca wouldn't notice her pain. Luckily, Rebecca got distracted by Meg and when she looked back at Annie, Annie had forced herself to start smiling again. "Well I think you did the right thing," she said. "I mean, if it were me—"

"And let's thank God it wasn't, considering your temper." Rebecca laughed, somewhat nervously.

"Hey. What's that supposed to mean?" asked Annie, feeling hurt. Before Rebecca could answer, however, Meg interrupted, laughing maniacally. "Bad temper! Bad temper!"

Rebecca stared blankly at Annie, who shrugged her shoulders. She lifted Meg in the air. "Want one? Going cheap. Free even!"

"I don't think I want this one." Annie laughed. "You know Meg doesn't like me."

Confirming this, Meg's face screwed into a scowl and she growled at Annie.

"Enough, little one," said Rebecca. "I brought you into this world and I—"

"Rebecca!" Annie gasped.

"What? Oh sorry... Sometimes I forget myself." She turned her attention back to Meg. "Come on and say hello to your Aunt Annie."

"Hullo ent Ninny," Meg said, and Annie and Rebecca exchanged glances.

"Think she does that on purpose?" Annie asked.

"This one? Probably. Of course, Meg doesn't like anyone but Minnie Mouse." Rebecca brushed a wisp of fine baby hair from the child's forehead. Her voice dropped to a whisper.

"We're going to have to eat something before she really gets bad."

"Of course," Annie said.

Meg between them, Annie and Rebecca headed to the food court. All the while, Annie was treated to such scintillating information, like how six-year-olds don't eat green food. Annie tried to be patient and be a good, listening friend as they got their food and found a table at the crowded food court.

"Anyway," Rebecca said, shoving a french fry into her mouth, "I spend my life talking about *Bubble Guppies*."

"Bubble who?"

"Oh forget it. I'm boring myself. Tell me about the world. Didn't you have a date last night?"

"I don't know if you could call it that," said Annie. "It was torture."

"Oh, come on. It couldn't have been that bad."

"I don't get dating. I don't think I ever did."

"That's because you're looking at it the wrong way, Annie. It's all very logical, really. When you're looking for the right partner. You look at the elements of a person, the elements of what you're looking for in a connection, and it all begins to add up. It's like math."

"I don't like math," Annie said and Rebecca smirked. "Besides, there's nothing romantic about what you're saying. You're making dating seem even less appealing."

"When you focus on what it's meant to accomplish—"

"It's not how you find real love. It's not how you find the magic…"

"It's how you find the *right* partner."

Annie made the choice to ignore what felt like a jab from Rebecca. "Dating is something people do between falling in love. That's not real love. Real love—that's what happens when you have a random encounter in an elevator. Or at the ATM. Or in a cemetery…" She trailed off, surprising herself. *Why had she said that?*

"A cemetery? That's a little ridiculous, even for you," Rebecca teased.

Annie wasn't insulted. She was too panicked for that right now. She had no idea why that word "cemetery" had popped out of her mouth. She definitely had not wanted to tell Rebecca where she'd been earlier. Rebecca would not have understood why she had to go see Jason like that. And she definitely would not have understood her conversation with the strange boy she'd met there. The boy with the silly ironic T-shirt and the single eyebrow raise that had, out of nowhere, made her flush with, strangely enough, a flicker of lust. She let out a slight cough. "Okay, well, maybe not a cemetery. But come on. You have to admit that dating is a waste of time," Annie said. "Love should just, I don't know, happen. It should just grab you and not let go…" Like the love she had for Jason. The love she somehow could not let go, despite everything that had transpired.

Rebecca seemed determined to not let the dating thing go. "Tell me about this date last night. What about him exactly was so revolting? What was his…fatal flaw?" She finished the last bite of her chicken sandwich and neatly balled up the wrapper.

"Well, if you must know. He twirled."

"Twirled? You mean like ballet?"

"Uh no. Like a crazy person. Every two minutes he was all like…" she said, and demonstrated by twisting the front of her hair with her index finger, a crazed look in her eye. "I mean—

who could concentrate. I can't remember a single other thing about him."

Rebecca looked down and began absently opening up several packets of ketchup, leaving them in Meg's reach. Meg, seeing the error of her mother's ways, donned a demonic look of delight.

"What was he like otherwise? Was there anything redeeming about him? What did he do for a living?"

"What does it matter?"

Rebecca sighed. "Annie, if you're always so hard on men, how do you ever expect to land a Mike of your own?"

Annie was frustrated. "Look, Becca, you know I love you. But I've told you time and again that I'm not looking for a Mike—and that's no offense to you. What you have works for you. It would never work for me. It's just so... well... normal. You know? Rational. I couldn't live like that."

"You can't be normal?"

Annie shook her head. "What I *want*, what will make me happy, is what it's like in the movies," she said, wistfully. "It's the *magic*, Becca. I need the magic. Otherwise, I mean, what's the point?"

Rebecca shook her head. "Magic doesn't put a roof over your head or provide for your children." There it was again. That quick, sharp hurt that stabbed her heart when it came to the prospect of the child she could have had with Jason. "Romantic magic is overrated, sweetie."

Annie didn't like when Rebecca talked down to her. Like Rebecca had all the answers and Annie would see her way of thinking when she "grew up" or something. She wasn't going to get into that now. Romantic magic was overrated? How could anyone see things that way, when falling in love, being deeply in love, was everything? How could two people see the world so differently? She knew from experience she wasn't every going to be able to win against Rebecca's pragmatism. "Let's agree to disagree on that, okay?" But she still went for one small stab of her own: "I mean, if you ever had it, you may feel differently."

Rebecca did not seem to wound. "It's just that we've been through this so many times before. And you've been through so much... can't you see that you're just not going to find that kind of magic? That it doesn't exist? I mean, it really is all very logical, if you can let yourself look at it that way. When it all adds up, that's when it's right. It's crazy to think..."

"To think what? I had it once." Jason was magic. That love was magic. When it worked it was magic...

"You *think* you did."

The women sat quietly for a moment or more before Annie spoke again. "Look, it has to happen sometimes. Not all relationships are about being complacent. About settling. I'll take my chances. And I can promise you that I won't be playing house with Captain Twirl when it happens for me."

"That's not what I meant. It's just that. You know. You just can't keep living like you are. I'm worried about you. You know... since... since..." The pure concern on Rebecca's face showed she wasn't faking being worried, but Annie didn't want to think about that right now. About what Rebecca knew and what she didn't know. About what had happened with Jason after their relationship went to hell. About what had really happened that horrible night... About Annie's part in it...

"I've moved on. Care to join me?" Annie snapped.

"Fine. Let's move on then," Rebecca said, then quickly changed the subject. "So did you hear about that party tonight?"

Annie felt a flash of excitement. "Why—you coming out?"

"I'd love to try. It would be nice to be around adults and have only Mike hanging on me for once," she said. Rebecca looked over at her daughter, who was building a fort with her chicken nuggets, gluing them together with layers of ketchup, which had permeated every crevice of the child's hands and was starting to seep up her arms and onto her clothing. "Give me that!" she scolded, taking away the ketchup and causing Meg to erupt. She looked at Annie with tired eyes. "What if I were to pay you? Would you take her then?"

Annie laughed and then helped Rebecca clean up the mess. "Hey, I'm sorry, Becca."

"Sorry for what?"

"For attacking you like that."

"I didn't notice," Rebecca replied, and Annie knew she was lying.

"I just hope I'm not becoming crazy like the rest of them," Annie said, nervously.

"You are not the rest of them," Rebecca said.

"Are you sure?" she asked, because she was generally terrified of the women in her family and the decisions they'd made for generations.

"If you're asking me if I think you're turning into your nutso grandmother, the answer is no."

"You're just saying that because you think I'm already there."

Rebecca didn't respond; Annie took the silence as an admission and began to quietly obsess. Was she as crazy as her grandmother, the woman who was her mother's *real* mother? As crazy as her own mother? Is that "crazy" what ultimately had turned Jason off her? What had compelled her to *turn* him off her?

"I am sure," said Rebecca. "Speaking of... I wasn't going to tell you this today, but I saw your mother recently." Annie knew that Rebecca still stayed in contact with her mother, even though Rebecca knew she was unhappy about it. She didn't understand why her best friend felt compelled to associate with that person even after Annie had decided to break free from her toxic oppressiveness and hadn't talked to her in more than a year. But as long as Rebecca didn't harass Annie about it, she let it go. "She's really worried about you, you know. She asked me to tell you to please call her, with the anniversary of your dad's death coming up—"

"Okay, thanks," said Annie, dismissively, annoyed that now she was going to get harassed over it.

"Don't you think it's time..."

Annie could feel rage welling up inside her and she fought to keep calm. "You don't know everything about it. It's complicated sometimes...mothers and daughters..."

They both looked absently at Meg. Now Rebecca spoke. "She also said—"

"Look, I don't want to talk about this now," Annie said. "I really gotta run." She gave her friend a quick kiss on the cheek. "See you tonight?"

Rebecca smiled. "Sure."

"Whut bout me, ent Ninny?"

"Well, look at that." Annie smiled. "Perhaps we're making some headway here after all," she said, and she bent down to kiss the child. As Annie approached, Meg began to scream as though her fingers had been caught in a blender set to "frappé."

"It's just a phase, Annie," Rebecca said, picking up Meg and lightly bouncing her on her hip. Annie wasn't sure if she was talking about Meg's attitude or Annie's own descent into madness. "Sure it is," she said, and she darted off.

chapter seven

---

the present.

Phyllis and Reg Weinstock lived on the top floor of an apartment building on Waverly Place with a wraparound terrace, four large bedrooms, and at least three fireplaces.

"How can anyone afford to live like this?" Hugh marveled out loud as they entered, thinking about how much he had to shell out a month to live in their crappy apartment.

"Because some people do actually take steps to improve themselves," Charlotte snapped back. "*Executive Feng Shui*, Hugh. You really should read it. East for Zest. That's what it's all about."

"Yeah, yeah," he said in reply. Hugh knew she meant well, that her enthusiasm for these things was genuine and that she really did want the best for him, so he just shirked it off as they headed into the apartment.

"Phyllis published it, you know," she said, then quickly got distracted. "Just look at this place! This furniture! So lush!"

Hugh wasn't as impressed with the opulence of the place as his photographer's eye was with many of the architectural details, like the pressed-tin ceiling, which he thought was especially cool. But being Hugh, he also couldn't help but wonder who had lived here before. He started to invent a scenario involving an heiress who had been murdered in a crime of passion by her lover when Charlotte interrupted him by tugging on his arm.

"Guard that Sancerre with your life," she said, pointing to the bottle of wine he carried for her, which he had learned on the 7 train on the way over had been a $40 investment. "And be sure to keep it cold," she continued before walking off.

He wasn't sure how he was going to be able to protect the wine and also keep it cold, so he hid it in the back of the refrigerator behind a giant jar of bread-and-butter pickles. Just as he had moved a six-pack in front of the pickles to help further obscure Charlotte's wine, he heard a voice on the other side of the refrigerator door.

"Hugh! How are you?" He closed the door to see a woman with a mop of frizzy brown hair and bright red lips smiling at him. He knew that face had a name. He couldn't remember it.

"Hey...you... How's it going?" He stuck out his hand to offer a polite shake, but she pulled him into a tight hug.

"Come here, you silly thing, and let Margie give you a kiss!" she said, and planted a waxy kiss on his cheek. When she pulled away, she squinted down at his shirt, and read: "'This is not my idea of a good time'?"

He raised an eyebrow at her. "It's Garbage," he said with an impish smile, implying the band but knowing the reference was going to be obscure and raise some questions.

"It is indeed," she replied, seeming more indignant than the T-shirt should have warranted. She took a few steps back.

Oh God, the eyebrow thing. He must have done the eyebrow thing. When was he going to learn?

Her annoyance didn't last long though. "I can't believe you finally made it out of the house. I thought you'd never show your face again after that mess you made with Sheila," she said.

Was anyone ever going to forget about that? So what if he had fallen too hard and ended up making a fool of himself. Surely he wasn't the only person in the history of the world who had come undone over a woman before. Or many of them, as his romantic history demonstrated...

"Come," she said. "There are some people here I know would love to see you!" Then he realized that this was a party full of Sheila's friends and he started to panic. Margie seemed to pick up on that. "No, no, she isn't here tonight," she said soothingly.

She looped his arm in hers and dragged him over to a group of people he didn't want to see. He had nothing to say to any of them. All he could do was smile, nod, and pray for an out. When the other women squinted at his shirt and made faces at him, he started to feel like wearing it, at least in this crowd, had been a mistake. When a girl in a blue sequined top joined the group and directly asked him, "Where's Sheila?" he knew he had to make a break for it.

"You know, I have to go to the..."

"Right down the hall." Margie nodded in the direction she meant. "Go ahead. I'll wait right here."

"Great," Hugh said, and as he walked off, he could hear Margie lash into the girl who had asked for Sheila. "Jesus, Brandy! Why'd you have to go and remind him of her? I was totally working that."

"Oh come on? Him?"

"He's sort of cute..."

"He's sort of psycho," Brandy said, and both girls erupted into gales of laughter.

Hugh could feel his chest start to tighten as he ducked into the bathroom. He felt around in his pocket for his inhaler and immediately relaxed knowing it was there. He worked on his breathing as he continued to try to calm himself.

So what if Sheila had never seen *Say Anything* before and didn't understand his ill-conceived "Lloyd Dobbler" boom box stunt on her fourth-floor fire escape in his thrift-store-bought trench coat? Does it make *him* psycho if she didn't get how deeply romantic that gesture was? And did she even appreciate how tough it was to find a boom box like that anymore? And had she really needed to call the police over that?

He waited a few minutes before emerging again. Margie, true to her word, had stayed in place waiting for him, so he stealthily crept in the other direction. Hugh swiftly looped his way through the various conversation clusters that had formed in the apartment, dodging Margie's glances around the space, until he skillfully slipped into a bedroom and climbed into the closet for a moment's reprieve.

Just as he had closed the closet door behind him, two people engrossed in conversation entered the room.

"How is it possible you've never seen *Airplane?* Surely you can't be serious?" a woman's voice asked.

"All I know is that you're looking pretty damn hot tonight," a man's voice replied. The tone was smarmy. It made Hugh cringe. Who spoke to women like that?

"No. You're supposed to say…" the woman said back. He didn't understand why the woman would put up with him. Why she would let this guy talk to her like that. "You're supposed to say…."

Then something clicked. There was something about that voice he recognized. It sounded like *her*. Like that girl in the cemetery. But how could that be?

The man started hitting on her again. "So why don't you say me and you——"

"Well, aren't you the sweetest," she began, but it seemed like she'd had enough. "I thank you, but I must be getting back to my friend. I left her with a real bore. You know how dreadful that can be."

Yes! It had to be her! He wasn't sure why he was so excited.

"Aw, come on, baby. We just got here. Why don't we sit down for a while? Get acquainted?"

Hugh pushed up against the door to try and catch more of the conversation. He wondered with a sense of anticipatory delight whether or not the woman was going to attack this guy with words like she'd attacked him earlier that day.

He heard her clear her throat, and she began speaking sweetly. "That would be lovely except my doctor says it's not healthy for me to associate with, um..." Then her tone took on an edge when she said, "What am I trying to say here...?" And went downright angry when she shouted: "Assholes!" The bedroom door opened, then slammed shut, then opened again.

"What did you just say to me?" he called after the woman.

"Must go!" she shouted back from the hall.

"Hey, get back——"

Right after they left, Hugh's leaning inadvertently pushed open the door and he face-planted on the floor. He picked himself up. He was definitely intrigued; he decided to go after her, lurking like the creep he apparently was as he did. The last thing he wanted was for her to see him stalking her, so he tried to remain as stealthy as possible as he tailed her.

He watched her duck into the kitchen and throw her arms around a very large man, whom she kissed square on the mouth. This made another guy, whom he surmised was the one who had been hitting on her, quickly leave the party.

Next, he watched as she leaned into the fridge, reached around, and pulled out Charlotte's wine. He gasped as she stuffed it into her purse, along with a corkscrew and a glass. Following her out of the kitchen, he witnessed her bumping into Charlotte. The tiny woman smiled, while Charlotte sized her up and sharply turned her back. She stuck out her tongue at Charlotte before heading out onto the terrace, skillfully opening the wine, and pouring a large amount into a glass. She gulped it down and then quickly refilled.

He continued to watch her for several moments, taking smaller sips of wine while taking in the skyline. Then, without warning, she quickly turned around and darted back into the apartment. Not looking up, she barreled into Hugh.

"Excuse me," she snapped, haughtily, as if the crowd was supposed to have parted for her.

Angry's a good look for this one, Hugh thought, though he was sure she'd be even prettier if she smiled. He tried smiling at her; it didn't work. So he spoke.

"Don't call me Shirley!" he said.

"I didn't... What are you..." Her faced reddened. "Oh... you heard that?" She started to look uncomfortable.

He felt bad. "*Airplane*. Such a great movie."

"Sure..." she said and started edging away.

"No—*surely!*" he quipped back at her, stupidly.

"Uh...."

She was walking away from him. He had to think fast. "Hey how's your head?"

That got her attention. "Sorry?" she said and stopped, now facing him.

"You know..." He smirked and tapped himself on the back of his head where the lens had hit her. "Your noggin?"

She scrunched her face at him. "I don't know what..." She trailed off and it gave Hugh the confidence that she was starting to recognize him.

"You *are* the cemetery girl, right?"

"The cemetery..."

Why had he done that? He had known enough women in his life to know they did not like to be labeled like that. And yet, he kept going. "From earlier today? At the cemetery? You were sort of pissed off."

She folded her arms across her chest and stepped in closer to him. She was as high as his chest, maybe a little smaller, and she paused to read his shirt. He watched her face as her expression changed from annoyed to confused to warm... and there it was... the smile. Even prettier than he had imagined it would be. He felt a jolt, a shock.

"That's Garbage," she said.

"*Surely* it is," he said. The jolt that had seized him ran from his heart to his pants, when she extended her hand to him.

"I'm Annie," she said, as she placed her hand in his.

He looked down at her improbably small hand, feeling like he still couldn't believe she was for real.

"Hugh," he replied, surprising himself that he was able to speak his own name. "You got it. No one ever gets it."

She nodded. "To be honest, this isn't my idea of a good time either."

"Then why are you here? A boyfriend?" he said, and the jolt now turned to panic. Of course a girl like this had a boyfriend

"Uh, no. Not right now," she said with an absentminded bite to her bottom lip.

There was something about this woman, something that terrified him and put him at ease all at once. He felt like he

65

must have met her sometime before—not in the cemetery, but that he had actually already *known* her. He somehow felt amazingly connected to her. And just as that feeling came over him, he tried to quash it. He tried to talk himself out of feeling that way because nothing good ever came from feeling that way. From feeling too much too quickly, his usual pattern. But it was so intense. It could not have been one-sided. Something definitely surged there in the air between them.

Annie pulled the bottle out of her purse. "Join me?" she asked, and he smiled. "Good." She scanned the room. She spotted a used wine glass on a nearby table and poured it out onto the carpet. He gasped. "Relax. It's not like it was red wine."

He had to admit, she made a good point. She filled the glass almost to the top with wine and handed it to Hugh. As he pulled the glass to his face, he noticed a lipstick print on the rim, which made him cringe. He didn't want to offend her though, so he turned the glass around and sipped from the other side, praying he wasn't going to contract cholera or some other awful thing by drinking out of a dirty glass.

Annie shrugged her shoulders. "Trust me, that was piss," she said, pouring more wine into her glass. "This is the good stuff!" she said, before clinking his glass with hers. "Come on," she said, heading to one of the apartment's three fireplaces. She sat down and invited him to sit with her.

"So how do you know Reg?" she asked him.

"I'm not sure," he replied.

"What? Did you and your T-shirt crash this thing?"

"Ha, no. I'm here with a friend of mine."

"Oh?"

"Yeah. A girl friend—I mean not a girlfriend. Just a friend who's a girl. You know. Not a *girl*-girl."

She pursed her lips. "What's a *girl*-girl?"

"Oh forget it," he said, and she giggled when he blushed. "So you're a lot nicer tonight," he said. "Why?"

"I was awful today, I know. You just caught me at a bad time."

"So how's the bump?"

Annie rubbed her head. "In good company." She laughed.

"Why? You mean you get hit by rogue cameras a lot?"

"More than you'd think," she said. "In fact..."

"Yes?"

Annie edged up closer to him and he could feel himself almost sweating. He backed away slightly, but then leaned in closer again. "When I was a kid, I was one of those catalog models. You know what I'm talking about?"

"Sure."

"Well. Once during a shoot, I stood up so quickly, I smashed the back of my head on one of those huge reflector thingies...?"

He nodded. "Yeah, you mean a diffuser? Umbrella?"

"Sure. Whatever. Anyway, I was practically bleeding to death but my shoot wasn't over and my mother made me stay and finish. Even though blood was gushing out of my head! That bitch. She just kept re-bandaging, you know? Anyway, I ended up fainting and got rushed to the hospital." She stopped to take a sip of her wine and looked up at him. "I almost died."

"Oh my God, really?"

"No."

Hugh was taken off guard for a moment or so before realizing that he'd been had. "My goodness!" he squealed.

Annie burst out laughing and so did he. She squinched her face at him. "You talk kind of funny. You're not from around here, are you?"

"No, not originally."

"So where—no wait. Let me guess. Canadian. Right? Of course you are." She nodded. "Not very bright, and friendlier than anyone should ever be."

Hugh laughed. "Close," he said. "I'm from Michigan. I mean, that's where I grew up. My folks are...were...from England."

"Yep, I thought you seemed a little gay."

"Gay?" He raised his eyebrow at her, reflexively. She looked away, immediately. Damned eyebrow. He hated himself again.

She then exhaled deeply and started speaking to him again. "All British guys are a little gay," she joked.

"I can tell you, I'm a lot of things, but gay? No way."

"Then how come you haven't made a pass at me yet?" she challenged.

At just that moment, Charlotte approached, and Hugh's heart sank. Dutifully, he stood to greet her and Annie followed his lead.

"There you are," cooed Charlotte, saccharine as a diet soda. She looped his elbow in both of her arms and trilled, "I've been looking for you for hours!"

He hated when she talked like that.

Hugh turned to Annie, who had already managed to get herself involved in another conversation. He couldn't help but feel frustrated by her interruption. "Hi, Charlotte. Have you met Annie?" he asked, desperate to get back to talking with her before she ran off with someone new.

"Hey Annie," he tried. "Annie?" He tapped her several times before she turned her attention back to him. "This is Charlotte. My roommate?" he said.

"The not a *girl*-girl," she joked. Hugh laughed; Charlotte glared. "Delighted to meet you," she said, and turned back to the other conversation.

Now he saw Charlotte scowl as she peered into Annie's open purse, spotting the nearly empty bottle of her prized wine sticking out the top. She took a deep breath to calm herself before she spoke. "So I just found out there's another party uptown that's apparently a better scene than this one," Charlotte said, never taking her eyes off the bottle. She tugged on his sleeve. "Let's go."

"That's okay," he replied. He could feel himself smiling stupidly at Annie, but he couldn't help himself. "I think I'll stay here."

Charlotte now glanced back and forth between Annie and Hugh and shook her head. "Oh no. No, no. Come on, Hugh. Let's get out of here while you're still in one piece."

"I can take care of myself," he snapped.

"No, no you can't. I mean, come on." She started looking around the room and continued in a loud whisper, "Didn't we talk about this? Weren't you going to take a break from women for a while?"

"You worry too much," he said, brushing her off. "Go and have a good time. I'll be fine. Promise."

Charlotte hesitated for a moment but gave up. "Okay then. See you later, I guess."

But before Charlotte even got the words out, Hugh had already turned to the other group, where the conversation had just come to a curious halt, everyone regarding Annie with a blank stare.

Hugh, impulsively, in a prince-charming-to-the-rescue maneuver grabbed Annie's hand and led her back out to the terrace. At least he felt that he had "rescued" her judging by the look of relief she gave him. They stood together for a while, in silence, enjoying the view and Charlotte's wine.

"I really am sorry I was so horrible to you today," she said after a while. "I guess you didn't deserve that."

"Please don't sweat it. I mean, you're sorry? What about me, lurking around like that. Asking you crap that's none of my business."

She nodded. "You have a point."

"So who was he?"

Annie smiled coyly at him. "It's still none of your business."

He couldn't believe that out of all the guys at this party, the prettiest girl in the room was talking to him. Something was happening to Hugh, he knew, but he also knew that he had no business feeling this way about anyone. Not right now. He had promised himself, promised Charlotte, that he was going to take a break from women. That he was going to look, and that meant *into himself,* for a while, before he leaped into love again. So even when Annie gave him her mobile number and told him to text her at the end of the night, he was sure he wasn't going to use it.

chapter eight

---

ten years ago.

Annie emerged from the shower in a clinging silk robe, her wet hair wrapped in a towel. She felt a sting of annoyance that Jason was still asleep in the bedroom. Where plastic horizontal blinds had once hung, now thick tapestry curtains blocked out the sunlight. Okay, maybe it wasn't possible to know the time of day in this room with the curtains closed, except there were also the giant red numbers that blared from the digital clock on his night table.

"Jason?" she called softly, but he didn't move. "Jay?"

Annie walked over to the window and let in the morning sun. It bounced on their new queen-sized, iron-framed bed. Jason still didn't react. She sat on the bed next to him, worried that this could be Jason being lazy or it could be him being depressed. Sometimes when he didn't work for a few days, it brought him down. She leaned in and planted a soft kiss on his bare shoulder. That's when she noticed a caked water ring on the mahogany night table beside him. She scraped at it with a fingernail as she called to him again, trying to hide the frustration she felt at his being inconsiderate about the furniture again. "Come on, love," she cooed. "Time to get up. Get dressed."

Jason finally stirred from underneath the plush bedding. He pulled her under the covers with him as she laughed. "Come on! No!"

He slid her underneath him with ease, parting her legs with his torso, her robe now open, exposing her body. "Do you know how beautiful you are?" he asked her, his warmth enveloping her.

Annie could feel her need for him rising like heat throughout her body. She looked at the clock. It was after 7:30 already. She had to shut it down. "Stop that. I am not," she said, and she deftly rolled out from under him. She pulled the blankets up over his head. "You're a horn dog. Come on, you've got to get up."

He sat up next to her now, pulling her robe down off her shoulder and planting soft kisses on her skin. "You are the most beautiful woman I have ever known. And I am going to cover your luscious body with kisses now."

Oh, how she loved the feel of his lips, at once soft and rough, a delightful texture that made her skin tingle when he grazed her with them. "Oh Jason..." She was about to lose herself in his passion, her passion. The electricity of them—of what they were together. But there was work to be done. Play later. "Come on, stop now. It's late. I have to get to work. So do you..."

Jason continued to kiss her. "This is my job now, isn't it? I serve only you."

"You have to..."

"And besides, it's slow this week. I called Manny last night and he said he probably can't use me 'til Thursday anyway," he said, and he burrowed his head in her neck.

All at once images popped into her head—the rent bill, due in a few days; the electric bill, already a month overdue.

She had divided up their financial obligations, giving him a handful of bills that were less urgent to pay, but if he didn't pay them, there would be no electricity. No cable TV. They wouldn't die if he didn't work, but she couldn't take it on all on her own.

"That's not good enough."

He continued to ignore her, now laying her down again and tugging away her robe. He climbed on top of her and once again she struggled to get out from under him. "Please stop, okay? If Manny doesn't have work for you, you have to find it somewhere else. We need you to have work. I'm doing well," she said, and in fact she was. In two short years she had managed to advance from entry-level to landing a few of her own big clients at the ad agency where she'd worked since she'd graduated from college. It was a source of joy and discord at once in their marriage, and she sometimes forgot to tread carefully when it came to the subject. "I'm doing well, yes. Very well. But it's not fair, you know? I can't be expected to support us all on my own—" she said and his face flashed dark, just for a second. She'd crossed the line, just for this moment. Then, without missing a beat, his eyes lit up again.

"I'm your husband now. By law, it's my job to keep you satisfied, till death do us part," he said, and began to kiss her neck and tried to enter her.

Annie took a deep breath and she wriggled out from under him. "Well, by the law of this household, we go to work. Both of us." She jumped out of bed. She picked a shirt up off a nearby chair and threw it at him. "Put this on for now," she said, trying to sound playful. "You'll get yours later."

Jason yanked the shirt off the bed where it had landed. "Yeah. When you come home at ten o'clock again?" he snapped, just under his breath. He pulled the shirt over his head.

Annie was annoyed now. "Oh come on. That isn't fair, and you know it. I'm putting in a lot overtime, sure, but I'm doing it for us. For our future. When I get ahead, *we* get ahead."

Jason smiled slyly at her. "Head—yes! That's what you're getting!" he said. Then he leaped off the bed and threw her over his shoulder. Lightly, gently, he laid her down on the bed.

"Jason, come on! Jason really stop now. Jason—" she tried but had to give up. "Do you know how much I love you?"

chapter nine

circa 1943.

"Bless me, Father, for I have sinned. It's been two weeks since my last confession."

"Maggie, my child, what's kept you away so long?" There was a playful lilt in his tone. Something almost accusatory, beyond missing a week between confessions. Something almost teasing. He was flirting with her again.

Maggie gulped. She'd been spending all her free time with Walter, and doing a very good job not thinking about Phillip while she was at it. Phillip should not have been flirting with her like that. He should have been encouraging her to spend more time with Walter, and less time with him. He wasn't available. Why did he behave with her the way he did? What did he think was going to happen?

She didn't address his question. She pressed on. "In that time, I yelled at my father. A lot. I used the Lord's name in vain so many times..."

As she prattled on about all her "sins," he hmmmed and ummmed and encouraged her to keep speaking. He was, as was his job, trying to bring her comfort. But with Phillip, it was anything but comfort. Her association with Phillip, her attraction to him. It was dark. She had to get over it. It burned hot, but truly was a winter without end. The frozen core of Hell in Dante's *Inferno*. A one-way ticket to damnation.

But with Walter... Walter really did bring her comfort. And excitement. And passion. So much passion.

Father Phillip chanted his prayer of absolution, concluding with, "Okay, my child. Please say three Hail Marys and three Our Fathers, and try, if you can, to have more patience with your own father. It's not his fault."

That, she well knew. Her father had been through so much pain in his life. The War he'd fought in before she was born. It had left an indelible scar on him, one which had never healed. One that ultimately drove his wife, her mother, away.

She felt better after talking things through, and she thanked Father Phillip and wished him well. She then moved to a pew in the back of the church to pray her penance. She took out the glass-beaded rosary her mother had given her on her Confirmation Day and began her prayers. But while she prayed, her thoughts drifted to the place where they mostly drifted to these days. When she wasn't at church.

To Walter.

Their first date had been pure magic, though there hadn't been anything fancy or exceptional about it. He'd taken her to a quiet Italian place in the neighborhood. Other men she'd dated before Walter had tried to dazzle her by whisking her away into Manhattan in taxicabs, to fine restaurants, the theater, social clubs. It was all about the flash. But not with Walter. And she got the sense when she was out with him that she could be anywhere with him—that the sparkle that shone had nothing to do with anything but them being together.

"Good evening, Mr. Randalls," the host had said when he greeted them at the entrance.

Walter waved that salutation away. "Antonio, please. It's Walter. Just Walter."

"Very well, sir," the host said, and grabbed a couple of menus off his stand.

Walter shrugged his shoulders at Maggie. She loved his humbleness. How basic and uncomplicated he was. A strong complement to the complicated mess Maggie Ellis could be. He gently placed a hand on her lower back as they followed the host to a quiet table in the back of the restaurant.

"Funny thing about Antonio," Walter said, and tore at the loaf of fresh bread between them, "is that I used to have to call him 'Mr. D'Amico' when I was in school. I was friends with his son, Salvatore. All through grade school and high school, actually."

"Oh?" Maggie said. She looked around the restaurant. "Does he work here too?"

Walter's eyes went dark for a moment and she immediately regretted the question. She already knew the answer. "I'm sorry," she said, her eyes downturned.

"No need to be," Walter said, his breezy tone returned. "It's pretty much par for the course these days, right? A lot of my buddies have enlisted, and a few of them... Well..."

She surprised herself by reaching across the table and grabbing his hand. "Not very ladylike," her mother's voice chided in her head. Her mother was gone, but her influence remained. Why couldn't it be the other way around? When Maggie tried to release his hand, though, he clasped on to hers, and tightly.

"I haven't enlisted yet," he said. The word "yet" hung in the air between them.

Yet...

"I mean, I think I probably will, you know, before they come for me. But Stan needs me right now, so..."

"I get it," she said, wanting to sound supportive, and hoping to God she didn't sound as possessive as she was feeling.

I've only just found you. You can't leave me. You just can't.

The waiter came and took their orders, taking the heat off the conversation, if only temporarily.

"Let's not talk about that now," he offered. "Let's talk about you, okay?"

"Sure," she said, and hesitated. What was she going to be able to tell him about her? About her boring job in the factory? About her obsession with the young priest?

"Tell me about your family," he said.

The worst topic of them all...

"Oh, that's so boring..." she lied.

"All families are boring," he said, and took a bite of bread. "How about you bore me with yours, then I'll bore you with mine?"

"Well..." she began. "Well, my father. My father..."

"Your father, who art in... Heaven?" he teased.

She shook her head. His corny joke relaxed her, but not enough. "No, he's alive. I mean sort of..." She stopped herself. She wasn't ready to share. Not yet. Not with him. "My father was something of an impresario. Do you know what that is?" He shook his head. *Good*, she thought to herself. "Well, how about a showman? Basically, he used to run a Museum of Oddities before the War."

"You mean a freak show?" he asked, looking intrigued. She bit the inside of her mouth to keep from smiling. She had him.

"Sure, some people call it that."

He blushed. "Oh, sorry. Was that insensitive?"

She shook her head. "No, it's fine," she said in a comforting tone. Just then, the waiter came and delivered their entrees. Maggie took a bite of her Chicken Marsala and savored the flavor. So decadent. It had been quite some time since she'd had a meal like this.

"So," he asked, his head titled in anticipation.

"So..." she drew the word out. She was enjoying this... this keeping him on the edge like this.

"So?"

"So my mother was a performer there. The Tattooed Lady, actually."

"No!"

She swallowed in order to keep herself from breaking out laughing. "Uh, yes. Totally," she said, and shoved a hunk of bread into her mouth to keep from losing it. "They fell in love and got married. In fact, the ceremony was officiated by Tiny Tim himself. Ever hear of him?"

He smirked at her. "You're kidding."

She shook her head. "Nope. I was conceived and born at the, what did you call it? The *freak* show?"

At that, a staring contest ensued. For what could easily have been minutes, he probed through her with his beautiful eyes and she nearly choked to death on all the laughter that was threatening to force its way up through her. Finally, she cracked and a giggle escaped.

"Oh my God! I can't believe you! I mean... I believed you!"

She burst out laughing then and he joined her. "My mother, the Tattooed Lady?" she chortled. "I can't believe you bought that."

When the laughter quieted, he set his eyes on her again—this time with a deep sincerity. "So? Your father?" he asked gently.

She took a deep breath. She didn't want to tell him anything, but there was something about his eyes when he looked at her, some invisible sense between them that no matter what she did or said, everything was going to be okay.

"He hasn't been the same since…" she started to speak, and found it hard to continue. But she found it harder still to resist his sincerity. Her desire to open up to him took over, and it was amazing. As soon as she started talking, the words just came. She wasn't choked by fear or emotion or anything. Everything she always held inside flowed freely from her. Never before had Maggie connected with another human being like she did with Walter, and it seemed to calm the intensity of the attraction. It didn't diminish it; it simply transformed it into something more than random currents in the air.

After dinner they walked arm-in-arm down the sidewalk. It didn't bother Maggie to share secrets with him she'd only really shared with Phillip. But with Phillip, the reasons were different. With Phillip, with *Father* Phillip, it was because her own father had spurred her to think and do terrible things that she needed to confess.

With Walter, it was freeing. There was no judgment. There was no penance required. All of the pain she had kept inside felt somehow released. The wall she had erected to protect herself from the shame of her family and its secrets seemed to disintegrate in his presence.

Out of nowhere, Walter stopped and grabbed Maggie's arm. "There!" He beamed, pointing.

Maggie looked up just as a shooting star streaked across the sky. She watched with pure delight, wondering if there was any way this man, this night, could become more magical. When he leaned in and kissed her, softly, adoringly, he took her breath away.

Walter stroked Maggie's cheek with the back of his fingers. "Do you even know how beautiful you are?" he asked her.

She closed her eyes, trying to impress every nuance of this moment into her memory, as she couldn't imagine there could ever be a more perfect moment.

Except since that night there had been so many incredibly perfect moments. Her life had become a living dream. Her job had become less drab. Her anxiety over the state of the world at war seemed to melt away. Walter had become her salvation.

He was the man who had changed her *everything*.

chapter ten

---

the present.

Hugh looked down at his watch. He had arrived super early and had managed to secure a seat at the bar in The Campbell Apartment, a swanky bar located inside Grand Central Terminal. He'd ordered a club soda. He didn't want Annie to think he was a drunk, especially considering all the wine they had consumed together the other night. So there he sat and waited, in a sea of custom-made suits, feeling quite underdressed in his black jeans and an old blazer that used to belong to his dad.

He hadn't texted with Annie, but apparently either he or she had tapped the date and time, 6pm, and location of this rendezvous into the calendar app on his phone, along with her name.

Minutes passed as he sat wondering how he actually got here; a type of bar he never went to, to have a drink with a pretty girl he had somehow managed to meet twice in one day. But by the time six-thirty came, he found himself hoping he wasn't the victim of a prank. His chest started to tighten now and he brushed his hand against his jacket pocket to make sure his inhaler was there. Why would a woman like that waste her time going out with a guy like him? She was sophisticated.

Professional. It certainly wasn't the first time he'd fallen into a trap like this…

He sipped at his club soda and worked to relax his breathing as his thoughts slipped to Alicia. She would be about Annie's age now? No. She was a few years older than Annie, for sure. Annie just carried older. Something about her. Something in her life. She just felt older.

The truth be told, he hardly thought about Alicia anymore these days, although the "burn" she'd given him still hurt when a passing thought or memory, or even a recent event, brushed against it. Like meeting a new woman. Was Annie going to be another one like her? The fact that she was now about a half hour late seemed to indicate that maybe she was.

He was starting to feel embarrassed and stupid and ready to leave just as Annie bounded through the front entrance. He watched her scan the room, then make a beeline for him. Okay, maybe not a prank. But what then? What could she possibly want from him?

"Hello! Hello!" she bellowed and she planted an air kiss on each of his cheeks, then unapologetically usurped the barstool directly to Hugh's left.

"I'm so glad you made it—"

"Oh my God, I have had one fuck of a day, you have no idea," she interrupted. "Do you know what a fucking imbecile my boss is? *Do* you?"

Was he expected to answer her? Hugh cocked his head.

"No, of course not. How could *you* possibly know?!"

Wait? She didn't think he was stupid, did she? He shifted uncomfortably on his bar stool. "Oh well I'm glad you made it. I wasn't sure—"

"Ugh! I can't even speak, I'm so mad! That fucking mother fucker!"

Hugh coughed club soda all over his hand and the bar. Annie absently handed him a clump of napkins and kept talking. "Idiot. Him—not you. But you knew that already."

Hugh tried to reply, then Annie slammed a clenched fist down on the bar. "Drinks here!" she shouted at the bartender.

"What can I get you?"

"Grey Goose martini, straight up. Extra olives." She turned to Hugh. "I haven't eaten all day," she said, as if to explain. "What're you having?"

Hugh felt a little thrown. Her energy felt manic and way too charged for him. "Me?" he asked, somewhat confused. "Uh, the same for me. I'll have the same."

"Well, come on, now, buddy. Get with it. Off you go!" she barked at the bartender, who left to fix the drinks.

Hugh felt uneasy. The sweet, silly storyteller from the party the other night was apparently now gone and the raving bitch from the cemetery was back, and he definitely didn't want to spend the evening with her. "Will you excuse me a minute?" he asked.

"What? Okay. Whatever," she said.

Hugh got up and headed to the bathroom, where he called Charlotte from his cell phone and told her he'd call her by ten if he needed her to bail him out. When he returned, Annie's mood had shifted again.

"Well, hello," she seemed to purr. "Welcome back. Please sit down. Let's drink, shall we?" She flashed Hugh that crooked smile that had started to grow on him. "Great shirt!"

He couldn't remember what he was wearing for a second. He squinted down to read "The Truth Is Out There" on the black *X Files* T-shirt he wore under the blazer.

"Great show. Really great show!" she said, sounding like she was trying to convince herself more than him. "Tell me, please, how was your day?"

He stumbled through a report while she nodded and sipped from her glass.

"Anyway, never been here before," he said, as he finished. "Nice place."

She nodded. "It used to be a real apartment, you know. Some guy named Campbell lived here."

"Right." He laughed. He took a sip of his martini and nearly spit it out as it choked his throat.

"Whoa, there, little fella!" Annie chuckled. "You'd better stick to the soft stuff for now. Hey, bartender? A beer for my little friend here?" she asked, and then placed her hand on Hugh's and whispered, "Baby steps."

"So some guy named Campbell lived *here?*" he asked when the choking finally subsided.

"You bet! Railroad magnate. And then during the Great Depression, he lost all his money and went berserk and killed his family. Right in this room!"

Hugh gasped. "No!"

Annie nodded and continued. "Oh yes," she said. "The Port Authority somehow ended up owning his apartment. And they decided what cooler haunt for a hotspot than a crime scene. Get it? *Haunt?*" Annie raised and lowered her eyebrows repeatedly, in the manner of a Vaudeville comic. "Get it?"

"Oh, man. I can't believe it. You're kidding again, aren't you?"

"Well, yes. About the murder thing. But the other part is true. Google it if you don't believe me."

"You sure do like to tell stories," he said, feeling at once duped and charmed. Alicia never told stories, he'd give Annie that.

"Perhaps," she said, taking a sip of her drink. "But my own life is so boring. You're better off that I do."

Hugh scratched his chin. "Why do I find that hard to believe?"

She shook her head and motioned to his T-shirt. "So what you're saying is that you don't really like *The X-Files*. That you're just nosy."

"I think both can be true."

Annie took a breath before she spoke again. "Okay. Here's the short version: I grew up an only child on Long Island. My parents... well, my mother... was insanely religious. *Insanely*! And my dad..." she said, then finished her drink, motioning to the bartender to bring her another. "My dad died a few years ago. And I don't talk to my mother anymore."

"I'm so sorry. Is that because—"

She waved him off. "It's okay. My dad and I really didn't have a relationship anyway. He wasn't a bad guy. He was just, well, simple. Apparently he'd sustained a head injury in Vietnam. Something that should have killed him, but didn't. I guess he was sort of, I don't know, braindead? But not dead. Just not, well, with it. It was like living with a child instead of a parent. Sometimes it was sweet, sometimes it was exhausting. Anyway, whatever he was lacking in being firm and strict, my mother more than made up for."

"Is that why you don't speak to her?"

She exhaled. "Let's just say she didn't agree with my divorce and stuff and what with my dad going like that and..." Annie stared off into the distance a moment. She looked back at Hugh. "My mother's all 'fire and brimstone.' That kind of Catholic. Honestly, I just can't deal."

"That's so sad," he said, and impulsively reached for her hand.

She snatched hers away. Why had he tried to touch her like that? When was he ever going to learn?

"Not that sad. I can think of a lot worse. Like how they would still be messing me up if they were still involved in my life."

Annie then knocked back Hugh's martini and switched to wine. Hugh ordered another drink. He found himself drinking more than he ever had in his life to try to keep up with her.

"You know, I think my parents messed me up," he said, surprised his words came out as clearly as they had. "I mean, don't get me wrong. They were happily married. Maybe too happily. I sometimes blame them for me screwing up all my relationships—kind of like 'how are you going to aspire to *that?*' You know? Crazy-making."

"Parents will do that to you," said Annie.

Hugh nodded and they sat in contemplative silence once again. "Charlotte says I shouldn't be looking to get involved with anyone right now," he blurted.

She pursed her lips. "I think Charlotte is right," she said, almost too quickly.

But that's not what he wanted. He did want to be with her in that way. She intrigued him. Affected him. He was so attracted to her. Why did the words always come out in the wrong order when he tried to talk to women about what he wanted? "Oh, but I was going to say... but..."

"But...?"

Then he lost his courage. "Nothing, nothing. I mean I guess she's right, but..." he began, trying not to look at her with the longing he was starting to feel for her. "But..."

Annie shook her head. "I don't know you that well, but from what I know about you, I mean, I guess what I learned about you and that girl Sheila at the party..."

"Wait? What did you learn?"

She waved his question away and kept talking. "And for sure from what I know about me, I don't think either of us is in any position to get involved in that way right now," she said. "It's too bad because you are kind of cute. But hey," she said, and took a drink, "I like you, you like me. No reason we can't be friends, right?"

Annie raised her glass and Hugh clinked it with his.

"Right," he said, and they both fell back into a contemplative silence.

Out of nowhere, she started laughing. "*Say Anything*, huh?"

His breathing started to strain again. "How did you know about that?"

"When you were talking to your roommate—the not-a-*girl*-girl?—those other people I was standing with were talking about you and that Sheila girl, who was apparently a *girl*-girl, from how they described your fixation on her." She delivered this information in such a disarming manner, not accusing, not ridiculing, just sort of matter-of-factly. It relaxed him.

"I told them I thought it was kind of romantic and sweet of you, which seemed to shock them silent. So I was actually going to go on the attack before you grabbed my hand and pulled me away like you did. Anyhoo..." she said, and sipped her drink. She started laughing again.

He could have been horrified and probably should have been. He didn't see anything funny about the lengths he'd gone through to try to win Sheila back, or that people were discussing it like that. He could feel his chest begin to tighten again. But when Annie started to sing the lyrics to "In Your Eyes" under her breath, he couldn't help but see just how ridiculous the whole thing had been. He surprised himself by laughing along with her.

Soon they were both in full-chortle mode, each taking turns mocking Hugh and his silly stunt.

"Were you wearing anything under the trench coat?" she asked, choking back a laugh.

"Uh, yeah. My best parachute pants," he said, nearly stammering to get the words out before the giggles consumed him again.

"Well at least those would have helped aid a soft landing had she tried to push you off the fire escape…?"

Eventually they laughed themselves quiet and the silence started to unnerve Hugh. "So… no boyfriend then?"

Annie paused before shaking her head. "I've dated since Jason, which I'll tell you because you're so nosy. But things… I don't know. I can't really explain it… They just have a way of going awry all the time."

"In what way?"

"I don't know. I guess things sort of, well, happen."

"Like…?"

Annie shook her head. "Maybe another time," she said. "In any case, the exes always make crazy replacement choices. Ridiculous actually."

"What does that mean?" he asked. He took a swig of his beer and took a chance leaning in so he could hear her over the din in the bar. He was happy when she didn't shirk away. In fact, she took the cue and leaned in closer to him.

"Well, like the last guy I dated, this guy named Jerry. He left me for an elephant."

Hugh choked again. "I'm sorry? A what?"

Annie handed him a napkin. "You're not that good at drinking," she joked, and he shook his head, trying to breathe as she downed the rest of her own drink. "Anyway, as I was saying, Jerry left me for an elephant. A woman with tree trunks for legs and," she looked at him over her eyebrows, "a highly menacing ass."

Hugh had gotten to a point in his stupor that he doubted that he even spoke or understood English anymore, but he wanted to try and stay with her. "Can an ass be menacing?" he asked, and he could tell by the look on her face that his stupid eyebrow had gone and cocked itself again.

Her expression was dead-serious, and she gulped before she responded. "It can when it's as wide as the day is long..." she said, and they both erupted into laughter.

The hours seemed to fly by like minutes. Hugh didn't know if it was the alcohol or Annie that put him at ease, but he really felt like he could talk to her. Like he could share with her.

"I was married once, you know? Al-EE-shah!" He felt immediately embarrassed. He had in no way intended to bring up Alicia this night or any night, and now the memory of his horrible ex had taken it upon itself to pour right out of his mouth, and with a convoluted slurring, no less.

"Um, God bless you?"

"Ha. No, that was her name. Alicia," he said, and took a drink. *In for a penny, in for a pound*, as his dad would have said. "She was a real bitch."

"I'm shocked!" said Annie, clearly feigning being scandalized.

90

"What, because I said *bitch*?"

"Because I don't see you as the having-been married type. I mean, married, maybe. But divorced? Uh-uh."

"Yeah, well... People get married a lot younger back home than here. Anyway, she was older and she left after a few weeks for some money guy. And I don't mean that in the *Swingers* way." Hugh motioned for another round of drinks.

Annie smiled. "Great movie." she said and she sipped. Then she nodded. "Yep. More her type."

"Why are women like this?" he wondered aloud. "I mean, seriously."

Annie seemed to consider his words before she spoke again. "Was she involved with someone before you?"

"Sure."

"Serious?"

"Seemed that way."

"Well, maybe she was just using you as a safe harbor—you know, to get her 'legs' back?" She looked away. "I'm sorry. Women do that sometimes. I imagine men do it too. It's not nice, but it happens."

"Is that what happened with you?"

"Something like that," she said, sipping again. Pausing. "No. No not really."

Hugh waited for more information, but it didn't seem she was giving any more away.

"Anyway, after that, it's pretty much the same as you. Lots of short-term, semi-serious flings, I guess. Charlotte calls me a 'serial monogamist'—whatever that means. After Alicia, I just had a lot of quick failed relationships that ended badly."

"Well, that's kind of what it means."

"Kind of like you? What happens with you?"

She stared off into space and was quiet for a few moments before she answered. "No. That's not like me."

Why did everything she say confuse him? "I guess in hindsight the relationships didn't really make a lot of sense."

"Just broken people trying to force all their jagged edges together?"

Hugh smiled. "Yeah. Now that you put it that way."

"Well, we can only move forward from here, right? Forward is the only way there is to go."

"Good point," he said, and sipped his beer.

"Good. Maybe you should go print it on a T-shirt," she said with a snort and they both broke out laughing again.

When they quieted down, Hugh said, "You know, it's weird. I really feel like I can talk to you."

Annie giggled. "God only knows why!"

"Yeah, because you're a New York mega bitch!" he joked. Now she glared at him.

"I'm sorry. I don't know why I said that. Charlotte always says things like that. She doesn't really trust New York women. I mean, not for me at least."

"I see…"

"But she doesn't think for me."

"No. Of course she doesn't."

He smiled at her, which seemed to warm her, and now she smiled back.

"I guess because of the 'friends' thing," he said. "No pressure to impress, right?"

"It's nice, isn't it?"

"It kind of is," he agreed, and they clinked glasses again.

"So, uh, can I ask you…" Hugh started.

"Ask me what?" she answered.

"About your marriage? What happened with him?"

"I... I don't know if I'm ready to share about that yet," she replied, and gulped down her wine. "He's dead—as you probably figured out. But we were divorced already, which I'm not sure if I told you or not. I don't know... I'm getting a little confused now..." She stopped to drain her glass. She looked to him, smiling sadly. "Let's just say he was also much older and wasn't always that nice to me. Let's leave it at that?"

"It's cool. Some other time then."

"Maybe," she said, and her face went dark. He couldn't help but get the sense that something horrible and dark had gone down in that relationship, and he fought himself to press her further, even though he felt almost desperate to know what had made her go so dark so quickly like that.

Before he had a chance to learn more about what had transpired with the pretty small girl and the monster husband, the bartender brought over the bill and ended the moment. Hugh reached over to pick it up. Annie snatched it out of his hand and said, with a cackle, "For the love of God, no! Let that prick boss of mine pick up the tab."

Annie paid the bill and they finished their drinks. They got up and headed for the exit. "You need to use the bathroom?" she asked him.

He did, and badly. "Actually..." he began, but before he could answer, Annie already sprinted for the bar's only tiny bathroom. "Hey!" he called, and darted after her.

Annie was panting by the time they reached the bathroom. "Oh, I'm sorry. Are you really that desperate?" she asked.

"Oh yes."

"Okay, then you first," she said. But as he moved toward the bathroom door, she hip checked him and bolted in front of him, blowing him a kiss before slamming the door in his face.

When they left the bar, neither seemed that interested in going home, so they walked for a while. When they came across an all-night Associated supermarket, Annie lit up.

"Come on." She pulled at him. "I want to show you something!"

Hugh peered through the window of the grocery store and looked back at her. "What—you mean in *there?*"

"Come on!" What could she possibly have to show him in the grocery store after cocktails? He couldn't help but be intrigued, though he thought it best not to show that—in case he fell victim to another one of her jokes, so he played bored and annoyed as best he could. He doubted he was pulling it off very well. Annie tugged him by the sleeve and dragged him inside.

"Here we go! Ready?"

"Uh... Yes?"

They walked down an aisle. He couldn't imagine what she was so hopped up about.

"Okay, now." She beamed. "Listen. Do you hear that?"

Hugh was confused. "All I hear is Muzak."

"Isn't it wonderful?!"

Was she trying to play some kind of joke on him? Embarrass him by seeing if he'd buy into it? She didn't waver. Instead, she started singing along to "Magic" by Olivia Newton John, at the top of her lungs. She smiled at him and squeezed him into her breasts.

If he wasn't there, he would never have believed it. He remembered this song vaguely from his mother's Olivia Newton-John phase when he was a kid, but surely no self-respecting person actually knew the *words* to that song? And *all* of the words at that. Hugh didn't know what was more ridiculous: the music? The performance? She was definitely drunk. Not in a way that embarrassed him, though. In a way that he was intrigued. What was coming next?

"I do *so* love this stuff. If we're going to be friends, you should know my secrets."

Hugh stared back at her. "This is a dark one."

"Doesn't everyone have dark ones?"

"Not like this..."

Annie ignored him. "Sometimes when I need to clear my head, I just come in here—well, not here, specifically, but you know what I mean—I pretend to be shopping for food and just let it wash all over me."

"Okay..."

Annie grabbed a shopping cart and waved him on. He felt drunk enough to follow her anywhere.

"You think I'm crazy, I know. But there's poetry in this stuff! So soothing."

Hugh looked away. He didn't want her to see that he was smiling. "Uh, sure. Whatever you say."

"I'm serious! I also do always make it a point to come into these places alone," she said, then grabbed him by the hand and looked him dead in the eyes. "But I don't mind being here with you," she said.

He smiled, charmed by her. There was no reason to pretend otherwise. "I'm glad we're friends," he said.

"Oh sure you are!" she snapped back and began to ride the cart like a scooter.

The song changed again and thankfully this time it was one he recognized. "Red Rain" by Peter Gabriel. A less humiliating Peter Gabriel song. Hugh found himself enjoying himself. In spite of himself. Annie seemed to be enjoying the song, too. "Yeah, sometimes a crap one sneaks into the mix. I usually don't complain. I just suffer it."

"Are you kidding me? This is actually a *good* song!"

"Oh well, if you say so..." she said.

He impulsively grabbed her by the shoulders and looked her right into the eyes, and spoke the lyrics to her. *"I come to you, defenses down...."*

"...With the trust of a child..." she said back to him.

Electricity surged between them. He could feel it so intently. He felt an undeniable urge to kiss her, but just as he leaned in, she pulled away, letting out a small cough. He was embarrassed now, and disappointed. How could that moment only have existed for him? Maybe Charlotte was right. Maybe he was nuts.

"Speaking of menacing asses, what's with that Charlotte girl anyway?" It was as if she'd read his mind. Sort of.

"Oh, come on. That's not nice. Besides," he said, and smiled mischievously. "Where I'm from, we call that 'corn-fed.'"

"Here we call it—"

"Okay, that's enough." He laughed. "Look, she really is a nice girl."

"If you say so," she replied. He just laughed and shook his head. "So... You ever... You know... Tap that?"

"Cripes! I would never go there!"

"Aha. Too menacing." Annie began scooting again.

"No, it's not that," he said, shaking his head. "Charlotte's always been there for me. When my parents died. Even before that, when I was just a geek in high school. She's like, you know, like a sister to me."

"Ah. I see," she said. She stopped the cart and turned to face him now. "Does she know that?"

Before Hugh could answer, Annie rolled away again, now keeping her eyes on him. Not watching where she was rolling,

Annie crashed into a Rice-a-Roni display arranged in a stack and knocked it over.

"Hey, what the hell..." came a man's voice from the next aisle.

"Run!" said Annie, and Hugh raced after her, past the wrecked display, and out the front door. By the time they exited, they were out of breath and laughing hysterically— until they nearly slammed right into Charlotte and a group of her friends.

"Where have you been?" Charlotte demanded.

"Wow. Hello," said Annie, as though stunned, and looking at Hugh to get his attention.

"I have been looking for you since you called me hours ago," said Charlotte.

Now Annie and Charlotte stared each other down. Hugh shifted from one foot to the next, nervously looking back and forth between Charlotte and Annie. He was mortified.

"I'm sorry, Annie. I guess I owe you an explanation. You see, when I first met up with you... I didn't... I..."

"I get it. You called her. From the bar," Annie said. The disappointment in her voice crushed him.

"Yes, as a matter of fact he did," Charlotte snapped. "Said you were as mean as you were the day he first met you and he was scared of how much worse the night was going to get. He called me to rescue him," she explained, almost too smug.

Embarrassed, Hugh looked down and Annie looked away from them all. "Hey. That's okay," she said. "I mean, I guess I was pretty bad. I deserved that. Well, I have to go anyway. Big meeting tomorrow. Goodnight," she said, and stepped on her tiptoes to kiss Hugh on the cheek.

Hugh watched as she walked away, feeling more longing inside than he cared to admit. He was so lost in her leaving, in fact, he did not hear Charlotte whisper under her breath: "Goodnight, angry bitch."

chapter eleven

---

the present.

Annie met Rebecca for Japanese at a restaurant in her neighborhood the next night. She arrived first and ordered a sake martini. Smooth, cold, and delicious, it went down much more quickly than a regular martini, and took the edge off the hangover caused by all the drinking she'd done the night before. The drinking she'd done with Hugh at the Campbell Apartment and the bottle of wine she'd polished off watching *Joe Versus the Volcano* for what could have been the tenth or eleventh time. Tom Hanks and Meg Ryan—that was the kind of magic she was looking for. Not really the stuff of fairytales but a breezy, bantering connection between oddballs.

The kind of magic she'd never been able to find. She wondered if Hugh knew this movie. If he liked it as much as she did. He seemed to like the obscure things she did. He seemed to look at the world the way she did. Another bantering oddball... A fit when nothing else ever quite fit...

Don't be ridiculous. She dismissed the thought and downed the rest of her drink. *You are not getting involved with that person. He is way too sweet for you. You will eat him alive.*

By the time Rebecca rushed in, she was already on her second cocktail. "Sorry I'm late," Rebecca said, and slid into the chair at the opposite side of the table. Her hair was in a ponytail and the only makeup she wore was mascara on one eye. Annie made another check on her imaginary list of why it was better not to have children. "What's that?" she asked, nodding to Annie's half-empty glass.

"Sake martini. You want me to order you one—"

"Oh no, no. 'Martini' and 'mother' don't mix," Rebecca said, probably not meaning to sound smug, but sounding that way all the same. "I'll just have a green tea."

"You missed a good party the other night," Annie said, not really believing at all that Saturday's party had been so great. Except that she'd met quirky, funny Hugh. Who turned out to be a big pussy anyway, so whatever. Still, she didn't feel like letting Rebecca off the hook.

"Yeah, couldn't get a sitter," Rebecca said with a weak smile.

"So why not just come by yourself?"

"Oh no, I couldn't do that to Mike. Leave him alone on a Saturday night?"

Annie tensed. Wasn't that what she had done to Annie? She let it go. "Well, it's just as well you didn't make it," Annie said, now thinking of Hugh and the adorable way he looked at her when he listened to her. That night and last night. So attentive. So interested. Maybe not a pussy after all. Maybe a puppy? And the way he raised his eyebrow when he called her on her crap… in the cemetery and then again at the party. It sent a jolt through her when he looked at her that way. She blushed. "I kind of met someone."

"Oh?"

She couldn't decipher if Rebecca's tone was that of interest or judgment so she decided to tread cautiously. "Well, yes and no. I mean, we met at the party. It's so weird, but before the party. At..."

Annie quickly stopped herself. She couldn't believe she'd almost told Rebecca *again* that she'd been to the cemetery to visit Jason. She had to get a grip. She took a long sip of her drink. "Forget it. Anyway, we spent the night——"

"Oh, Annie." Rebecca gasped. "No. Please tell me you didn't..."

"If you would let me finish talking. We spent the night *talking*. And then we went out. Last night. And talked. Again."

"Huh. Okay. Well, what's he like?"

Annie felt herself warming on the inside, and she knew it was more than the booze at work. When she thought about Hugh, she felt happy. Not insecure or desperate or tentative as she had with other men since Jason. She felt, well, good.

"He's very nice," she said. "And cute, in a dorky kind of way. He likes taking pictures and apparently has this weird thing about T-shirts." She trailed off, thinking about how funny his shirts always were. Subversive and sweet. She'd never known this type of guy before. He intrigued her. "But I think we decided to be just friends, you know?"

"Friends?" Rebecca said after a short pause. "Well I guess that's an improvement."

"What's that supposed to mean?" Annie asked, even though she already knew the answer.

Rebecca shot her another smug glance. "I think you know." Annie rolled her eyes, and Rebecca ignored her and picked up her menu. "You order yet?" She didn't look up for an answer.

"And then his roommate showed up," Annie prattled on, "and she kind of shit all over the night."

Rebecca raised her eyebrows. "He has a girl roommate?"

101

Not a *girl*-girl. She thought about how Hugh had squirmed at the description he had tried to make and she laughed to herself.

"So what?" Annie looked away from Rebecca and spotted an older couple at the sushi bar. In their late fifties or so. The woman said something and the man gently tapped the tip of her nose with his index finger. It was such a sweet gesture. She wondered how long they'd been together that the man still regarded his partner with such affection. She wondered if Jason would still have treated her with that kind of affection if they had made it. If she hadn't ruined it, alienating him like she had...

"Hello? Earth to Annie?"

"Oh sorry. What were you saying?"

Rebecca stared blankly at her. "You were telling me that you were having this great time with the dorky T-shirt boy and that his roommate just showed up."

"Right...?"

"And I asked you if you thought it was a coincidence?"

"Well, no," Annie said, now starting to feel embarrassed; also a little angry. Forget about the puppy. Now he was a pussy again. "No, not a coincidence at all. He called her."

"Ah," sang Rebecca, and she went back to her menu.

"What's that supposed to mean?"

"Oh nothing. Whatever. I mean, what do you care? If you just want to be friends with the guy..."

"Yeah. But some friend if he doesn't even want to hang out with me—without that horrible girl."

"You don't even know her," Rebecca said, just as the waitress came by to take their order.

"The tri-color sashimi. Please," Annie said, and pushed her menu to the center of the table.

Rebecca read from hers. "I'll have the teriyaki salmon," she said, and placed her menu on top of Annie's.

"No sushi tonight…" Annie said.

"Uh, no," Rebecca said, her eyes downcast.

"And no cocktail?"

Rebecca let out a long sigh. "We're trying again, okay? I didn't want to say anything yet because it's so early. But yes, we're going for number four."

"Jesus," Annie said. Again, she didn't really have issues with children and people having children. Though every time Rebecca was pregnant, it made her think about the time she'd been pregnant. And how horribly that had turned out…

"Let's not talk about it now," Rebecca said, and Annie was relieved. Not even Rebecca had known about her pregnancy by Jason and she wanted to keep it that way. "Let's talk about the roomie."

"Oh her," Annie said, an intended scoff in her voice. "Yeah, I hate her."

"Hate her? You don't even know her," Rebecca said, pouring her tea from a small pot into her cup.

"I don't have to know her," Annie said. "I know her type. Classic liquid."

"Huh?"

"You know. Liquid. Not a solid. Will assume the shape of any vessel…"

Rebecca held her forehead in her palm. "You and your vessel issues."

"This is different. This girl has no form of her own, you know? No shape. She just pours herself into whomever she wants to connect with. No real substance. No soul."

"This about a girl you met once."

103

"I could spot it from a mile away. And I've met her twice. Remember—also the other night at Phyllis's, which had you gone to that party, you would also know."

"And had I gone to the party, you wouldn't have spent so much time with the guy, what's-his-name. See? Everything for a reason." Rebecca placed her napkin on her lap and opened her chopsticks. "What's his name anyway?"

"Hugh." The sound of his name made her heart flutter and it confused her temporarily, until Rebecca reacted.

Rebecca laughed. "For real?"

"Why? What's wrong with his name?"

"Nothing. Sorry. He just sounds, I don't know... gay?"

"He's not gay! He totally hit on me."

"Oh he did, did he?"

"Yes, actually. He even tried to kiss me. In the grocery store." Annie's heart raced at the thought of that moment. Of Peter Gabriel playing in the background. Of trying so hard to play it cool when all she'd wanted was to feel his lips brush against hers. But it could not be. It was not going to be.

Rebecca slapped her forehead with her hand. "You took him to the grocery store? On a date?"

"I told you. It wasn't a *date*-date. It was just friends. Hanging out. Laughing."

"And almost kissing."

"We didn't kiss."

"Okay, whatever you say," Rebecca said as the server arrived with their entrees. They each took a bite of their food before Rebecca spoke again. "So if you're just friends, does it really matter that this girl is in the picture?"

Annie believed that it did. "I'm worried this girl is going to be in the way."

"Okay, but again, in the way of what? If you just want to be friends—"

Rebecca's blunt pragmatism was annoying her now. "I *do* just want to be friends." She started to tense up. "I can't deal with another failed relationship right now, and he just seems like such a nice guy. Yes, I like him. But I don't want to destroy him, like I do. You know…"

Rebecca shook her head. "You don't destroy them."

"I destroyed Jerry."

"Jerry had all the complexity of a rock. He couldn't understand you. That's not destroying a person. That's just, well, kicking a rock."

"Did you ever see what he landed up with after me? Massive Marlene? I broke him."

"Rocks don't break. I think you're reading too much into what happened there. As you sometimes do…"

"Look, things end badly when I get involved with men, and you know it. If I don't start anything with him, it can't end badly. You see?"

Annie was proud of her conclusion, though Rebecca seemed less impressed by it. "Well, why don't you just talk to him?"

"I guess I could do that," Annie said. If they were friends, she could trust him, couldn't she? She could tell him some of her secrets. She'd never tell him all of her secrets, but maybe just a couple of things? She lifted a piece of salmon sashimi into her soy sauce then placed the entire delicious slab of heaven into her mouth.

"Of course you can do that," Rebecca said, punctuating her sentence by waving her fork in the air. Because that's what friends do. They talk. Like us."

Annie smiled. "Like us."

They silently savored their food a few moments before Rebecca spoke again. "Speaking of talking, I have something for you. From your mother..." Rebecca reached into her purse and pulled out a long black velvet jewelry box, which she then pushed toward Annie.

Annie knew that box. That box had been in the family for generations. And she wanted nothing to do with what was inside that box, or the person who had foisted it on her. She pushed it back.

"No thanks."

Rebecca, more insistently now, pushed it back. "You're going to have to talk to her sometime."

That annoyed her. "Really? And why is that?"

"Because she's your mother. Annie, she's so worried about you. Also, I, uh... I think there's something she wants to tell you. Something sort of—"

"She's a sanctimonious monster. I have nothing to say to her and nothing to hear from her," Annie's stomach started to turn. Maybe it was the alcohol and raw fish on her hungover-queasy stomach, but more likely it was the stress that her mother, even the idea of her mother and everything she stood for, placed in her. And she felt bitter and betrayed that Rebecca always seem to side with Bridget, despite everything that had gone down in the Jason situation. From the wedding and into the marriage. To the end of the marriage. The disastrous and terrifying end of the marriage...

Rebecca squeezed her eyes shut and took in a long breath. "Okay, suit yourself," she said. "Just take the box."

Annie rolled her eyes. "Fine." She took the box and quickly slipped it into her purse. A Pandora's Box that held all the reasons for the dark secrets in her family. A reminder of everything she'd tried so hard to hide from all of these years, now thrust into her life like a knife in her heart.

chapter twelve

---

the present.

Hugh felt giddy about his night with Annie. He didn't want to be so happy about it, but how could he help himself? Sure, he had been horrified by her at first, but he was then charmed. She was so pretty, yes, but she was also so easy to talk to. She had made him laugh about things he never thought were funny before—about things he'd previously taken too seriously. It was like she'd lifted his shame layer and tossed it aside. Saw right past the stupid things he sometimes did and said, and made him comfortable to just be himself. He rationalized this was because they'd decided to be just friends, as they'd agreed to be, but he couldn't help but wonder if he'd have the same sense of calm in his excitement if they had decided to be more.

Charlotte, on the other hand, seemed quite horrified by Annie. "Oh Hugh… Hugh, Hugh, Hugh," she muttered his name a few times under her breath after he'd excitedly given her some highlights of the evening. Not even the scary parts—the funny parts. Still, she wasn't having any of it.

"What?" he asked, feeling sort of irritated.

She shook her head. "Don't you get it? What she is?"

"No. What is she?"

"Wow. You really don't see it, do you? No wonder this always happens to you." She clicked a few tsks apparently waiting for him to speak, but he had no words for her. "Well, I'll tell you then. I think that's what we do, going forward. To spare you from getting hurt all the time, especially as you've apparently decided to ignore my advice to be alone for a while—while you worked all this out on your own."

He sighed. "Just tell me."

"Well…" she stalled, and he impatiently waved her on with his hand. "Well, this Annie? She's kind of a barracuda."

A barracuda? This confused him. She seemed to have a temper, yes. But he didn't get a sense of "predator" from her. More like a creature that had been preyed upon, or so it seemed to him. He wanted to know more. There was definitely a defensiveness about Annie. A defensiveness about something broken. He wasn't quite sure what, but there was a vulnerability there. A vulnerability he felt compelled to protect.

"A barracuda? You don't even know her. I mean—"

"Hugh, do I have to explain everything to you? This is the kind of woman who just goes after what she wants. And when she gets bored, she leaves it and moves to the next challenge. Just like Alicia. She's just going to be using you to get over something. Just like Alicia."

That was sort of what Annie had said, too, wasn't it?

"Don't you ever learn? She doesn't give a fig's fart about anyone but herself."

"A what?" Hugh didn't quite know what a "fig's fart" was, but it was clear Charlotte didn't think highly of Annie.

"Forget it. Just stay away from her," she warned.

He tried to defend Annie, but Charlotte wasn't finished yet. "Manic pixie dream girl."

"Huh?"

She rolled her eyes. "You really don't know anything. It's an archetype. In films. The cute, crazy girl that drags the nice guy kicking and screaming into love with her?"

He shook his head.

"Okay, how about self-absorbed angry bitch? Can you grasp that?"

Annie wasn't a bitch. Charlotte was wrong about that. He was sure of it. Angry, yes. But she was protecting something. Annie hadn't told him any of the details of what had happened with that guy Jason Scott. And she did have a pretty good sense of what Alicia had done to him—using him to get her legs back. But... No. Impossible. She wouldn't bother explaining that to him—how he'd been used—if her intention was to use him that way. It didn't add up.

"All I'm telling you, as your friend, is that I think you'd be doing yourself a huge favor if you backed off from her. Maybe just for now. Just so you can get some perspective is all." She placed her hand on his shoulder. "I don't want to see you hurt again, and that's all I can see coming from this," she sighed. "Okay—now I've said too much."

How was Annie going to hurt him? "But we're just friends."

At that, Charlotte hurried off into her bedroom. Hugh followed her and when he got to the door, she slammed it in his face. He sat there for a minute or so, and then got annoyed with himself for standing there like an idiot and he headed back to his own room. Harold and Maude swirled through his legs as he walked, and he shut the door behind them.

When he sat down on his bed, both cats jumped up to join him, rubbing themselves against his face. The affection became too much as he struggled to breathe. "Dammit, you guys," he wheezed, as he leaned over and pulled his inhaler from his night table drawer. "I don't know how to get you away from my face." Both cats rubbed up against his face again in response and he started wheezing again.

Once he got his breath back, he opened his door and kicked out the cats. Harold went willingly, but Maude paused and stared back at him from the bed for a while as he tried to shoo her out. She took a long yawn and satisfying stretch, digging her claws into his new white duvet, and she hopped off the bed.

Hugh wasn't allergic to the cats. Sometimes their hair got to be too much for him, but even he knew that what was really giving him trouble breathing was the stress of the conflict with Charlotte. He hated being in a fight with anyone, but especially with Charlotte. She was like his sister. The only family he had. He needed to keep that bond safe and protected, or else he'd have nothing.

Once he'd calmed his breathing, he slipped the inhaler back in his drawer. It was early to be going to bed, but he was exhausted from last night and a little hungover. After burrowing deep under the covers, he let his mind wander.

Even though they'd been gone for years now, Hugh still thought about his parents often, and mostly before he drifted off to sleep. But there was a particular time when he especially thought about them. Every time he met a new woman, he couldn't help but wonder: *Is she the one?*

It was the relationship his parents had shared that sparked these thoughts. Is this why he craved relationships so much? After all, hadn't he sometimes been disgusted by the way his parents couldn't seem to ever keep their hands off each other?

Hugh remembered a time he yelled at his parents for mortifying him with a PDA. It was his eighth birthday and they had taken him to see a baseball game. In the parking lot, on the way back to the car, Henry took Grace in his arms and dipped her, and Hugh's ears burned in embarrassment as he was sure everyone was watching them. When his dad essentially started to make out with his mother, right there in the parking lot, he couldn't contain his humiliation any longer.

"Will you cut it out already!"

He remembered his father's face had filled with rage. "You ungrateful little wanker!" he'd shouted, but Grace cut him off.

"He's just a little boy, love. He doesn't mean anything by it."

Henry just sneered. "He should watch his mouth," Henry said, and Grace nodded to show that she agreed.

Hugh just stood there, more embarrassed and confused. His father had never shown that side to him before. He had always been a kind and caring man towards his son, and Hugh was worried that maybe his father had stopped loving him.

Later that night, Hugh's mother came into his bedroom and sat beside him on his bed. "Honey, I think we should talk. About today."

"I'm sorry, Mum. It was bad of me to get angry like that."

"Oh, my sweet boy," she said as she hugged him to her, "there are just some things you can't possibly understand yet. Like what goes on between a woman and a man."

"What do you mean?"

"Well, sometimes people have to go through a lot to be together. So when they finally manage to be together, well, they take it very seriously."

"I guess I can understand that."

"I'm not sure if you can. Not yet, sweet boy. But someday you will." She sighed. "When you grow up, you'll learn that there's something called passion. And then there's another thing called compatibility. And these are two very special things that grown-ups strive to find in partners. For some people, passion is everything. For others, well, others prefer the calm of compatibility."

"Compat—you mean like getting along?"

"Yes. Anyway, it's a rare gift to find both of these qualities in someone—let alone even one of them. So when you are blessed enough to have both, and you fight so hard to have it, you have to celebrate it each and every day and in any way you can."

"Like getting all mushy like that?" he said, pursing his small lips in disgust.

Grace let out a small laugh. "Exactly. But there's more. You see, many times when people decide to get married, they do so because they're settling. Do you know what I mean by settling?"

"Like making yourself think you're happy when you don't get what you want."

"Precisely. And it's a tragic thing indeed. I had a sister who married some boring old codger. We all knew this was someone she never could possibly love. And she knew it, too— which is why she had married him."

"I don't understand—"

"Sometimes grown-ups make very silly decisions. And it's true, Estelle married Mr. Jenkins *only* because she knew she could never possibly love him. No love, no risk; no risk, no hurt." She took a thoughtful pause and her eyes rested on his. "But then…no love."

"Why would anyone *not* choose love?"

"What happened with Estelle was that her heart had been so badly broken by a previous relationship, by a passion she felt for a man, that she had simply decided to give up."

"I'm never going to do that, Mum. I'm never going to settle."

"I know you won't. Just remember that you need to hold out. And don't ever give up, no matter how badly your heart gets broken. Eventually you will meet the one who makes everything make sense. She may not be what you expect, but when you realize you've found her..." She trailed off and got a dreamy look in her eyes.

"How will I know?" Hugh nuzzled up to his mother and she gently stroked his hair.

"I can't explain it. You know how it is with me and Daddy. It's just a feeling that you'll get—a feeling like you've never had before. It wasn't there right away for me. But when I realized it... I can't explain it. It was...just...magic..."

"I hope I meet her tomorrow!" Hugh beamed.

"Well maybe not that soon, muffin. Just remember that you are a very warm and intelligent boy. You need to find someone who can share your warmth and intelligence and peculiar sense of humor." He was peculiar? His mother thought he was peculiar? "And if you can find all that in a partner who you are also madly attracted to, then you'll have everything."

"And then I'll make out with her in the parking lot when I'm old?"

Grace giggled again. "Yes, sweetie. When you're *older*. Even when you're old, you'll still want to make out with her in parking lots, or wherever the mood strikes." She kissed her son on the head. "This I promise you."

"Goodnight, Mum," Hugh said as he ducked under his blankets, ready to dream of his true love.

"Goodnight, sweetie," she said with a soft kiss as she tucked him in.

As Hugh drifted deeper into sleep this night, his thoughts drifted to Annie. About her smile. Her wit. She and he were not the same, but they were certainly compatible. And she was pretty, no doubt. He'd been drawn to her even in the cemetery.

Could she be... The One...?

Hugh's eyes flew open and he bolted up in bed. He had to stop his crazy romantic brain going off the rails again, the way he had with Alicia. With Sheila. The way it had every time he met a new woman. He and Annie had decided just to be friends, and that was that.

But he could still think about her, right? Friends thought about friends. And if he had other thoughts… well, those were just thoughts. He wasn't going to act on them.

He wanted to text her. What harm could a text do? Lots. Texting her would show interest. It would let her know he was thinking about her, more than a friend would or should be thinking about her.

Texting her would be a very bad idea, he rationalized, and he forced himself again to just try and get to sleep.

chapter thirteen

---

the present.

Annie staggered into her apartment. She'd been living in her place for so long, she never noticed the cracked paint anymore. The rough, dirty linoleum floors. A slum, really. The walls were bare, but the space was incongruously furnished with oversized, lush sofas and chairs, high-end tables and lamps. An area rug in the living room that easily cost six months' rent in a space like this.

The furniture was from a different space. A different life. The cast-off clothes that obscured it. The empty takeout containers and wine bottles. So many empty wine bottles. Those were from this life.

Annie kicked a path in a blanket of old newspapers and walked to the living room, where she placed her purse on the elegant coffee table almost entirely obscured by haphazardly stacked papers, magazines, and mail. She sat on the sofa, right on top of the outfit she had peeled off in front of the TV when she had gotten home the night before, and put her feet on the coffee table.

Hugh hadn't texted her all day and she was really sad about that. She hadn't really expected him to, had she? Sure it had been a fun night, but it didn't end well—his fault, not hers.

Their relationship, such as it was, wasn't going to the next level, so why did she care? Zoning out as she tried to figure it all out, Annie noticed the light flash on her ancient answering machine.

No one called her on this line anymore. Only her mother had. She didn't even know why she kept it. She panicked.

Only her mother had…

This was not a call she wanted to face, but why shouldn't she? She could listen to the message, hit delete, and never call her back. That's just what she decided to do as she darted across the room and hit "Play."

"Oh hey, it's me. It's Hugh. Hugh Jeffries." Annie's heart shocked her when it skipped a beat. "Look, I wanted to apologize for last night. For Charlotte showing up like that. I just didn't know where things were headed. And when we talked… dammit I'm such an idiot. In any case, if you want to talk, here's my landline number," and he gave it to her—but why? "I know you're probably wondering why I called you on this number. Uh… It's kind of a long story. Anyway, if you think you might want to forgive me, please give me a call."

She felt a glow of warmth emanate.

He called… He actually called…

She picked up the phone and dialed the number he'd left.

"Hullo?" he answered on the third ring, sounding sleepy.

"Hey, it's Annie. Is it too late to call?"

"No, not at all," he said.

"I woke you up, didn't I?"

"Uh no. I wasn't expecting to hear from you so soon," he said. "Girls never call back right away."

That made her nervous. Why did she call him back right away? Had she not learned anything about dealing with men? *But this isn't a guy, this is a friend*, she rationalized. It was okay that she'd called back right away, and she was going to make that abundantly clear to him. "Well, I'm not a girl. Not a *girl*-girl. Just a friend, remember?" She still hated how she sounded and wanted to hang up immediately, but when he started talking, she realized she wasn't the only nervous party on the line.

"Right. Well, I just wanted to call and tell you how sorry I am about last night. Kind of a crappy thing to do to a friend."

"I guess I can forgive you. But don't try and spook me with that M.A. again like that."

"M.A... M.A..." he struggled. "Menacing ass!" he chuckled. "That's not very nice, you know."

"I know. But I'm not very nice."

"Somehow I don't believe that," he said. "I think you're much nicer than you want to be." This warmed her for a moment, but the moment passed quickly. If only he knew how wrong he was about that. If only he knew that she destroyed lives.

It was time to play it cool again. "Is that so?"

"Maybe not. But it's what I think."

She laughed, masking her nerves. "Fair enough. So how was your day?"

"Not bad. Just worked. The usual. You?"

"Boring day, then kind of an excruciating dinner with my friend, Rebecca."

"The one with the demon child who hates you?"

"Yep."

"So why was it so excruciating. Kid put a curse on you?"

"No, the kid was mercifully at home. Though I kind of feel like Rebecca did..."

"Uh oh. What happened? She's giving you the kid?"

Annie laughed. "No. Nothing like that. Forget it. It's stupid anyway..."

"Tell me."

"She gave me something from my mother. I guess it's got me confused..." It felt like he hesitated a moment too long and it made her uncomfortable. She broke in to the silence. "What?" she said, feeling a little defensive.

"Well... maybe you should talk to her. You know, your mother?"

"You have no idea what this woman is like. I am much better off without her kind of crazy in my life."

Annie cradled the phone between her ear and shoulder and pulled the box out of her purse. She opened it to reveal a diamond cross sparkling against black velvet.

"I'm sorry," he said. "I guess it's hard for me to understand. I really miss my mum."

"So do I... miss my mom," she said. Of course she did. Sometimes at least. "I mean... She isn't all crazy. But the Jesus thing is way out of control. I mean with that, it's like she *knows* she's crazy. But it's like... I don't know... I guess it's like she's okay with it." She took the necklace out of the box and stroked the cross between her fingers.

"Aha! Kind of a *comfortable* madness?"

"I guess. Yeah. Something like that."

"Well, that's not so unusual. Everyone has one of those, you know."

"You may be on to something here," she said.

"Think about it. We all have a little crazy that we rationalize makes sense because it feels good, right? Like for me, it's cemeteries."

"And supermarkets for me."

"And serial monogamy!"

119

"And children..." she trailed off. Why had she brought that up? She never brought that up with anyone. It hurt way too much to think about, let alone discuss.

He laughed. "Wait. I thought you hated children?"

She paused as she calculated how she was going to answer him. "Well... I wouldn't say hate. I'd say I have some difficulty with them."

"You want to talk about it?"

"No," she said so abruptly she was surprised he didn't react at all. She placed the cross down on the table and headed to the kitchen still cradling the receiver, this time to deftly open a bottle of wine.

"Hmmmm," he said. "What if you were to deal with your mom like that?" he offered. "You know? Just manage her madness—like it's an addiction or something?"

"Look, it's not that simple," she said. It was time to change the subject. "Hey, did I ever tell you that we were the only non-Italian, non-Hispanic family in the entire neighborhood that had a Mary on the Half Shell in the yard?"

Annie poured nearly half the bottle into an oversized glass.

"I'm sorry... A Mary on the what? You mean *Mary* Mary. Mother of God?"

"Yes, that one."

"Don't get it."

"It's pretty simple. Go to the Internet—right now. There yet?"

"Getting there. Okay. Now what?"

"Hmmm... Try searching for 'Our Lady of Guadalupe statues," she instructed.

"Okay. Loading..."

"Well?"

She took a large gulp of the wine and headed back to the living room.

"Hang on. I have crappy Internet. Takes forever and... Whoa-ho! Ha! Now I get it! Mary on the Half Shell. It's like she's standing in a clam shell!" he exclaimed. "That's funny."

"I can't believe you've never seen one of these. Don't you live in Queens?"

"I guess I never noticed," he said.

"You should congratulate me for giving you a 'religious experience,'" she joked, and lifted the cross necklace again. It was beautiful, sure. But everything it symbolized is what had brought her to the end of her marriage, and nearly to the end of her "sane."

"Hey, speaking of religious statues and religious experiences in general..." he hedged.

"Where could this possibly be going?" She was getting nervous again. What? Did he want her to go to church with him? Was he religious? And religious enough for her to tolerate?

Annie placed down her wine glass and stood in front of her hall mirror. She held the necklace up to her neck.

"How would you feel about going on a cemetery crawl sometime with me... get a taste of my wacky madness?"

"I can't believe you hang out in cemeteries."

"I can't believe you hang out in supermarkets. So?"

"Okay. What the hell," she said. "Text me tomorrow."

"Later—"

"Wait. You never did tell me why you called on the landline," she said. As soon as he started explaining, she hung up the phone with a giggle. She had to keep him on his toes a little bit—even if he was going to just be a friend.

She stopped laughing when she caught sight of the necklace again. Annie opened the clasp and placed it around her neck. The cross sat in an almost perfect position, just at the start of her décolletage. It was undeniably beautiful, yes, but it was also an eerie reminder of who she was—where she came from, how she had made her choices, and how she had ended up here, in this dump of an apartment. With a terrible hole in her heart, and an unforgivable stain on her soul.

chapter fourteen

---

circa 1943.

Spring seemed to always be in the air whenever Maggie was around Walter Randalls. There was an undeniable magic about him, a glow. He emanated tranquility, serenity. Things sorely lacking for her at home. The painful pit of hell her home had become in recent years.

Along with that, there was a purity about him. An essence of sincerity. He made her feel when he was with her that there was nowhere else he'd ever want to be, and she believed it completely.

Everything about Walter embodied perfection for Maggie. His exquisite chin. His shoulders so square, his build, so strong yet slim. Not to mention the way he made her feel. He made her want to be better, and, at the same time, he also made her feel she was perfect. It was crazy. That, and the fact that she knew on some level deep down inside that there was no way this was going to end well...

But there was today. All they had was today. And on this day, after he'd surprised her by arranging to take the afternoon off, he'd brought her down to Crocheron Park, where she was again surprised and equally delighted that he'd already set down a blanket, spread with a lovely lunch of luscious finger foods—cheeses and fruits and tiny, prettily iced cakes. And a bottle of wine.

"This is amazing," she cooed.

"What? You mean you've never been here before? It is sort of nice, I guess," he joked.

She punched him lightly on the arm. "Not the park, dummy." She giggled. "This. All of this."

"This?" he asked, making a sweeping motion with his arm. He smirked. "Nah. This is nothing." He pulled her into a soft cuddle. She nuzzled into his neck. The scent of soap and mint. Fresh and clean and pure as rain. She was in heaven. Clearly she had died and somehow managed not to land in hell. She absently fondled her diamond cross.

"No. This is everything." She smiled.

"You're pretty easy." He laughed. "Well, come on," he said, and he pulled away from her and sat on the blanket. He waved to her to join him.

She sat beside him. "My parents used to bring me here," she told him, as he poured her a glass of wine. "When it opened. Do you remember how excited the town was about it?"

He handed the glass to her and poured another for himself. "You forget, I'm not from around here," he said.

"You're right. I do," she said, not fully understanding on some level that he hadn't always been a part of her life, and then also, out of nowhere, feeling a wave of playful mischief rising in her. "So you don't know the story?"

"About the park? I guess I don't," he said, and picked up a strawberry. Delicately removing its stem, he placed it in her mouth.

She bit down on it, an explosion of sweetness. For a second Maggie reconsidered telling him her story, but she couldn't resist. She chewed and swallowed. "Well, long ago, there used to be a family. The Crocheron Family—"

"Like the park!"

She nodded. "Exactly. The Crocheron Family was the first to live in the area. This guy John Crocheron, a farmer, moved his family here in the late 1600s, and I guess they just grew and spread out from there."

"Okay...?"

"There were some congressmen down through the lineage, an assemblyman. Even a gambler."

"Also a politician." He laughed.

"Well, no. That guy raced horses. But the home and property did host a ton of politicians in its day, especially in the 1860s and 70s."

"Why then?"

"Boss Tweed."

"Ah."

"So if you don't know anything about the park and the grounds and the house, you probably don't know that Boss Tweed was murdered here?" she hedged.

"You don't say?"

"Oh, sure. It was a terrific scandal."

"What happened?"

"Well, you know how corrupt politics are these days?"

"Uh, the War...?" Walter gave her a sexy sideways smile.

"Right. It was a really bad scene back then. Tammany Hall is still around now, but in Boss Tweed's day, it was lawless."

"One might argue that today..."

"One might. Or one might just shut the heck up and let a girl finish telling a story."

His eyes wrinkled and sparkled as he laughed. She fought to catch her breath and regain her composure. Those eyes, and the way those eyes looked at her. Walter took her breath away.

She took a sip of wine and relaxed. "Anyway, there were a lot of people against Tweed and his politics, one of the main opponents being Phil Crocheron. He was master of the house around the time of Boss Tweed's demise, and even though Tweed was on the wrong side of the fence for him, he still spent a lot of time with the Crocherons. Crocheron's wife was great friends with Tweed's. You know how that goes."

Walter nodded, and Maggie continued. "Except Crocheron was getting tired of putting up with appearances for his wife's sake, and, politically speaking, he had had quite enough of Tweed's meddling and bullying. He had a plan to take New York back."

Walter leaned in. "I'm listening..."

"So one weekend, after a particularly insulting week, he arranged a hunt at the estate. A man hunt..."

He cocked his head. "You mean to tell me that Crocheron and a pack of his cronies—"

"Crocheron's cronies! That's a mouthful!"

"That Crocheron and his men...?"

"That Crocheron and his 'cronies,' as you so cutely referred to them, chased Tweed all over these grounds until they finally caught up with him. Phil was poised to shoot him in the head, but then his wife, armed with a bow and arrow, finished off Tweed with a shot right between the eyes!"

"Unbelievable! What about her friend?"

She ignored him, continuing on. "Yes, unbelievable is right! And that's what most of the men involved in the hunt thought, too. They were so angry, in fact, that Mrs. Crocheron had been the one to finish him off, they killed her, too. Like a pack of wild dogs. She was drawn and quartered, right there in front of her husband and kids and right..." She hesitated and looked around. "And right on that spot, right over there," she said, gesturing with her thumb.

Walter whipped his head around. "No!"

"No," she said, and nonchalantly tossed a grape into her mouth.

"What do you mean? Not on that spot?"

"I mean no, all of it," she said, trying not to laugh.

"This is funny?"

"The story? No, not at all. That you believed it? Yes!" And she burst out laughing.

He shook his head. "I can't believe it. I can't believe I fell for another one of your stories."

"Well, some of the story is true. I mean, there was a Crocheron Family and this was their estate. And there was a Boss Tweed and he used to hang out here. And he is dead."

"Murdered at least?"

She shook her head. "Sorry, no. Pneumonia. Prison."

"Damn."

"You're mad at me?" she asked.

He chewed on his lip. Now she felt bad.

"You are, aren't you? Now you think I'm nuts, don't you?"

He shook his head. "You know, when I brought you here today, I was going to tell you I loved you," he said.

Her heart sank; she had taken it too far.

"Now all I can say to you is...is..."

She placed her hand in front of her mouth. She had messed it up between them. She'd taken it too far. She somehow always knew she would. "I'm sorry. I'm so sorry..."

127

"All I can say to you is that I don't think I have ever loved you more."

She was stunned. "But I thought..."

"I have loved you because you are incredibly beautiful. But smarts and imagination, too? Now I'm doomed," he said. He kissed her gently on the lips and she savored that moment for a while, the soft feel of his lips against hers in the warmth of the afternoon sun.

"Being with you, Maggie Ellis..."

"Yes?"

"It's pure magic," he said, and she got chills all over her body. "This thing we have. It's magic. You know that, right?"

She could feel heat rising in her, warming her heart, her face. She placed a hand up to her cheek in an attempt to cool herself down. "It is," she said, not at all afraid to admit that what he felt, she shared. She just couldn't believe he felt for her the way she had for him.

"I mean, everything," he continued. "Like that shooting star that other night. Remember it?" His face was as bright as that of a little boy on Christmas morning. "Remember the star?"

"The shooting star."

He fed her a grape. "It's a magical thing all right," he said. "When you see one, it means that the universe is about to shift."

"It is?" she asked. He reached back into the bowl.

"The universe... Wooooooo..." She tried to sound like she was mocking him to hide the fullness of her excitement.

As he fed her another grape, this time she seductively licked the tips of his fingers before he pulled them away. Once she swallowed, she said, "So you're saying the one we saw the other night..."

He nodded. "Yes. That was a sign that very soon, our worlds will change forever."

She nuzzled into him. "Uh-huh," she said. "And do you know how?"

Now he took her fully under his arm, reaching with his other hand into the picnic basket behind her. She didn't see him smile or know that his fingers grazed a small black velvet ring box he'd hidden away in there.

"We'll just have to wait and see," he said.

chapter fifteen

---

the present.

As Hugh walked through Annie's neighborhood trying to find her building, he was sure he would be mugged at any minute. He worried about leaving the Zip Car he'd rented parked on the street, but also about his camera in the trunk. Though he wasn't sure if the camera would be safer on him than it would be in the car. He started to get anxious and felt his inside pocket to ensure he'd brought his inhaler with him.

He must have copied down her address wrong. Plugged the wrong address into the GPS. This neighborhood was all concrete and storefronts in shambles. Not at all the kind of neighborhood he'd imagined Annie living in. He was sure he was being pranked.

Annie's building was made of brick. Many at the entryway were cracked. A freshly sprayed "Fuck you" (the black paint still dripping from the words) greeted him in the foyer as he scanned the buzzer board looking for Annie's apartment number. Annie had claimed to be an executive in her firm—advertising he thought she'd told him. Was that another lie?

When the buzzer sounded, he darted inside. The lobby was just as rundown as the facade. The tile floor was black with filth at the corners of the room, a filth that seemed to seep up the walls. The dirt and neglect of years. He scanned the lobby looking for an elevator, but seeing none, he bounded up the stairs to the third floor, hoping all the while that this wasn't going to be a modern version of the "Inferno," with every level of the experience growing worse before getting to the frozen core of hell.

Annie's floor matched the squalor of the lobby and may have been a touch worse. An enormous insect darted across his path to the other side of the hallway as he quickly made his way to Annie's door. He knocked frantically, desperate to get in before that "thing" scurried back at him.

"Oh thank God—is that you?" Annie called from the other side, sounding panicked.

"Uh, yeah...?" he answered, sort of reflecting her panic, but the door stayed closed.

"You have to do me a favor."

He forced a cool, "Okay." He was feeling frustrated with her, but also panicked about the bug.

"Look around out there. Tell me. Do you see a doorknob?"

Did she think he was stupid? Did she not know that giant hungry insects lurked in her hallway? "Gee, let's see," he said, sounding as "hick" as he could. "Now what does a doorknob look like again?"

"Don't be a wiseass. I'm serious about this. Look around on the floor out there and see if you can find a freaking doorknob."

Hugh looked to the door where a knob should be. There was no knob. He then noticed a shiny brass object several feet away and picked it up. "Got it," he said, turning it in his hand.

"Can you put it back on?"

"Right!" he said, with more enthusiasm than planned, and screwed the knob back in place. He pushed open the door and there stood Annie, barely wrapped in a short silk kimono that clung to her curves. He felt a surge shoot through him, seeing her standing there, practically naked and wet.

"Oh, thank God you're here. I thought I'd be stuck for days. Come in!" she said. "Take off your jacket."

He complied and she chuckled when she saw his shirt. "'WALKER'? Really? So very sensitive."

Hugh was happy about the T-shirt choice he'd made, but he didn't want her to see how dorkily happy he was to have made her smile, so he forced himself to look away—though immediately regretted that decision as he glanced around her apartment.

The surge of lust he felt seeing Annie in her robe quickly flipped to horror as he took in his surroundings. She seemed to sense his dread and she giggled uncomfortably.

"Sorry—I'm not ready yet. I was, um, cleaning," she said, running her fingers through her wet hair.

The lust returned as he watched her do that, and gave him an urge to also touch her hair, but then it disappeared again when he slipped on a pile of magazines and nearly hit his chin on her cluttered coffee table.

"Cleaning...?"

"Are you okay?" she asked.

"Uh, sure." Not okay. What kind of adult person lived like this? His disgust quickly flipped back to lust, however, when she stood over him. She was short, but her legs were long. He swallowed hard.

"The cleaning lady didn't make it this week. So... uh... Can I help you up?" she asked, and as she bent toward him, her robe slipped open enough to expose her cleavage.

He choked and looked away. "I'm good, thanks," he lied, worried she'd be able to detect the nervous shaking of his voice.

She didn't seem aware of having practically flashed him as she headed into her bedroom. "Why don't you take a look around?"

"Uh, okay," he said, not really sure if he wanted to see the rest of the space, but he walked around reluctantly. The bathroom was filthy, complete with a mildewed shower curtain. In the kitchen, stacks of dirty dishes cluttered the kitchen counter, the table, and even a nearby windowsill. He had a momentary urge to pick up a sponge, but the terror of what could be hiding out between the plates chased him out of the kitchen and back to the living room.

"Oh hey," she called. "Look out for Mr. Badass!"

Mr. Badass? Who was Badass? Not a rat. Please not a rat. Hugh then got something underfoot and inadvertently kicked it. A rock? Rocks didn't hiss, and whatever this was most certainly did.

Hugh looked down to find an irate-looking box turtle on its back, swimming its legs through the air. He bent down and flipped it over just in time for Annie to emerge from the bedroom dressed in a short skirt and tank top.

"Mr. Badass!" she cooed. "I see you've met Hugh!"

(Hiss!)

"*This* is Mr. Badass?"

(Hiss!)

She nodded and got down on the floor to play with the little reptile. She said she only wanted to only be friends with him—so why was she down on all fours like this? Looking over her shoulder at him. Was she doing this on purpose? She had to be doing this on purpose. "Yes. He's my little exterminator. You know. Queens?"

Maybe the ones it could see from its two-inch-off-the-ground vantage point. How did she think he was helping with the swarm of roaches, no doubt scampering throughout the piles of unwashed dishes in the kitchen?

Hugh quickly found himself not caring, however, when she got off the floor, then sat in a chair and pulled on a pair of high-heeled, thigh-high boots. He swallowed hard as he slipped himself back into his jacket. She grabbed a light sweater off the chair and met him at the door. She looked hot, for sure, but not appropriately dressed for a cool day in the cemetery.

"That's what you're wearing?"

"Have you seen what you're wearing?"

"It's at least appropriate. I'm staying in themes."

She cocked her head at him.

"What? *Walking Dead* is definitely a theme," he said.

She chuckled. "So what's wrong with what I'm wearing?"

"Uh nothing. Forget it." He surmised that if she got too cold he could simply wrap himself around her to keep her warm. Then he quickly dismissed the thought. *Friends. Just friends.*

"Ready?" she asked.

"You bet!" he said, with perhaps more enthusiasm than was warranted, but he was desperate to get out of this filthy slice of hell.

He bounded to the door and began tugging away at the doorknob, not thinking in his panic to escape that he might unwittingly strand them again by knocking off the knob. But the doorknob on the inside fell off in his hand. He looked at Annie, sweat now forming on his upper lip. His chest tightened. He felt for his inhaler, but he didn't want her to know that he needed it. He didn't want her to think he was weak, so he tried to quiet his breathing on his own.

She didn't seem to notice him struggling. "Yeah, you can't pull at it too fast," she said. She leaned her face up against the door and looked through the peephole. "Oh good—knob's still on out there," she said. "That's key." She turned to Hugh and flashed him one of her coy, crooked smiles. "See what I did there? Doorknob? *Key?*" she asked and cracked herself up.

Now Annie grabbed a wrench, a screwdriver, and a pair of pliers "stored" on a bench right by the door, and managed to work all three at once, somehow still having one free hand to pull the door open. "Voila! And we're off!" she said.

chapter sixteen

---

the present.

Hugh and Annie weaved through the stones in the bright sunshine. They walked closely together—close enough to be touching, but he wouldn't dare lay a hand on her. Perhaps also aware of their proximity, Annie drifted away from him and sighed. "So, explain it to me again. What exactly is the point of this?"

Before he was even able to get his mouth open to answer her for what he felt was about the thirtieth time she had asked him this same question, she lost interest and gleefully ran over to read the inscription on a nearby stone.

"Hey, check this out!" she said, grabbing him by the arm. "'As flowers are made sweeter by the sunshine and dew, so this world is made brighter by the likes of you.' That's it! That's exactly how we're going to win that new foot-odor fighter account!"

Annie kneeled down and dumped out her bag, then futilely rifled through the mess. "Fuck! You got a pen?"

Hugh shook his head. "But don't worry," he said. He lifted his camera and pointed it at the stone. He took a shot. "I'll text you a JPEG," he said.

She smiled at him. "Thanks," she said. "Looking for material?" she asked.

He nodded. "My portfolio."

"Fancy," she teased.

"Maybe I'll show it to you sometime," he said, instantly regretting the offer. He never shared his portfolio with anyone. Well, not his personal one at least. Charlotte had been begging him to share it with her for years, but it was off limits, even for her.

"I'd like that," she said, and they held a glance perhaps a moment too long. Hugh became uncomfortable and so changed the subject.

"You like stories," he said definitively, now walking in front of her. "You're always telling them." Annie folded her arms in front of her and looked up at him. Man, was she cute. "Well, you'll like this then. The idea is to read the names and dates and then make up stories about the people buried beneath."

"I see. So you don't actually *know* anyone here... and... when did you get into this bizarre hobby again?"

Did she ever listen to anything he told her? "When my parents died," he said, trying to be patient.

"Oh right. Sorry," she said, clearly getting the point.

Now he felt bad. "Don't worry about it," Hugh said, and they walked several paces in silence.

"What were they like?" Annie asked. "Your parents?"

He turned to her and she was looking up at him now with true sincerity. Her pretty eyes were full of questions. She did care about things outside herself. He knew for sure in that moment Charlotte was wrong about her. "Actually... They were kind of great. More in love than two people should be allowed to be."

137

"Is there a limit?"

"Good question."

"What was their story?"

"It's kind of long."

"Short version?"

"They were from England. Neither of their families wanted them to be together. Mum came from money. Dad didn't. So when she got pregnant with you know who, they came here. I mean, not here. They just left England for Michigan."

"Huh."

"Anyway, they didn't speak to their families at all. Then, after about twenty-five years, my mother finds out that her mother died."

"I'm sorry."

"And suddenly decides it's time to see her father again."

Annie yawned. "Oh?"

"Bored already?"

Annie smiled and yawned again. "Sorry. Long week. Tell me, please."

"So my parents ask me if I want to come, but I'm still so messed up about Alicia... Anyway, I say no and drop them off at the airport. That's the last time I saw them." The guilt he'd felt for not having gone on that trip still stung so much. If he had been with them, would things have gone differently? He was starting to panic now. She placed her hand on his arm and he felt immediately calm.

"Because...?"

"Car accident. My grandfather, a guy I never spoke to in my life mind you, called me with the news. The next thing I know, Charlotte's helping me get a passport rushed over and blammo. I'm in England—and I had never even left Michigan before."

"Really?"

"Really. I'm not really a 'cutting edge' kind of guy. Sort of a little retro, in case you haven't noticed."

"Yeah, I noticed. But what does that have to do with anything? You mean to tell me you never left Michigan before coming here?"

"Nope."

"Not even for vacation?"

"I like things to stay as they are. Retro. Not really good with change," he said, shaking his head. "Not good with change" was truly an understatement. Dreaded change more than anything else would be more accurate. But he was trying to get used to change. And this adorable creature in his life was surely a change he wanted to embrace…

He moved closer to her; she pulled away.

"Oh God. That's terrible. I mean… Not the sheltered Midwesterner thing. Well, that is a little bit. But what happened to you. I'm sorry. I am so sorry. So bad to lose people like that. So sudden…" she trailed off, and her eyes went dark.

A loss. A significant loss. He could *feel* that in her now. It was so weird how he could just feel what she felt. Loss and guilt. He had to know what happened to her. One day she would tell him.

"It was bad for a while. I mean… I wish you had met my mother. She was so… I don't know. Can't really explain it. My grandfather was kind of a bastard, though. It's a good thing Charlotte came with me… Did I tell you Charlotte was there?"

She immediately let go of his arm. "No, actually. You didn't mention it."

"Well, yeah. She was there and she gave that guy a piece of my mind."

"She gave *him* a piece of *your* mind?"

"That's not what I said."

"It is. It's exactly what you said."

"It isn't what I meant."

She rolled her eyes in reply, which shamed and enraged him. "What I meant to say was, she gave him a piece of her mind. He wanted my parents buried in London. She told him absolutely not. Honestly, I would have been fine either way, but Charlotte is better than me at making things happen, you know?"

She walked a few steps ahead of him. "If you say so."

"I just went along with whatever she said. Pissed my grandfather off like you could not believe." He took a breath. "And when he told us that if we took my parents back to the States that I wouldn't get a dime for my time or travel, and I wouldn't be welcome back there in that city, and that there would be no inheritance for me, well, Charlotte went ballistic. Right in the middle of proper afternoon tea!"

Annie stopped walking again and turned to face him with a sly grin. "Really. That must have been uncomfortable."

"I thought so too, you know, at the time."

"And now?"

"Now I see why she did it. She told that old bastard that we wouldn't take his money if he jumped off the Tower Bridge for it. I was amazed. Looked like the guy was going to burst a vein in his forehead! But that was that. We took my parents back to Michigan and we got on with our lives."

Annie was quiet for a few minutes. "She sounds like a pretty good friend, this Charlotte."

"Yeah," he nodded. "She can be."

"Huh…" she said, and trailed off. "Do you ever look for people who died the exact day you were born? Now that would be eerie!"

Just then, a gaggle of Canada geese descended upon the cemetery. As if on cue, Annie shrieked. "Oh fuck! These are Louboutins!"

"Your boots. Yeah. That seemed like not the best choice…"

"Don't just stand there judging me. Do something!"

Hugh was relieved when he remembered a Discovery Channel piece he had caught once about Canadian geese, and how they could be herded. He knew what he had to do. He could rescue her! And when he did, maybe she'd change her mind about just wanting to be friends with him. When he saved her, maybe she would give in.

"Come on, little duckies." Hugh laughed. He called to them and began to walk in circles around them, his hands extended outward, "fencing" them in.

"What are you doing?"

Hugh ignored her and went about his business. "Come on now—away you go. Save yourselves! You don't want to see what this woman will do to you if you relieve yourselves anywhere close to her silly boots."

Hugh giggled and glanced over at Annie.

"You are a freak, you know that?" she screamed out to him over peels of uncontrollable laughter.

"So I'm told," he said.

But was she laughing at him? With him? It didn't matter. He could only imagine what an ass he must have looked like, but he didn't care. Whatever he was doing was distracting her. It was making her happy, and that's all he cared about. That glimmer of dark he sometimes saw in those eyes could be captivating, but he wanted to see her pretty face smile, because when she smiled that crooked grin, it lit up her eyes and made them sparkle, and he couldn't think of anything more beautiful than that…

Get a grip, he thought to himself, and turned his attention back to the geese.

"Uh-oh! Here they come again!"

He then got the idea he wanted to mess with her and started herding them in Annie's direction.

"What are you doing? Get them away!"

He laughed. "Okay, crap monsters. Looks like she's never going to warm to you," he said, and herded the geese away again.

They turned their attention back to the stones.

"How's this for a story?" she asked, pointing to a stone for The Brothers Novotony. "One brother buys the farm in nineteen seventeen. And the other hangs on until nineteen sixty-five. And yet, they're buried together."

"So what's the story?" He was eager to know what she'd come up with.

"The story is that there is no story," Annie replied. "At least not for this poor slob, Stanislav. I mean, what kind of a life did he have? His older brother dies nearly fifty years before him, and he still gets buried with him?"

"Okay…"

"You'd think this poor bastard would've gotten married and had a family or something. Where are his wife and children?"

"And why this twisted devotion to a brother he hardly even knew?" he asked.

"Precisely," she said and smiled again, clearly proud of herself.

"Fun, isn't it?"

A shroud of concern fell over her face. "I feel bad for him. We should do something."

"For a guy with no life? Who died before we were born?" He cocked an eyebrow at her. She looked away immediately.

Why did he never remember about the eyebrow? Why could he not control this silly "condescending" reflex Charlotte had told him again and again that women hated?

She took a long breath and looked back up at him. "Yes."

Aha! She did have a heart. He knew she did. Now he knew for sure that Charlotte was wrong.

"I know," she continued. "When's his birthday?"

"October nineteenth?"

"Okay, here's what we do. We come back here for his birthday and help him celebrate."

"Deal," she said, and they began wandering around again.

Something caught his eye. "Whoa—watch out!"

"What is it? More crap?" She looked panicked.

"No," he said, then bent down to collect what he'd spotted. He came up again, now balancing a lady bug on the tip of his finger. "Look who you almost took out."

"A ladybug."

"A ladybird beetle, actually."

"Whatever."

"Did you know that these little guys can flap their wings as fast as eighty-five times per second?"

"Oh good. Now we're on the Discovery Channel."

"And that this baby will eat about a thousand aphids and other such insects in its lifetime?"

She gave him a playful, bored look. "This may be my all-time favorite story—"

143

"There's also an old superstition that a ladybug is good luck. And that rescuing a ladybug is actually a pretty good omen."

"I didn't know that," she said, resting her chin in her hands. "Please, go on," she joked, the sarcasm apparent.

He smiled and gently took her hand. He placed the ladybug on the inside of her wrist. "For luck."

They gazed at each other and Hugh felt an almost desperate urge to kiss her. He had to bite his lip to ease the ache. Getting himself back in check, he led her to a nearby tree and delicately removed the ladybug, placing it on a branch.

He could feel her eyes on him; he didn't know what to say or how to act.

"Come for dinner Friday night?" he finally blurted out, regretting the words as soon as he'd uttered them.

"Is that a good idea?"

She tensed. She didn't show it, but he could feel it. It was starting to amaze him, how clued in to her he felt. He breathed in and tried to keep his cool. "Why? Charlotte will be out."

"I'm not sure..."

"Dinner, Annie. Just dinner. Friends eat dinner together."

She relaxed. "I think I can swing it. Sure."

As the day went on, and they moved from stone to stone, Annie began playing his game even better than him. Of course that's what she did. She made up stories to hide herself from the rest of the world. There was a significant wall there, but he could feel something behind it. A secret. He wanted to know it so much. He was sure that when she was ready, she would tell him.

Eventually Hugh stopped listening to her as she went on with a hundred outrageous scenarios. It wasn't that he didn't want to listen to her; he just couldn't concentrate anymore. For now, he was mesmerized, just watching her beautiful crooked mouth curve around every word.

chapter seventeen

---

the present.

Annie came home to the answering machine flashing again and she smiled. She realized she still needed to ask Hugh why he liked using the landline instead of her cell phone. The whole retro thing maybe? It didn't matter now. She was giddy about the day they'd had. She couldn't remember the last time she'd had so much fun with a boy—with anyone really. Weird as it was that her most fun day in she couldn't remember how many years had taken place in a cemetery. She didn't care about that now. Hugh was goofy and strange and quirky. A delight. She loved having him in her life, if only as a friend, and she was so curious to know what he had to say after having only just dropped her off. So, without hesitation, she pressed "Play."

"Annie. This is your mother."

Panic shot through her and she immediately hit the "Pause" button. It had been two years since she'd heard her mother's voice. Maybe slightly more than two years. And now here that horrible woman was, back in her life. Annie bit her lip as she stared at the light, still flashing.

But only if she let her back...

Why did she need to let her back in? She was doing fine without her mother. Better, even. What could her mother possibly have to say to her at this point? What would anything matter?

Annie considered that last thought. Of course it was true. Of course she'd grown enough not to allow her mother's words, her antiquated Holy Roman Empire ideas to bother her any more. She was stronger now. Defiant, she supposed against that part of her that still feared her mother and all she stood for, she hit "Play" again.

"I know you don't want to talk to me, but I'm worried about you," she said, as Annie could easily discern, slurring through a mouth thick with chocolate. "About your salvation." Annie now winced as she squeezed the diamond cross between her fingers. "I'm not sure if Rebecca told you, but I spoke with Monsignor Phillip. He told me that it's not irreversible. There's hope for you. You can be forgiven, if you repent. I know a little something about this. I have something to tell you. If you'll please call me back. Call me back, Annie?" Annie was shaking now and fighting back tears. All of the horrible memories of that night rushing back on her. She wrapped her arms around herself for comfort. "Please let me help you. You need help."

The message mercifully ended. She'd never forget the last time she'd seen or spoken to her mother. Her mother shouting through the supermarket at her as she fled down the snack aisle, away from her. "I know what you did!"

You only think you know what I did. You'll never know what I did...

Annie rushed into the kitchen to uncork a bottle of red wine, no small feat with her hands shaking as she tried to maneuver the corkscrew. Challenge accomplished. She was a pro. She took a dirty wine glass out of the sink and rinsed it under the tap. She shook out the water and replaced it with wine that she filled to the top of the glass. Before she left the kitchen, she downed half the glass in in one swallow. She filled it and grabbed the bottle with her free hand before heading back into the living room.

She dropped herself onto her couch and turned on the TV. She flipped through the channels and found that *Harold and Maude* was on, coincidentally at the scene in the cemetery when Harold first spots Maude. Annie giggled. How could she not? Isn't that sort of how it was with Hugh? A young quirky guy meets an older woman in a cemetery… Okay, she wasn't that much older. Probably just a few years. But still…

She reached over for her purse and pulled out her cell phone. She placed it on the table in front of her. Her mother wasn't going to be able to find her on that line because she didn't have it. Unless Rebecca gave it to her. Which if she did, she'd shut Rebecca out of her life too. But maybe, just maybe, Hugh would text her…

Annie snuggled back into the couch cushions and took another long sip of her wine. The more she drank, the less she focused on the movie and the more her thoughts drifted to Hugh, adorable Hugh, and how, well, happy she was to have such a breath of fresh air in her life. His sweetness. His kindness. His sincere intent in listening to every stupid thing that fell out of her mouth. He took her mind off everything… mostly.

There was no way she was going to get involved with him on any other level, though. There was no way she was going to ruin this, whatever it was, that she had with him. There was no way she was going to destroy him like she'd destroyed Jason and so many others.

Annie was happy she'd agreed to have dinner with Hugh the following weekend, both because she loved spending time with him and also because it meant she was legitimately busy. So busy she wouldn't have time to call her mother back or speak with the nosy old priest.

They could both go to hell.

chapter eighteen

---

the present.

When Annie arrived at Hugh's apartment her hair was in a messy bun, with strands flying out all over the place. Her clothes, possibly professional-looking that morning, were wrinkled and disheveled. She still looked pretty as hell. He wanted to brush her hair out of her face so she could see, and so that he could see more of her. But friends don't touch friends that way so he resisted.

She was weighed down by the bottles of wine she desperately clutched to her small frame. The brown paper bag they were in was ripping open at the bottom and one of the bottles had dropped nearly to her knees.

"Cripes. Let me help you with that."

"Cripes?" She mocked and grinned.

"Just hand me the bags."

How many people did she think would be eating with them? "Holy cow—what did you bring here?"

"I know. I'm such a sot, aren't I?"

"Well, heck. I'm not sure what a sot is, but if it means needing a liver transplant in the next five years, then yes. You're a sot."

"Oh ha, ha. I couldn't remember what you said were making, so I wasn't sure if I should bring red or white."

"Two of each—so we each get one of our own?" he teased.

She chewed her fingernail. "Something like that."

Hugh lifted a champagne bottle out of the bag. "And this one?"

She shrugged her shoulders, and took it back from him. "I guess I felt like a little bubbly."

"I guess we'd better get started on the drinking then."

She handed back the champagne bottle. "Just put this and the whites in the refrigerator and let's see what you've pulled together here. I'm fucking starved!"

Annie walked around the apartment, taking everything in. "Clean," she quipped.

"Yeah, I kind of like it that way."

She walked over to the loveseat and just as she did, Maude jumped down and darted into Hugh's room. "Nice cat," she said.

"Maude only really likes me," he explained.

"Huh," she said. Then she ran her hand over the top of the loveseat. "Nice couches."

Hugh started to feel defensive. "They're from my old house. My parents—"

"Hey, chill out. I wasn't being sarcastic. I get it. Re-trooo," she said, dragging out the word. "They're kind of cute," she continued. "They remind me of dollhouse furniture. I actually really like them," she said, and she flashed a smile. "This is beautiful. *Vhat is dat, velvet?*"

"Huh?"

"*Coming to America?*" She rolled her eyes. "Some retro boy you are."

He laughed, instantly remembering the film. "I saw it. That's the part when James Earl Jones comes into the barber shop wearing that lion."

"Ha! Yes!"

"Good movie. I didn't think anyone our age ever saw it."

"I see a lot of weird movies."

"Me too," he said.

"I figured," she teased.

"What's that supposed to mean?" he asked.

She pursed her lips. "Nothing I guess. I mean, you're just a little, I don't know… peculiar? I mean, in a good way. In the best possible way."

Peculiar.

Hugh shrugged and sat down next to her. She started picking up magazines and books from the coffee table, considering each for a handful of seconds, then tossing them down with bored disinterest. Until she got to Charlotte's *Corporate Feng Shui* book. She opened it and looked up at Hugh. "Why are you reading this? This is ridiculous," she said. "We did the press for this and I didn't even read it."

"Not mine," he said. "Charlotte's."

"Ah, that figures," she said. She then leapt off the couch Mary Lou Retton-style and headed back into the kitchen. "Well, doesn't this look delicious." She poked a wooden spoon into the pot.

"It's like you live here," he joked.

He could feel her tense again, even if her words were cool. "Ha, no. I didn't mean…"

He felt bad. "I didn't say that it was a bad thing." He smiled, and she smiled back. He was happy to feel her relax again.

Annie grabbed two bowls from the table Hugh had set for dinner and filled them right from the stove. She placed them down at the table as Hugh opened one of the reds, poured two glasses, and joined her.

"Bordeaux glasses?" she asked, impressed.

"Ah, yes. Wedding present. You know the difference?" he replied, also impressed.

"I have vessel issues."

Hugh laughed. "I'm not exactly sure what that means, but it's nice that you noticed. Not many people do," he said, remembering how Charlotte had insisted they leave them behind. He took a bite of food. "Okay, so what's a vessel issue?"

"Silly, I know. It means drinks don't taste right if they're not in the proper glass, you know?"

"Uh... what?"

"Okay, so a martini," she said. His throat burned just at the sound of the word, and he absently brushed his neck with his hand. "Ah, so you do remember!" she laughed and he pulled his hand away. "Okay, so a martini needs to be served in that stemmed, upside-down triangle shaped thingy or it's undrinkable—"

"And even then!"

"White wine in a long-stemmed glass with a slender bowl. Red in a wide bowl," she said, holding up her glass. "And the bigger the wine, the bigger the bowl. These are not glasses for a pinot noir."

"You're kind of a pain in the ass, aren't you?"

Annie drained her glass again. Hugh picked up the bottle and poured another glass for each of them.

"Yeah. I know," she said.

Hugh froze, his attention now fixed on a spot on the wall.

153

Annie started talking to her glass. "No, Annie. You're fine. Really..."

Hugh continued to ignore her, completely still except for a light shaking of his head and a look of horror shooting from his eyes. "No... not now... not now!" he exclaimed. He could feel his chest start to tighten. "Please not now..."

"Not now what? What the hell's gotten into you?" Annie whipped her around as Harold darted around the room. Something must have clicked for her because she then quickly pushed her chair out from the under the table and threw up her arms. "Raid! Stat!"

Hugh fought back a laugh and raced into the kitchen, producing all the different varieties of Raid he had accumulated, as none had ever been able to ever properly eradicate the water bugs.

Annie was as cool as a general devising a strategy. She carefully corked the rest of the wine in the bottle and flipped the conveniently now-empty wine glasses over. Then she grabbed two cans, one in each hand, and twirled them around in her fingers as if they were pistols and she was a gun-slinging sheriff. Like she was in the Old West and this was *High Noon*. Then her expression changed to all-out killing machine. "Die, you fuckers!" she screamed. She let out a banshee scream and began spraying like a madwoman.

He was sure at any moment she was going to do a triple back handspring. She did not.

Hugh was beside himself laughing at the ferocity of this tiny blond warrior. And then she hurled a can at him. "Look alive, soldier!" He caught it just before it clocked him in the head. "To your left corporal!" And he obeyed. She was spraying. He was spraying. It was like a video game. "Kill the bastards!" Annie screamed like a lunatic. Finally, all the enemies were felled, writhing away on the floor. The cats, knowing a predator when they saw one, had long since scampered into the bedroom.

Hugh scanned the room and took in the dead sprawled all about them. The aftermath of a great battle. Like the scene in *Gone With the Wind* when Scarlett O'Hara arrives in Atlanta to retrieve a doctor to birth Melanie's baby, and all around her are dead and wounded soldiers strewn about the streets in ever-endless numbers as the camera rolls back. It was too much to bear. They both broke out into hysterics.

Hugh thought only for a second that with all the chemicals in the air and the laughter how odd it was that he wasn't having any trouble breathing.

"I can't even see you," he said, waving his hand in front of his face.

"Oh God, this is really bad, isn't it?" she called back to him.

"Where are you?"

"Just follow the scent of..." she said, squinting to read her can, "Super-strength."

Finally, Hugh made his way to her. Her hair had fallen out of its messy bun and stuck out in a million directions. There was murder in her eyes. She smiled at him. "I guess dinner's over." She blew her hair out of her face.

There was something about Annie in that post-massacre moment that sparked Hugh. He couldn't hold back anymore. He kissed her, at last. She didn't fight him. She kissed him right back. And even though they were no doubt just a little high from the bug poison that lingered in the air, there was no question about it: The chemistry was there.

Annie and Hugh tore at each other and landed up in Hugh's bedroom. Being with her, like this... He couldn't imagine a time in his life that there would be anything else he'd ever want to do.

When it was done, they collapsed together in a jumbled heap. Then Annie rolled on to her back, pulling the duvet up over her chest, much to his disappointment. But just as she did, both Harold and Maude jumped on top of her and started to purr. This was a happy place, and even the cats knew it. They hated Charlotte, but they seemed to love Annie.

Then seemingly out of nowhere, Annie jumped up. Hugh felt a surge of panic. "Where are you going?"

"Oh don't be so nervous," she said, and she darted out. Two minutes later she was back, with the corked bottle of red and a couple of fresh glasses. "I saved the wine!" she said. She filled the glasses, first handing him one. She placed hers down on the table next to the bed. "So what was dessert?" she asked.

"Refrigerator, middle shelf," he said, and she ducked out again.

A minute later she returned with a small cake and a couple of spoons, and jumped back into bed. "You don't care if we eat this here?" she asked.

Of course he did…but of course he didn't.

Annie leaned over and reached for her wine glass. She picked it up and placed it to her lips, ready to take a big swig. She looked down at her glass just in time to see that a giant waterbug had drowned in it.

"Dammit!" she screamed, and spilled red wine all over his pristine white duvet cover.

Again, Hugh was horrified…but not really.

"I should have grabbed the white," she said, shaking her head. "That fucker couldn't have hidden so well in a pinot grigio."

Hugh smiled in spite of himself. "Sure."

Even though she had just barely avoided swallowing a giant prehistoric insect, and her face and hair were drenched in red wine, and she wiped away at her tongue with one of his pillowcases, he wanted to kiss her again. As insane as he knew it was, Annie compelled him. He wanted to know her inside and out, more than he'd ever wanted to know any other woman in his life.

chapter nineteen

the present.

Hugh couldn't believe his incredible luck. He had no idea how this had happened, but it did, and now he was feeling more bliss than he could ever remember feeling. The way her hair smelled. The softness of her breathing. It was like a dream. Of course he'd fantasized about being with her like this. But never had he imagined that it would come to pass. That she would ever let him get this close to her. That she would ever let him hold her like this. And yet, against what both of them had firmly agreed they were not going to do, chemistry took over and there she was, this naked and amazing softness in his bed.

He grazed her shoulder with the side of his thumb. He couldn't believe how soft she was, as compared to how "hard" she always tried to be. And the slight, peaceful smile on her face when he touched her like this... He had never seen her look so comfortable. Yes, she could be fun while manic and animated, but there was always that uncomfortable edge to her. That wall. That shield. But tonight, that had all slipped away. He was happy that he could do that for her, if, in fact, he *had* done that for her.

He lengthened his strokes, moving his thumb from her shoulder to her collarbone, stopping at the diamond cross that hung just over her clavicle. So out of place on her skin. Hard and rough. Cold and sharp. "Why do you wear this?" he asked, holding up the cross between his thumb and index finger.

For a moment, he could feel her tense. Her lips tightened and her face pinched back into that girl with an edge. He should have known better than to pry like that. But then, just as quickly as it had gone, her smile returned.

"Did I ever tell you I grew up in an oppressively Catholic house?"

"Uh, yeah. I think you may have mentioned it about once or four hundred times."

"But did I ever tell you just how ridiculous it was?"

Ridiculous wasn't exactly the word that came to mind, but he decided to indulge her. "Try me."

"Well, for one... I slept under a crucifix."

"That's a little creepy. Do you still?"

"Oh, ha ha. Could you imagine?"

He pursed his lips. "Actually..."

She gave him a playful smack. "Can you be serious here? I'm being serious."

"I can be serious."

"Alright then. Hey, did I tell you that my mother was anti-Barbie?"

"Um, no. Did anyone ever teach you how to finish a story?"

"It's relevant. I promise."

"Well..."

"It is. So here's the thing. My mother hated Barbie, HATED her. But not for all the typical reasons—body

159

distortion, anti-feminist, would fall flat on her face with those boobs if she was a real woman, objectification, blah blah blah. It was because the woman who invented Barbie was Jewish, and therefore Barbie must also be."

"That's a little freaked up."

"Yeah, that is *fucked* up. Except that for my mom, tolerance of other groups is okay, but you definitely don't cross the line with actual association."

He laughed. "I guess she wouldn't want to know you were associating with my Anglican ass then."

She seemed to ponder this. He got annoyed at himself. Why couldn't he just let her speak? She was finally opening up to him, and here he was, talking all over her. Idiot.

"I'm not really sure, actually. Anyway... I always wanted a Barbie doll and so badly. I used to watch the other girls play with their Barbies at recess, and sometimes if someone brought an extra one, they'd let me play."

"Not sure how this...?" *Shut up shut up shut up!*

"Give me a chance."

"Sorry." He planted a soft kiss on her forehead. "I went to a pretty upscale Catholic school where most of the kids came from money, so when they got bored of the Barbie clothes, they'd just toss them. Well, when they did, I'd snatch them up, take them home..." She buried her face in his chest and he started to get excited again, just feeling her breath on him. Then she looked up at him. "I can't believe I'm telling you this. I never told anyone this..."

"What's so bad about this?"

She paused. "Well, at night, I used to pull Jesus off the wall and dress him up and pretend he was Barbie, you know, in the clothes..."

"Wait—what?"

"Yeah…"

"Yeah. That is super creepy. I don't think I can talk to you anymore…"

"Come on! I was a kid. How could I help it? That darn thing scared the crap out of me. And Jesus looks magnificent in a sparkly ball gown."

"Wow, you're going to hell," he said with a laugh. When she looked away, and her shoulders started to shake, he realized he'd been had again. "Wait a minute… You're kidding, aren't you?"

She turned back to him and stared him in the eye, looking dead serious and hurt. And then she broke out in a laugh. "Of course! I mean, come on? Jesus Barbie. Can you imagine the marketing plan for that one?" Her tone then changed from bedroom to boardroom. "'Barbie has a strong, proven platform. And if it's a following you want, well, it doesn't get any bigger than Jesus...' Man are you an idiot." She gave him a playful tap on the forehead.

At that he rolled on top of her and started kissing her. God it felt so good to have his mouth on hers. His body on hers. His skin against hers.

Just then there was a loud knock on the bedroom door. "Nuts," he said. "Hang on." Hugh jumped out of bed, grabbing a sheet to cover himself. He opened the door ever so slightly and stuck out his head. "Hey, Charl. What's up?"

She looked pissed. "What's up with *me*? How about what's with the kitchen?"

He felt bad. He had totally forgotten about the mess they'd left. It seemed like another lifetime at this point. "I'm sorry. I'll deal with it tomorrow," he said.

She relaxed. "No, I'm sorry. I didn't mean to snap at you. It's just that I had such a shitty night. You know what? Let me grab a beer and I'll tell you about it..."

"Uh... I can't... I've kinda got..." How was he going to explain this? If she wasn't still mad at him over the mess in the kitchen, she'd surely be mad at him now for having a woman in his room. Except...

"You've got a *girl* in there!?" she asked, almost too gleefully. Was she drunk or something? Why wasn't she mad at him? She must have been drunk. She craned her neck to try and look around him. "Who is it? Not Margie? She likes you, you know..."

Hugh could feel the heat rise in his cheeks as he tried to block her from rushing into his room. "I'll tell you later," he whispered. But then his excitement overcame him and he blurted out, "It's Annie!"

"Annie? You don't mean..."

"Tomorrow, okay?"

"Sure," she said, and she walked off.

"Man, that was awkward," he said, as he joined Annie back on the bed.

"Why? You've never had a girl over before?"

"Ha! Sure. But, I don't know. She doesn't seem to like you all that much," he said, immediately regretting his words.

"Well, that's at least mutual," she said. Then she pulled away from him.

"I didn't mean to hurt—"

"Yeah, that's not so easy to do. But now, what I really want to know is..." she began, and then dropped her voice to a husky whisper. "Are you going to show it to me?"

Now he was excited all over again. "I think I've shown you quite a lot tonight."

She rolled her eyes. "Honestly. No, horndog. Not your dick. Your portfolio."

"I don't think this is really the right time..."

"This is the perfect time."

He hesitated. This was like showing her his soul. Was he ready to show her his soul?

"Well?"

"Okay. Hang on," he said, and reached under the bed. He presented it to her, saying, "As you sophisticates like to say... Voila."

His heart raced as she opened it and started to look through it. "Not bad," she said, but her face didn't say that. Her face said that she was essentially unimpressed. This was a mistake. After a few minutes of this torture, she said, "Do you mind if I make an observation here?"

"Uh... Sure?"

"Okay, but don't get mad."

"Tell me."

"Well..." she stammered. "I think it's terrible."

"Terrible?" He tensed. He was surprised, though, that it ended there. He was still able to breathe, which was unusual when he was about to face confrontation.

"I mean. Oh God. That was harsh. Okay, I don't exactly mean that. I was just expecting something better from you, you know?"

"What do you mean 'better'?"

"Well... look at this apple."

"Yes...?"

She hesitated before she spoke, then looked up at him with those piercing blue eyes of hers. "It's just not art. That's all I wanted to say," she said, shredding his heart. "Don't get me wrong. It's not that I don't think you don't have an eye for photography, because I really think that you do."

"So what are you trying to say?"

"You kind of take pictures like…"

"Like a what?"

"Well, like an accountant."

"I don't know what that means."

"Yeah—you know. You capture all the lines and curves, but there's no feeling behind it. No passion. It's all just facts and figures—what's there and nothing else."

"I don't know what to say." He really didn't. If he wasn't so desperately attracted to her, he would have asked her to leave.

"What if you shot it with more shadows—or even rotting. Something like that?"

"Why don't we just drop it, okay?"

"Okay, fine. I'm sorry. It was none of my business anyway." She kept turning the pages. "You know, the only difference between 'artistic' and 'autistic' is you…"

"Huh?"

"Yeah, it's A-U-T and A-R-T… Letter U."

"So also an R."

"Yeah, I guess. Sorry. Just trying to make a bad joke," she said.

"That may be the worst one yet," he said, and she smashed him with a pillow.

They were quiet again as she continued to flip through the pages. And then she stopped. He looked at what had stopped her. Jason's headstone. The photograph of Annie bent over Jason's headstone. How had he forgotten it was in there?

She was quiet for a while as she gazed at it. He could sense a torrent of emotion welling up behind the wall, but when he looked at her face, it gave away nothing. "See, you can do it," she said. "More like this. I look at this picture, and I *feel* something."

"Do you want to talk about it?" he asked, trying to keep cautious.

"No."

An uncomfortable silence fermented between them. He didn't like it at all. He stroked her face. He looked into her eyes and whispered to her, "I come to you, defenses down..."

She smiled. "With the trust of a child."

"Still friends?" he asked.

"Still friends—*just* friends."

And again, she stabbed him right through the heart. Why the emphasis on the "just" friends? Hadn't this night meant anything to her? Just as he was about to ask, he noticed her become distracted by a "statue" sitting on top of the TV. Not a statue exactly, but something that had been crafted from an empty toilet paper roll. It took all he could not to laugh as he watched her screw up her face and try to figure it out. Then, without warning, she jumped up out of the bed, grabbed it, and held it up. "What the fuck is this?"

"Oh, you like that? It's me, of course."

"You're not serious."

"Oh yes. I am."

"This is *you*? Ha! Ha! Oh, Hugh. That's rich. Looks just like you!"

He decided to have a little fun with her. He shot her a deep, serious stare, quieting her down.

She now seemed genuinely uncomfortable, and he was delighted. "You didn't tell me you had a nephew or niece?"

He felt like he was about to crack. "I don't."

"But surely some child… who made this for you?" She gasped. "*You* didn't make this?"

"Why? Do I look like a crafter to you? More *crafter* than artist?"

"Oh, well…" she stammered. Now he was starting to feel bad for her.

"No, I did not make it. Charlotte made it for me."

"Charlotte… made this?" A small laugh forced its way out of her.

He went back to serious. "She did. It was a birthday present actually. This year. Why? What's the problem?"

She cleared her throat. "Well, it's very nice."

Hugh couldn't take it anymore. He burst out laughing. "Annie. It's a toilet paper roll. Decorated to look like a man. It's ridiculous."

"Yeah. It is kind of stupid," she said.

He pulled Annie underneath him and just as she tossed TP-Hugh to the floor, Harold immediately pounced on it and began shredding it with her paws.

chapter twenty

circa 1943.

Maggie pressed her face into Walter's neck and breathed him in. The warmth of him. The softness of the moment. She had never been with a man before, but if there was one thing she knew lying here in his arms, in the glow of the consummation of their love, she would never be with another.

As she pressed herself closer to him, the diamond cross she wore around her neck stabbed her lightly just above her breast and she let out a small "Ouch."

That cross. That gift from her mother. A cross that had been given to her mother by her own mother. A family reminder of where they had come from. A symbol of who they were. And also, a reminder of a woman who had abandoned her. A connection to her past that she couldn't let go.

She liked to think she'd found peace in religion. That Father Phillip wasn't the only thing that had kept her going to church in the years after her mother left them.

Maybe it wasn't the religion itself. There was something about being in church that gave her a sense of peace. She liked to think this was due to her strong sense of faith and deep sense of piety. But if she was honest, it was the grandness of the space that calmed her. The soaring ceilings. The stained-glass windows that were at least twenty feet or more high. If not for the correct reasons, being in church made her feel like the world was bigger than she was, and because of that, it was somehow okay that she wasn't always in control of her world.

And maybe there was something about wearing this cross that comforted her, in a strange way. Strange because there was no comfort in her mother having abandoned her. Having deserted her and her father. Leaving a cold husk of a family behind.

"You okay?" Walter whispered to her as he softly stroked her hair.

"Couldn't be better," she whispered back, and with his other arm, he pulled her into a strong embrace.

"I don't think it could be humanly possible to love you more than I do at this moment." He breathed the words into her hair.

Her mind still on her mother, she spoke absently. "Please never leave me."

"Oh my goodness, Maggie. You can't be serious?" he said, and he pulled away to look her in the eyes. "How could I ever leave you?"

"I mean it, Walter. I don't think I could stand it," she said. And she knew how deeply she meant it, even if he didn't. She couldn't take being abandoned again by someone she loved. She was sure the pain of that would kill her, or, at the very least, land her in an institution.

He pulled her close to him again. She never wanted to be out of his arms. "I would never leave you. You know that. I couldn't live without you," he said, with an intensity she had never before felt from him. But still she could not be sure.

"Promise?" she asked.

"I promise," he said, and he squeezed her closer into him. "And you?" he whispered.

"What about me?"

"Promise you'll never leave me," he said, and she felt like her heart might break at his words.

"I promise," she said. "Of course I do. You know I do."

"Good." He pulled away from her for just a moment. "Because then I'd have to kill you," he said, and they both laughed as they dove back under the sheets.

chapter twenty-one

---

six years ago.

Annie was annoyed when she entered her apartment. All the lights were on—overhead lights, table lamps. And it wasn't even dark out yet. While she had to admit a part of her loved seeing her apartment like that, aglow in the warmth of a home now filled with elegant things that she had worked so hard to provide, it was just so wasteful on Jason's part.

It seemed sometimes like he took everything for granted, especially lately. That they could even keep the lights on when they had struggled not so many years before to be able to do even that. She at once felt a sense of pride that she had been able to do all that for them—and resentment that *only* she had been able to do that for them. It wasn't his fault that business was slow. That he couldn't provide for them. That couldn't have been easy on him, already in his thirties and not going anywhere...

Her resentment quickly flipped into guilt. How could she resent him when he already felt so bad about himself? What kind of person was she?

"Honey?" she called. She placed her keys down on the entry table and picked up a pile of mail. "Jason?" Was he not even home?

"Just a minute," he called from the bathroom through the closed door. Why was the door closed? He never shut it—a source of constant annoyance for her.

She headed over there. "Ha! What gives? You never close the door! What are you up to...?"

"Just give me a minute!" he shouted, now sounding impatient. She was confused and pushed open the door.

"Jay..." she said, but her voice trailed off when she saw him there, kneeling over the toilet. The lid down was down and under his face was a mirror covered in white dust. "What are you doing?"

He glared at her. "What are you doing in here? I thought you were working late again. Jesus. Can't a man get any fucking privacy?!" At that, he got up, shoved her out of the room, and slammed the door behind her.

She was utterly shaken. He'd never spoken to her like that. Never treated her like that before. She couldn't believe what she had just seen. Cocaine? Where did he get the money? She looked around the room. She noticed an antique side table they had purchased together on a New England weekend not too long ago was missing. She started to panic. What else was missing?

"Jason, we should talk—"

He whipped open the door, his eyes crazed and sparkling like ice...

Why did his eyes shine like that? Now she knew why.

"Why don't you just mind your own fucking business!" he yelled through a shimmer of white dust over his upper lip. He slammed the door on her again, so hard this time that the framed picture of the two of them sitting in the sun by the waterfront that hung next to the door shook and nearly fell off the wall.

How long had this been going on? How many of her late nights at work found him like this? What else had he been up to? What else was he hiding?

"But you are my business..." she whispered, then sat by the door and cried quietly to herself.

chapter twenty-two

the present.

When Annie awoke, sunlight was streaming through the slats of the blinds. She looked over at Hugh, who slept peacefully, his long eyelashes sweeping his cheeks, his lips curled into a contented smile. She quietly breathed him in. He smelled sort of wonderful. Like something purely sweet but not saccharine. Something so...

She couldn't place it. She closed her eyes as she nestled down next to him. She considered waking him, but she knew once she did, there would be questions. Questions the photo he'd taken of her in the cemetery that day could not answer. She didn't want questions right now. She just wanted to lay here, next to him. She just wanted to _be_. She breathed him in again. He stirred for a second. She snuggled against his chest and closed her eyes. And then she breathed him in some more. There was something about the way he smelled that put her at ease.

Jason had had that about him. He'd always smelled so good. She remembered when she'd pushed her body up against his back at night, and she could brush her nose up against that special spot... the nape of his luscious neck where he smelled the sweetest. Security. Peace. Love.

Annie loved cuddling up behind Jason while he slept. When she climbed into bed, sometimes hours after him, he would always be curled up in the same position, as if he couldn't shift until he knew she was there. She crawled underneath the blankets and pressed her body up behind his. She fit against him like a key in a lock. But the highlight of it all came when she could touch her nose to the back of his neck and breathe him in. He smelled like rain. Clean and pure. That was the smell that put her to sleep each and every night.

Hugh couldn't be more different than Jason. Hugh was not her usual type, yet she could feel a pull to him. She felt so comfortable with him. Like she could be herself. Like he understood her somehow.

The sex had been so unexpected. Yes, she was attracted to him, but she hadn't wanted to take it to this level. Though now that she had, how could she regret it? He seemed to know her body so well, and just how to bring it alive. When they came together, it was as if they had always been together.

Hugh made Annie feel things she'd never felt before. In sleep, their bodies had clicked into place. Another key for the lock of her body. And a smell that was so fresh and full of promise. He smelled like spring. Fresh and full of hope. Alive.

Her eyes shot open. This was not what she wanted. This was not where she wanted to land with him. From here, things could only spiral. They could only go dark. If she let herself feel for him, then she would feel for him when she lost him. Dark and cold and crazy… she never wanted to be in that place again. She never wanted to feel that pain again. That pain that never left her. That dark hole in her.

Why had she allowed that line to be crossed?

She thought again about that picture of her. The way she crumpled over Jason's headstone. The pain she wanted to bury for so long but would never go away. Time had not erased it. It was all there in that photograph Hugh took of her. Somehow he had captured with his lens what she'd fought so hard for years to hide.

She gasped, the panic now setting in. She bolted up. It woke Hugh. "What are you thinking about?" he whispered to her while lightly stroking her wrist with his thumb.

What am I thinking about? About love and loss. About how being with you feels so safe, and how this will only end badly. In tears. In pain. In deep, unhealing pain.

It was the calm before the crazy. The memory of losing Jason. The fear of love and loss. Of not being able to recover again...

It was too much. She was not not *not* going to put herself through that again.

"I'm starving!" she said, and threw her legs over the side of the bed.

"We'll order in. Or whatever. I'll make you something. Just come back to me?" he asked, so sweetly her heart might break.

Dear Hugh. Sweet Hugh. The way he looked at her. The affection in his eyes. The hope. Those things that being with her would only shatter. Why did he have to look at her like that?

"I want to go home," she said, and his face fell. She'd already done the damage. She had to get away from him before she completely ruined him.

"Okay," was all he said.

chapter twenty-three

---

the present.

"But can I at least take you home?" Hugh asked as he watched Annie scramble around the bedroom, collecting her things and rushing to get dressed. She seemed tense. Jumpy. What had he said to her? What had he done?

She looked away from him. "That's okay. I'm a big girl. I can find my own way."

This wasn't at all how she had been the night before. Something had changed. "Maybe I'm being old-fashioned, but I wouldn't feel right…" he said, not really having anything more convincing to say. "Wow, I'm such a dork," he muttered under his breath.

Annie sighed. "You're not a dork."

"You weren't supposed to hear that."

She sat down on his bed to slip on her shoes. "Then why did you say it out loud?" she said, now seeming to relax.

"It wasn't exactly out loud."

She smiled. That sexy crooked smile. It melted him. A "Please?" slipped out and he wanted to punch himself in his own mouth.

She sighed. "Okay, I'll let you take me home," she said. "But first you have to feed me."

An hour later, they were sitting across from one another in a diner down the street from Annie's apartment building. The Olympus Diner, while not original in name, was an original establishment of this Eastern Queens neighborhood. This was apparent mostly in the never-renovated fixtures and finishes, and the ancient desserts positioned behind the greasy glass under the countertop where the cash register sat. Hugh couldn't have gleaned all of this from simple observation. Annie filled him in on the historical bits. And of course she had fabricated another story he fell for—this time about how the Russian mafia tried to take over dessert deliveries from the Greek mafia, and how the Italian mafia put an end to it all.

"They called it the Cannoli Wars," she explained. "Notice how the cannoli outnumber all the other desserts?"

He shrugged; he couldn't help but notice this was true. "Really…" he mused.

"Nope." She let out a huge guffaw.

"Oh, ha ha," he said. "You know, one day I'm not going to fall for your stories. I'm not always going to be this trusting."

The silence that ensued signaled that neither of them believed this. It also created an uncomfortable space no one knew how to fill until Annie opened her mouth again.

"I used to come here all the time. You know. After Jason."

A turning point? he thought. A hope that she would share with him. That she now trusted him enough to share with him. He stepped through the open door before it slammed shut in his face again. "What brought you out here—to Queens? This neighborhood?"

"My grandparents lived here. I mean, when they were alive. What about you?"

Deflected again. He was going to let her get away with it. At least for a little while. But he would bring her back somehow. "Calvary," he replied, wondering how he was going to be able to turn the conversation back on her.

"What? You mean the cemetery? You're kidding me."

"So, it's okay for you to follow dead people but me..."

"Point taken."

"Anyway, I guess it's weird. But that place is huge. Seemed like it would keep me busy for a while. I can walk there from my apartment." He put down his menu. He tried to bring the conversation back to her. "What about you? Seriously. I want to know more. You seem to make a good living. So why that apartment? The way you live." He reached across the table for her hand. "I have to admit it's not what I expected..."

Annie yanked her hand back away from him. "So about last night..."

Hugh felt excitement rise in him. Finally, she was going to open up to him; he didn't have to coerce her. He could just feel it. "I'm glad you brought that up."

"We're still friends, right?" she said, not looking up. "Still *just* friends? Nothing changes?"

Her words felt like a punch to the stomach. "I guess," Hugh replied solemnly, but quickly caught himself when he realized he may have sounded disappointed. "Uh, I mean, sure. Of course."

"Thank God." She flipped open her menu. "Well I'm starved," she said, and finally looked at him. "What do you feel like?"

Like a piece of shit, he thought.

He forced a confident smile. "Pancakes," he said.

After a mostly quiet breakfast, he walked her down the street to her apartment building. They walked in silence, Hugh awkwardly trying to figure out if he should try to clasp her hand or place an arm around her waist or shoulders. He wanted so much to touch her…but how much touching were friends permitted? He didn't know.

In a few steps, Annie stopped in front of a store window. The store was a haggard-looking second-hand shop featuring odds and ends on display in the window. Useless used garbage at irresistible prices.

"I got my wedding dress here," she said, with a faint smile.

Hugh peered inside. "In here? Is this another story?"

"My mother didn't want me to get married. I was very, very young then," she said with a sardonic laugh. "But that's not the only reason she didn't approve of Jason. Anyway, I pretty much had to cover all the expenses on my own."

"That's sad." There was no need for him to fake sincerity; he thought this was a genuinely crappy thing, and it made him mad that any parent could treat their child like that.

She shrugged. "It was okay. Sort of special, I guess. The dress was from the 1940s, and it sort of made me feel tied to my grandmother. Not the woman I knew growing up who had raised my mother. My *real* grandmother."

Annie drifted into her thoughts and he hesitated to bring her out of them. "Do you want to check it out?" she asked.

"Uh, okay…" he said, not really sure what the right answer was, but he followed her inside anyway.

They strolled silently through the aisles, where glassware and vases, old clothing and record albums, purses and shoes, mountains of jewelry and books all coexisted awkwardly. An elderly sales woman in a white satin turban approached them. "Can I help you find something?" she asked.

"We're good, thanks," Annie snapped back, apparently annoyed that someone had offered to help them.

Within minutes, after breathing in a considerable amount of dust and God only knew whatever else, Hugh could feel his chest tighten.

"Oh hey—look," she said, and he forced back a cough. "Look. It's your friend from the cemetery." Perched between her fingertips, Annie held a small ceramic ladybug.

"Cute," Hugh said, as a cough forced its way out. Once he started coughing, he struggled to stop.

"Are you going to be okay?" she asked, genuine concern in her eyes. It warmed him. Other women he'd know thought his attacks were faked. Alicia especially had accused him of being weak or trying to get attention—or, more often, of creating a distraction when he didn't want to face something—any time an asthma attack hit him. It hurt like hell. Why would anyone fake that sort of thing? Charlotte also believed he laid it on too thick when the attacks happened, yet Annie treated him with kindness. *Who's the real bitch here, Charl*, he surprised himself thinking.

"It's fine. It'll pass," he said, knowing that without his inhaler it was going to take a while for him to stabilize again. "Can I buy that for you?" he asked through a fit of more coughs.

She quickly placed it down again. "I don't think that's really appropriate," she said. "Come on. Let's get you out of here before you drop dead on me."

chapter twenty-four

the present.

A short while later, Hugh made it home. He had thankfully been able to start breathing again when they exited the musty old store; though he was both disappointed and relieved in a very confused way when Annie didn't invite him upstairs when they got to her building.

He felt instantly guilty to find Charlotte cleaning up the mess of the waterbug massacre. "Oh hey. Sorry. I was going to get to that. I just wanted to take Annie home—"

"Done," she said in a flat, considerably unfriendly tone. "Don't worry about it."

She finished wiping down the dining room table and headed for the kitchen. He stopped her, placing his hand on her arm. "Hey, can I talk to you about something?"

"Sure," she replied, still sounding somewhat curt.

"It's about Annie."

Charlotte's face went dark. "Okay…?"

He really didn't get what the big deal was—why Charlotte disliked Annie so much. "I want you to be honest with me."

"Aren't I always," she said, not looking at him.

"I need you to tell me how you *really* feel about her. Not about me and where I am in my life—not about me and my relationship issues. Just about her."

She blew her bangs out of her eyes and paused before speaking. "I don't know. I don't even know her," she said, shaking her head. "My gut just says to not like her. But, again, like I said, I don't know her. But I don't trust her, especially when it comes to you."

"Because I was thinking... I was starting to feel..." *What was he starting to feel?* "I think I want to be with her. You know. Involved with her."

"Oh, Hugh. I thought you were giving yourself time—not getting involved for a while. We all know you're not over the last one yet."

He opened his mouth to disagree, but she cut him off. "Come on, you know Sheila and I are friends. She showed me that lovesick tome you emailed her the other week."

He felt his face go instantly red. "She did?" He had forgotten all about that stupid email. In fact, since he'd gotten to know Annie more, he'd pretty much forgotten all about Sheila.

"Oh come on. That was before—"

She spoke over him without letting him finish. "I didn't want to tell you because I didn't want you to be embarrassed, but she's kind of a big fan of 'forward to.'"

"Whatever," he took off his jacket and hung it neatly. "That was *before*. That's what I'm trying to tell you. This is different. Everything is different now. With Annie... I can't explain it."

Charlotte pursed her lips. She shook her head and started to walk away.

"What?"

She turned to face him. "You want me to be honest then?"

"Yeah, I do..."

She took a deep breath. "Then it sounds like lust to me, plain and simple."

"Lust? But there was only last night..."

"Exactly. I mean, what else could there be? Can't you see she's not the one for you? She's nothing like you. She's nasty and rude. She'll eat you alive."

He really didn't get how Charlotte saw Annie this way. She wasn't mean. She had a turtle! Did Charlotte know she had a turtle?

"She has a turtle!" he said, surprising himself that he'd said it out loud. "I mean, you know, she has a pet. Mean people don't have pets."

She glared at him. "You do know that a turtle is a reptile? Cold-blooded?"

He thought about the way the turtle had hissed at him, but then seemed happy to see Annie. Well, he did practically crack its shell by stepping on it. He would have hissed at him, too.

No, she had it wrong. Charlotte couldn't see Annie the way he saw her. A soft soul in a hard shell. Like the turtle...

No, not like the turtle. Idiot.

Well, a little like the turtle maybe. She did have a hard shell to protect herself. How could Charlotte not see this? He'd have to explain it to her. She'd understand.

"No, it's not like that. I mean, she can seem like she's hard and mean. Cold-blooded, sure. But really she isn't. It's weird, but I can talk to her. I mean *really* talk to her. Like I can talk with you."

Charlotte's eyes flashed with anger, but she spoke calmly. "Just be careful. Please. Look after *you*. Try not to get too carried away. You're such a sweet soul. Please don't get carried away."

"I don't think there's any chance of that anyway. Not now at least. She's got some issues with an ex... Did I tell you she's also divorced?"

"Well, does it seem like she wants to take it to the next level?"

"We kind of talked about it. But she keeps insisting that we're still *friends*. Just friends. Then she gets all quiet, like she doesn't want to lead me on, you know. So I think she's looking out for me."

"I don't..."

"What? What do you think it means?"

"Honestly, I don't really know her that well to be able to tell. I mean, I don't want to hurt your feelings or anything," she said, and started heading into the kitchen.

He followed her. "What? Just tell me."

Charlotte grabbed a dry dish towel and she handed it to him. She then started handing him dishes off the counter drainer. He complied, taking dishes as she handed them to him, drying them, and putting them away. But he couldn't help but wonder what the purpose of the dish drainer was if he had to dry the dishes anyway.

"You must know by now that when women get all quiet like that, it's generally because they've lost interest. You know? No, clearly you don't know. They don't know how to get themselves out of a corner they've painted themselves into and..." Hugh hung on her words, waiting for her to finish speaking. "They hope the guy will pick up on the signals and break it off instead."

Just then she handed him one of the Bordeaux glasses and it slipped from his fingers, smashing into pieces on the floor.

"Shit!" he yelled, and rushed to the back of the door where he had the broom and dustpan neatly stowed.

Charlotte grabbed the dustpan and squatted on the floor where the shards lay as Hugh swept the broken "vessel" into the pan. He smiled thinking about Annie and her vessel issues. Though he remained genuinely confused. "But we're not *together*..."

"Jesus, Hugh. It's just a word."

chapter twenty-five

---

six years ago.

The apartment was dark when Annie came in. She thought Jason was home—she had parked behind his car. Maybe a buddy had picked him up? But to do what... She didn't want to think about what he was up to these days. Since that day she'd found him in the bathroom snorting coke, she felt like she didn't know him at all. Not anymore.

On the top step, she tripped on one of Jason's dirt-encrusted work boots and nearly lost her balance, her heart beating rapidly as she grabbed the railing just in time to save herself. It was only about ten steps to the bottom, but the staircase was steep. While the landlord had been promising for weeks to do so, he hadn't yet replaced the carpeting at the bottom of the stairs. Another thing that would fall on Annie's list, no doubt. The bare cement floor was where Jason was supposed to have kept his dirty boots, but he never seemed to listen about those kinds of things. Not really anymore. Not really ever.

She considered mentioning it to him when he got home, but the truth was, she was so worried about him. About his latest layoff. About how hard he was taking it. And the coke?

How long had she been so wrapped up in her work that she'd never even noticed it?

She headed through the apartment, flipping on light switches as she walked through the rooms. She stopped in their living room and plopped down on the couch, annoyed at the dishes littering the coffee table, until she looked up and into the kitchen. There, at the table, the silhouette of a man hunched sadly over the table. Her man. Sitting in the dark. Another bad day. She had to turn this around. She had to confront all this, before it got worse. It could only get worse.

She took a breath. "Jason?" she called. He didn't stir. "Jason!" she called so loudly she shocked even herself. That got his attention.

She took another large breath for courage then got off the couch and headed into the kitchen. "We need to talk. We need to talk about all of this."

He didn't look up at her, even as she stood over him. She placed her hand on his shoulder. "The other night..." she started, but her voice fell off when she felt his shoulder tense under her fingers. She knew she had to keep going. "The bathroom..."

He still didn't look up, but shrugged his shoulders to shrug off her touch. His face scrunched into a scowl. "I think we need to talk about someone not knowing how to keep her nose where it doesn't belong," he said, speaking through his teeth.

How dare he be angry at her? "My nose? Are you kidding me? And your nose belongs over a pile of cocaine?"

He slammed his fist on the table, causing her to jump back. She had nothing to say.

"Look I am in no mood for this. I have to go down to the unemployment office *again* and stand around all day with all those losers and—"

187

"This will get better. You will find something."

Now he turned to face her. "There hasn't been anything for months and you know it. You keep saying that everything's going to turn around and it never does."

"I'm just trying to be supportive."

"It's getting old, living with a cheerleader."

"Well maybe it's getting old being married to a coke fiend."

He cocked his head and smirked at her. "Then maybe you shouldn't be."

His words pierced her. They'd had fights before. Hurtful barbs traded about not wanting to be together. Yet there was something about his words now that didn't feel like something flippant said in anger. It felt serious.

"You're so much better than me," he snarled. "Maybe it's time you go find something better."

His words stabbed her. Had she made him feel like he wasn't good enough for her? Were the drugs her fault?

"Jason..." she said, and she hugged him from behind. "I'm just trying to be your wife. I'm trying to look after you. Like I promised when we got married. Maybe you need to go to a program. Maybe... I don't know... Maybe you're not strong enough to deal with this yourself."

She could feel the anger rise in him as his chest and shoulders clenched. "I need to what? What do mean I'm not strong enough? What the hell are you talking about?!"

Annie took a breath and tried to remain calm. She kissed him softly on the top of his head. "I'm just saying that sometimes you can be a little, you know, impulsive. You give into your urges."

Now Jason jumped out of his chair and pushed away from the table. He glared at her, his face purple with rage. "What the fuck did you just say to me?"

Annie tensed. She had never seen him like this before, and she was surprised to find she felt a little scared. But this was Jason. Her true love. It would be silly to be scared of him. If he heard her, he would calm down, and they could work this out together. "All I meant was that it wouldn't hurt if you got a little help."

"You uppity little bitch," he barked. "You really think I can't control myself?"

She bit her lip. She forced herself to speak. "Yes. Yes, I do think that."

At that, Jason lunged at her, taking her completely off guard. He got right in her face and when she flinched, he backhanded her so hard, she flew across the room and landed against the wall with an awful thud.

Pain shot up her back, and then all she could feel was nothing. Nothing until her body felt hot and flush with a prickling sensation she couldn't describe. Something that rushed over her, like a coating. Something that enveloped her in such a way that when he rushed over to her, she could barely feel his breath on her, his lips on her skin as he gently kissed her shaking hands. The sensation of his fingertips brushing away the hair at her scalp. She could, however, hear his words.

"Oh my God! What have I done? My little kitten. I'm so sorry. Please talk to me."

The coating then turned hard, into an armor. She could feel it seal around her. Outside she had changed. Inside she had changed. And no matter how much she was shaking, she forced herself to pull herself up off the floor. "I'm okay. I'll be okay."

"I'm sorry, Annie. I'm sorry. I'll get help," he said, taking her into his arms. "I promise I will. I will never hurt you again."

Jason went to the refrigerator and pulled out a bottle of white wine. He poured an oversized amount into a glass for her. "Here," he said. She pushed it away. She was too confused. He insisted. "Just to take the edge off. Too help you stop shaking."

She reluctantly complied. But he was right. The liquid, when it washed down her, did take the edge off. It quieted the pain. She took small sips at first but then downed the glass. She felt numb. Not better, not worse. Just calm.

The alcohol went right to her head and when she stood, she lost her footing and collapsed into his arms. He delicately lifted her into the bedroom.

chapter twenty-six

---

the present.

That night Annie woke in a cold sweat from a dream, feeling more unsettled than she'd felt in years. Why had she slept with Hugh? She had had everything under control before that, hadn't she? Yes, she liked him, but she could control it before. And now that panic had crossed into her dreams. Panic told her she was no longer in control of it. It was in control of her, and it could only mean a batshit spiral into bad from here. Just like with the others.

Just like with Tom, who would have left his girlfriend for her had she not called the girlfriend in a drunken stupor one night when he'd chosen to see the girlfriend over Annie, and Annie told her everything. While the girlfriend was with Tom. Who was breaking up with her at the time for Annie...

Just like with Jerry, who had been so nice and patient with her, and only left her for "Massive Marlene" when he discovered she was also seeing George...

Just like with George, who she threw out of her apartment in a drunken rage in the middle of sex because he'd called her "Kitten," and only Jason had ever called her that...

Just like with Jason, who...

No. She still couldn't bear the thought of what she had done there.

And there were so many others. Faces without names. Bodies without faces. She didn't know how to get close without getting hurt, or without creating hurt. She was broken. She was unrepairable. She wasn't going to get close again. She wasn't going to let it happen again.

She flipped open her phone and called Rebecca. "It's me. It's happening again."

"What time is it?" Even hearing the "groggy" in her friend's voice, she felt too panicked to hang up.

"It was a dream. I saw it in a dream. I was walking with him and we were laughing and having a great time, and then out of nowhere, he started walking really slow. I mean, *really slow*. And we weren't in step anymore. And I just kept talking and he was gone. I was there, in the street, by myself."

"Oh Annie..."

"Then all of a sudden, there he was again. Bounding up the sidewalk with this giant duffle bag on his back. But when he got closer, I realized it wasn't a bag at all."

A deep sigh. "What was it?"

"It was Charlotte! He was carrying her on his back!"

"Is that even physically possible? From what you've told me."

"Oh ha ha. It was a dream. Anyway, here's the scary part. He was panting and sweating and then he said to me, 'I couldn't leave her behind. I need for her to be with me. I hope that's okay.' Can you believe that?"

"Annie, this is just a dream. This is stuff you're creating in your own head. Please just try to be logical."

"No, this is a message. This is a *clear* message!"

"I don't get it."

"Rebecca, can't you see? I'm just the 'safe harbor.' The *transition* girl."

"Safe harbor? Honey, I don't think that any term could apply less—"

"He's going to fall for Charlotte. He may already be there…"

"Oh, come on. Why are you doing this? Why do you always do this?"

"Because I let myself like him. I trusted him, and I never should have trusted him. I always knew it would be her. I always felt it."

"If you just want to be friends with the guy, what does it matter?"

"I don't *want* to just be friends with him. It *has* to be that way. Don't you get it? I have to protect him."

"Honey, I'm sorry, but I just don't."

"It doesn't matter anymore. I'm telling you. I can feel it. He's going to land there."

Rebecca sighed heavily. "Okay. So what are you going to do about it?"

"*Do* about it? What can I *do* about it? It's over—or it's going to be. I told him all I wanted was to be friends. I felt so much for him and I didn't want to destroy him. And now he's going to turn his back on me. All because I didn't tell him the truth."

"So say something this time. Stop it before it gets too out of hand. Talk to him. If he matters that much to you, just tell him."

"I don't know. I don't think he'd understand."

"If he really cares about you, he'll understand." Rebecca paused a moment. "I still can't believe you slept with him."

"Hey!"

"I'm sorry, Annie, but this always happens. You sleep with them, and then you get nuts and you drive them away. I just wish—"

"I thought it was different this time. I mean, it *is* different this time…. I mean… I don't know what I mean."

"There's only one way to know if it *is*. Let yourself trust him. You have to level with him."

"But what if that pushes him away?"

"Well, then you have your answer."

"I don't think I could face that. I think I should just disappear. It would be easier…"

"Annie, you're going to have to face this. And sooner or later you're going to have to face everything—"

Panic seized her. She cut Rebecca off. "Okay, I'll try. I'll call you later," she snapped abruptly, then pressed the "end call" button and tossed the phone across the bed.

Annie wrapped herself in her arms. She stared at the phone. What if she was right? What if Hugh didn't feel the things for her she felt for him? What if he didn't understand her, understand her past? He certainly pressed her enough to know. But what if she did level with him? Would that mean losing him for good? It was almost too much to take.

She knew she was a broken person, a box of broken parts that no sane person would ever want to take on once they knew the truth about her. Why would Hugh be any different? Why *should* he be?

She burrowed into her blankets and buried her face in her pillow and cried. She couldn't do anything else for now, as much as she wanted to.

chapter twenty-seven

---

the present.

When his phone vibrated, Hugh turned down the volume on the TV. "Hey! I was watching that!" Charlotte barked from the other end of the couch.

A big smile came over his face when he saw who was calling, and he held up his phone to show her. He was so happy that Annie was calling, he didn't notice Charlotte's eye roll before she stormed out of the living room and into the kitchen.

"Hey."

"Hi. It's me."

"Hi, I know. Caller ID. I'm glad you called. I was just thinking about you—"

"Look, we need to talk, okay? Can you meet me tomorrow night?"

We need to talk...

"Is everything okay?" he asked, but he knew everything wasn't.

"I'm... I'm not sure."

Just then, Charlotte came back into the room. "What is it?" she whispered, and he waved her off. He jumped off the couch and headed into the kitchen, missing yet another eye roll from Charlotte.

"What's this about?" he asked.

"Not on the phone," she said. "I need to do this in person."

His heart sank. He had been on the receiving end of this enough times to know this wasn't going to end well for him. His eyes fixed on a "Bee Positive" sign tacked to the refrigerator, which Charlotte had made by pasting black and yellow buttons onto poster board. "Okay," he said, trying his best to sound cool, but feeling anything but.

"Eight o'clock tomorrow night." She gave him the name and address of a bar in Midtown and hung up.

He looked at the poster again. "Go fuck yourself," he said to it as Charlotte came into the kitchen.

"Okay...?"

Hugh snapped out of the place he had gotten himself. "No, I'm sorry. I didn't mean you."

She followed his glance. "Buzz-Bee then?"

"No. Sorry. It's... It's Annie."

At that, Charlotte put her arm around him, concern in her eyes. "Bad?" It was so bad. She was right. Charlotte was absolutely right. Dammit!

"She wants to talk," he said, and she pulled him into a hug, concretizing all the horrible concerns he'd had over the conversation before Annie hung up on him.

"Oh no," she said. "That's really bad." What Hugh couldn't see from his vantage point was the Cheshire Cat grin Charlotte now wore from ear to ear. "Oh, honey. I'm so sorry. I hate to say that I told you so..."

Hugh pulled away. "So I'm not overreacting? You also think..." All he could think about now was about being dumped. Every time. About how completely and utterly painful it was to be abandoned when you were in love.

How badly it had burned to come home after a weekend photography seminar to find Alicia had just left with all her things, without leaving as much as a note for him. He had to chase her down, calling her twenty times before she'd answered. "Sometimes it doesn't work out," was all she said when he'd finally gotten her to pick up the phone.

How empty and useless he'd felt when Sheila had decided he just wasn't the one for her, and how badly she'd wanted to get married and have a family and being with him was just wasting time for them both.

And so, so many others....

"Of course. What else could it be?" She pulled him back into her arms. "I hate to say, 'I told you so,' but honey, I really did."

chapter twenty-eight

the present.

When Hugh arrived at the bar, he didn't see Annie. This made him a little nervous, but also annoyed him—that either she wasn't going to show, or was going to show up late and in a frenetic tizzy like she had at The Campbell Apartment that night. He didn't realize that the sad, small form in the oversized sweater sipping a martini at the bar was Annie. His heart sank at the realization, but he was determined to stay firm. He approached her.

"Hi," he said.

"Thanks for coming," she said through a weak smile. Yeah, nice and phony, was all he could think. When she kissed him lightly on the cheek, he could feel himself recoil in disdain. He hadn't realized he was so angry.

"I'll have one of those," he told the bartender, indicating Annie's drink.

Then she giggled. She actually giggled. "Oh, but you can't..."

That infuriated him, but he was determined to keep his cool. "I said, I'll have one of those."

"Okay," and the bartender left to make his drink. She turned to him and invited him to sit.

"I'll stand, thank you," he barked, firm in his resolve not to let another woman stomp all over him ever again.

She shrugged. "Okay, well I guess you're wondering why I needed to see you."

"Right," he said, as cold as the kiss she had given him. If she was going to dump him, he certainly wasn't going to give her the satisfaction of letting her know that he cared about it in any way. "Well….?"

She gave him a tentative glance. "Maybe let's wait for your drink—"

"Now's as good a time as any," he barked back, shocking himself at his tone. If he had surprised himself, he certainly seemed to take Annie off guard. *Good. To hell with her.*

"So…" she stammered.

He was losing patience. "What do you want to talk about?"

"Okay, well, you know how things have gotten a little weird between us—you know, maybe since..." she trailed off as the bartender delivered Hugh's drink.

"Yeah," he said and took a long sip. It didn't burn at all. He was feeling way too angry to be able to feel anything else.

"There's a reason," she said. "At least for me." She stopped talking to take another sip. "Did I ever tell you about my grandmother—what happened..."

That was it. There was no way he was going down one of her rabbit holes with her again. "You know, I didn't come here to be led on by one of your stories. I gotta work tomorrow and I have plenty of other places I'd rather be right now."

"Okay, sorry, but... well... okay, well…" She squirmed in her seat.

Good.

He had had enough. "You know what—"

"I'm sorry. This is just really hard for me. I've never been really good at this kind of thing."

"Good, when you finally manage to spit whatever it is you have to say out of that mouth of yours, why don't you give me a call," he said and got up to leave.

"Okay, now I see," she said, taking him by the elbow but talking to her drink. "I know what's happening here."

Now he felt alone—like she wasn't there with him anymore. That she was some place far, far away. Whatever ability he had had to read what she was feeling, it was gone. He couldn't get anything from her. She was closed to him now.

Good.

That would make it easier to keep strong. "Well, if you'd be so kind as to inform the people in the room that aren't in your head…"

And then, without warning, she was back in the room. Her back was straight, her eyes bore into him. "I don't think we should see each other anymore. It's just that…"

"Yeah, no kidding. Let me see: We're not ready…"

"Well, yes and no. I mean, that's a huge part of it, but—"

He didn't know what possessed him to sit down, but down he sat, resting his elbows on the bar and looking her right in the eyes. Trying to look right through her. Not into her, but *through* her. Like she wasn't even there. He had to start to see himself on the other side of her.

"Uh huh," he said, trying to sound smug. "I see it now. An easy out. Okay, I had not expected that from you. But you know what. I'm going to give it to you. Go ahead. Whatever you have to say. It's as good an excuse as any."

"Wait, what? Hang on. I mean… I don't think I'm communicating here. I mean, yes and no, Hugh. That we're not ready is a huge part of it. You've really hardly ever been single in your life, and…"

What he couldn't hear were the words in her heart. The ones she couldn't say. The ones he used to be able to hear. All he could hear were the only words she could speak: "It's *not* an excuse."

"Yeah, whatever," he said. "I don't think there's anything more to get into here. I don't think we have anything left to say to each other."

He jumped up again and then surprised himself by downing his drink in one long swallow. This time he could feel the vodka in his brain like a mist. He felt like he wanted to fall over.

"Please," she said. "Let's not leave off like this. Couldn't we just talk it through?"

Then her hand was on him again and the mist cleared and the rage returned. "Okay, here's me 'talking it through.' Here's how I'm going to leave off." He glowered at her and tried as hard as he could to hurt her with his eyes. To make her feel as small and horrible as he himself felt. He logged off being himself, of being nice-guy Hugh, and decided to let the vodka speak for him. "So you know what? It's *not* alright. Okay? Not even close. I've had enough of this—of you women. To hell with you all!"

"Wait, no. I think you're missing the point…"

Hugh started to walk off. Without looking back, he called, "Take care of yourself," and stormed out.

The minute he left the bar he felt empowered. Vindicated. At last, for once and finally, he had won. He'd done the unthinkable. Just left her there by herself, with her alcoholism and her other demons. He felt better than he had in years! And better yet, throughout it all, never once did he feel like he couldn't breathe. He'd conquered it all, at last!

Except he had no idea why he was crying.

chapter twenty-nine

---

circa 1943.

Maggie stormed down the sidewalk. She had never been angrier in her life. Who did he think he was? How long did he think he was going to get away with lying to her like this? What? Was he just going to disappear one day, without warning?

She seethed at the thought as her hand continued to fondle the official-looking brown envelope she had taken off the entry table when she'd gone to visit his mother earlier that morning. She knew that he already knew what was inside. It wasn't as if the letter had been sealed. It had been opened and it had been read. It was dated and postmarked from weeks—WEEKS!—back. He knew about this and he had kept it from her. And she was not going to stand for that.

As she approached the barbershop, she took a deep breath. She fondled the diamond cross around her neck to try and soothe herself. She knew she had to calm down. She had to swallow her mother's inherited temper, the temper that had caused her mother to leave Maggie and her father behind without so much as a goodbye kiss or note. With every step she took, she swallowed it down. Because if she approached this angry, it *would* all be her looking crazy. Like she was overreacting. Even though she wasn't overreacting at all. Because he lied to her. He lied! She had never felt more betrayed.

She finally arrived and stood outside the window where she watched the lying liar comb and trim the long beard of a customer. She chewed a nail for a moment, watching him. The way he smiled as he chatted to his customer and Stan, who was working on another customer to his left. The way his eyes alone could brighten the room. His chiseled, expressive features.

Before she was ready, Stan noticed her, and she watched him tap Walter to alert him. And she watched Stan point outside at her and she watched as both men smiled, so happy to see her. But when Walter's eyes met hers, she saw something else there. She could feel it through the glass. A sense of unease, of dread. Who was he to be looking at her with such dread in his eyes?

She again swallowed her anger and forced a smile onto her face. As friendly as she could be, she motioned for him to join her outside. He nodded to her, removed the towel from his client's neck, and shook his hand. Then he motioned to Stan and headed outside.

"To what do I owe this delicious surprise," he asked, wrapping her in his arms. Those arms. The tight muscles like rope. She stroked them just a moment then willed herself strong and pushed away from him.

"What—" he asked.

"What is this?" she demanded, and yanked the envelope out of her purse. She started waving it in his face then shouted again, "Why didn't you tell me?"

Walter looked at his shoes. That he couldn't look at her only fueled her rage—a rage she felt at once both justified and ridiculous in feeling.

"I didn't want to tell you. I knew…"

"Knew what?"

He looked at her now, his face showing both guilt and a little fear. "I knew you would take it like this. Look, it's not about us. It's about something bigger. Something I have to do—"

"You said you would never leave me. You PROMISED me you would never leave me."

He looked back into the shop. Stan waved. They both awkwardly waved back. "Can we please talk about this later?" he pleaded.

She stared at him for a minute, and as she stood there, all she could think was that he had enlisted to get away from her. She was burning with hot madness and she knew it. Logically she knew the way she felt made no sense. But she couldn't bring herself to let logic win.

"Fine." She chucked the envelope at him. And didn't look back.

As she stormed down the street, she passed Smitty's. As if the whole Universe was out to mock her, the window was done up to salute all the young heroes who were fighting overseas for their country.

But it was when she saw a revolver on a black velvet pedestal stand in that window that she got what was possibly the craziest idea of them all.

chapter thirty

---

the present.

Hugh could feel himself falling apart. He had thought that by being strong, by taking the upper hand, that he could control whatever emotions would ensue when he lost her. If he was in charge of the loss, of course it would hurt less.

Now he knew better. It would never hurt less.

For the past week or so, he had spent most of his time holed up in his bedroom, thinking. He'd sworn he wasn't going to fall in love with Annie. And he was quite sure he had not. They weren't even a couple! And yet... why did he miss her so much? Why did he feel so horrible about what had transpired between them? Why had he gone totally batshit on her?

He knew why. He knew it going in to that bar. He was tired of being the sucker all the time. He needed to stand up for himself, and the time had finally come. He had guessed what she wanted correctly—and Charlotte had confirmed it for him. And if severing ties wasn't what she wanted to do, she would have said something. She would have changed the conversation. She would have told him. If she truly wanted him, she would have fought back. She would have tried to show him that he was wrong—that he had misread her intentions.

She didn't. She'd let him go. That was a sure sign that she had lost interest in him and was looking for a way out. Any idiot could see that.

But still, he missed her.

And still, there was regret. While logically everything had played out as logic would have it play out, he couldn't help but feel something was off. If something wasn't, why did he feel regret? He had always imagined if he for once in his goddamned life was the "dumper," and not the "dumpee," he wouldn't feel those awful pangs. That awful loss. So why did he feel them so clearly and so heavily now?

Hugh knew getting out and keeping busy was the only way to heal, but he didn't want to heal. He wanted to lie on his bed, mope, and listen to Peter Gabriel's "Red Rain," over and over again, because that song put him in a moment he so desperately wanted to live in, a moment of pure connection that he truly had never felt before and that he had intentionally severed.

I come to you, defenses down…

With the trust of a child.

He played it repeatedly on the stupid boom box he'd picked up to win back Sheila. So many stupid choices made. How many more stupid choices could one guy make?

Lost in the song, he didn't hear Charlotte come in. He didn't realize she was there for several minutes, watching him mope. In fact, he didn't know she was in the room until she walked over to the boom box and turned the CD off.

"Hey!"

"You're driving the entire building bananas with that track. And me. I can't hear it anymore."

He jumped out of his bed and turned it back on again, this time cranking up the volume.

"You can't keep doing this," she called over the music. "You're making yourself crazy over nothing."

That ticked him off. "What makes you think it was nothing?"

Charlotte sighed. Then she turned off the music, pulled the CD out of the dock, and snapped it in half.

"Hey!"

"Look, Hugh. I have seen you go through this hundreds of times. I can't bear it again."

He snatched the pieces of the disc out of her hands and tried to put them back together.

"You look like crap," she said.

He tossed the broken pieces in the garbage. "I feel like crap."

"Why don't we go out and grab a drink? Why don't you grab a shower?"

"I don't know…"

Just then Charlotte got distracted. Her eye went to a point at the other end of the room. She headed to the spot with a singular focus. He peered over to see what had distracted her. She bent over then came back up again with the remnants of TP Hugh, destroyed by the cats. She shot him a look of grave disappointment as she turned the shreds in her fingers, looking pathetically like she was trying to put it back together. Finally, she threw it down on the dresser in frustration. She looked at him again, tears in her eyes. He felt like the worst person.

"Char, I'm sorry. I—"

"There's an exhibit. I think we should go to the exhibit, then get a drink."

He shrugged his shoulders. "I really don't want—"

"It's Lichtenstein. You always liked him," she said, now joining him on the bed.

"No, not today."

They sat quietly for several moments until Charlotte finally spoke again. "For what it's worth… I am sorry."

Hugh didn't know what to say. "It's not your fault. You were only trying to help. The whole time, you warned me and I never listened. It's my fault, really."

"You can't blame yourself that the world doesn't understand you."

"You understand me," he said. She shrugged. "So if you understand me, can you please tell me what it is about me that's so repulsive? What is it that I put out there that makes women turn off me like they do?"

She pursed her lips. "Wow, you really are dumb."

"Oh come on now—*et tu*, Charlotte?"

She shook her head. "It isn't *you*, sweetie. It's never been *you*. Don't you see? It's your choices. These women. They're not right for you. You're always drawn to women with agendas. They just use you and—"

Cold-blooded…

Hugh surprised himself by bursting into tears. Charlotte pulled him into her arms. "No, I'm sorry. I didn't mean it that way. Shhh…"

Hugh tried to speak through his sobs, but he gave up. She drew him closer and stroked his hair. He started to relax into her embrace. But when she cupped his face in her hands and wiped away his tears with her thumbs, he started to tense. And when she leaned in and kissed him on the mouth, he jumped right out her arms. "No, Charlotte. We can't," he said. "Please. I don't want to lose another friend."

She pulled herself closer to him again. "Just trust me, okay? I've never hurt you before. I'm not going to hurt you now." She pulled him in close again and he let her.

209

"No. We can't..." But back in her arms, he was finding it harder and harder to resist this sense of security. This safe place...

"Hugh, my precious Hugh. I believe so much in *us*. Don't you understand?" She covered his eyelids with soft kisses and he let her. He let the comfort wash over him. And when she moved her lips back down to his, this time he didn't resist. He let her take him in in a long, languid kiss.

She pulled away from him and said, "Look at me. Don't you know that all I want is to love you? That all I've ever wanted is to love you, and for you to let me."

And with that, everything changed. Hugh had a jolt—a reckoning. He wasn't going to lose Charlotte's friendship. This was the kind of connection they had always been meant to have. One that was safe and comfortable and unthreatening. And now the friendship could at last move to the level where it was supposed to get to after all of these years.

No wonder why no other woman had made sense with him before. They'd all been wrong for him. That was why it never worked—of course! And as more clothes were removed and more soft, safe kisses exchanged, all Hugh felt was secure and loved. This was what he had always craved. What his mother had told him all those years to hold out for. That was what he had always had, in Charlotte. And now, at long last, he finally saw it. With Charlotte, he was finally home.

chapter thirty-one

the present.

For more than a week after her soul-crushing encounter with Hugh, Annie kept pretty much to herself, shut in by herself in her apartment, drinking wine and watching Lifetime TV movies. Mr. Badass was even starting to get sick of her. For a whole week, Annie had faked the flu and not gone to work. Her head could not function when her heart shut down. And it had been shut down brutally this time.

She had no idea how things had gotten so ugly when she'd met up with Hugh. She realized pretty quickly she wasn't going to be able to tell him how she really felt about him—how scared it made her. But not only hadn't he left her an opening, it was like he'd slammed the door in her face and clicked shut dozens of locks. How could it have gone any other way? The way he had acted toward her. Clearly he didn't care about her as she imagined he did. He obviously didn't feel the same way, and she would only have embarrassed herself had she told him anything about how she really felt. How had she so horribly misjudged him? What an idiot she was.

Yet despite what had gone down, she couldn't help but feel that something was off. She hadn't known him that long, but his behavior seemed totally shocking to her. He didn't seem to be acting like himself at all, and she had a pretty good idea why. Charlotte was influencing him. She was sure.

Still, she missed him. She hadn't realized just how much she had come to count on Hugh. How much joy their short involvement had brought her. How he seemed to understand her in a way no one else ever had. He made her feel normal. Being around him, she'd felt sane. But now he was gone, and she could feel her sanity spilling out all over the place until she was sure not a drop of it would be left.

At some point, on the sixth or seventh day, the phone rang. She was conflicted. Part of her felt hope. Hugh had called her on that line before. Maybe this was him calling to apologize?

The second ring sounded and she could feel the hope flutter in her heart. She started to feel less crazy. He was calling to apologize. Everything was going to start making sense again.

After the third ring, hope was replaced by dread. There had always been more bad news than good news recorded on that machine...

"Hey, it's Tabi. Call me when you get this. Great news. I know one of the waiters at Parchment and he got us a table. Can't wait to see you, sweetie!"

"What the—?" Annie was confused. Who the hell was Tabi? She hit the "Play" button again. She could feel her body tense as she listened to the woman's message again. A sick sense of dread rose from her heart and into her throat. "No," she said. "No, it's not that." She shook her head. "Has to be a wrong number."

She was well into feeling normal and making dinner when the phone rang.

"Hello?"

"Kitten. It's me."

"Oh hey. I was just starting dinner——"

"Good. I'm glad I caught you in time. I'm not going to make it home in time for dinner tonight. There's a union thing I can't miss."

That knot of dread tightened again. "Uh… Sure. So why don't I just make something and you can heat it up when you get home?"

"Oh, it'll be very, very late. I was planning to hit a meeting after. I'll just grab a slice of pizza or something in between."

"Right…"

"Don't wait up for me, kitten."

She felt like she'd just been kicked in the stomach. "Okay," she said absently. "But… Before you go…" She took a deep breath. "Do you know someone named Tabi?"

She shuddered at the memory of how she'd learned that Jason had found someone else, and how vehemently he'd denied it when she'd confronted him. The story he'd told about having a sponsor. About how it was perfectly normal for sponsors to treat the addicts they were looking after with such affection... to call them "sweetie."

It was six years ago already, but it still stung.

After the fourth ring, her message sounded, followed by a beep. Annie held her breath. "Annie pick up. I know you're there." Rebecca. "Your receptionist said you've been out sick all week. That must be some flu. Annie, pick up the phone." Her heart sank. Reality was reality. No matter what she thought, no matter what she wanted to believe, Hugh was done with her. "Come on." There was the sound of deep breathing. "I swear to God I'm going to come over there and rip you out of that bed... Annie? Annie? Okay, that's it. I'll be there in half an hour."

"Yeah, and how you gonna get in?" Annie said to the machine, surprising herself at how badly she was slurring the words.

"I have your keys," Rebecca remarked, as though reading her mind.

"Shit," Annie said, now feeling sober. She glanced around her apartment, disaster that it was, and started to panic that Rebecca was going to come in with a fresh lecture—one she didn't want to face. She pulled herself off the rug, fighting desperately to stop her head from spinning, and made a frantic but feeble attempt at straightening up. When she opened the trash can to throw things away, it smelled so vile she vomited right into it.

She quickly tied off the garbage bag and placed it on the floor, grateful that she had managed not to throw up on anything else.

Minutes later, she heard her front door locks clicking and Rebecca barged in. "Jesus Annie, how do you live like this?" she asked, and immediately started straightening things up. "This is disgusting."

"I don't know," Annie said, swiping at her mouth with the back of her hand. "Why are you here?"

Rebecca lifted Mr. Badass off the floor and placed him back in his tank. "You poor thing," she said through the glass as she watched him crawl on top of his heating stone. Then she looked at Annie. "What's going on?"

Annie looked away. "It's nothing. It's a bug. It should run its course soon."

She watched then as Rebecca scanned the room and all the empty bottles Annie had missed in her cleanup. "Looks more like a bender to me."

"Well—" Annie began, but Rebecca silenced her with a wave. "Is this really about *him?*"

"So what if it is?"

Rebecca shook her head. "You know, you can't keep doing this to yourself every time it doesn't work out. Sometimes it doesn't work out. Period. Move on."

Rebecca didn't get it. She never got it when it came to matters of the heart. Practical and unfeeling. She never understood and she never would. "See, that's what you said about Jason. But you never knew all the details. You never knew the real..."

Rebecca shot her a piercing glance. "I know more than you think."

Her words hit right to the heart. Annie quickly looked away.

"You have to stop punishing yourself like this," Rebecca said. "You can't keep doing this to yourself just because you lost—"

"But I found it again. You said it didn't exist and it does and I found it again. The *magic*. It was wonderful... And then I fucked it up. I ruined everything. Just like with Jason."

Rebecca took in a deep breath. "You *really* think Hugh was all that? So into you? As good for you as Jason before you 'fucked that up'?"

"I do."

"Then it's time to sober up. Go take a shower and get dressed."

"Why? Where are we going?"

"You'll see."

chapter thirty-two

———————

the present.

An hour later, Annie and Rebecca were back at the Waverly Place penthouse where Annie had first connected with Hugh. A raging party was well underway as they entered. Annie felt nervous. Lost. Panicked. The memory of her night with Hugh within these walls was unavoidable. And so, apparently, was Hugh.

Her heart shut down when she caught sight of him. Annie turned to Rebecca. "You didn't tell me he was going to be here!" She felt utterly betrayed.

"Better that he is," Rebecca said firmly. "You have to stop hiding away. You need to face things and you need closure. Go get it," she said, nodding at Hugh as he approached them, smiling uncomfortably.

"Oh God, I'm going to puke," Annie said.

Rebecca gave her a reassuring pat on the back. "I'm in the kitchen if you need me," she said, and turned to leave just as Hugh arrived.

Before she did, he extended his hand to her. "You must be Rebecca?"

Rebecca shook it. "Yeah. And you're screwed," she said, and left.

Hugh turned to Annie. The air was thick with nerves and anxiety, which she imagined were hers until he opened his mouth to speak. "Well… How are you? You're looking well." She couldn't believe how badly he was stammering. Why hadn't she ever noticed he stammered before?

She could barely even look at him, but she noticed he was wearing a plain black T-shirt, and she hated herself for feeling disappointed about it. No irony tonight. No sweet subversion. Just darkness. Just void. "Yeah, I guess I've been going to the gym a lot," she lied, scanning the room. There was no way she was going to admit to her steady diet of cabernet and throwing up takeout food these past couple of weeks. The situation was so painful, so uncomfortable. She tried to shield herself with disdain, yet all she could manage to dredge forth was a deep sense of longing. It was way too much to deal with and she had to get away from him.

"You know, I have to…" she said, already walking away.

"Of course. I'll catch up with you—" he called after her.

"Sure. See you," she said, and he darted off in the other direction.

Annie headed deeper into the apartment, scanning the crowd for one familiar face. She didn't even need a friendly one. As she got closer to the kitchen, she saw Charlotte. Resolving to take the high road, she decided to speak to her as she approached. "Charlotte, hello. How are you?"

Charlotte did not acknowledge her. Instead, she looked right through her. Then she smirked and walked off without a word.

"That bitch!" Annie said out loud to no one, but she was angry and confused and still a little drunk—and the filters that barely worked when she was sober could certainly not be trusted at a time like this.

She stormed off and finally found Rebecca in the kitchen, telling her with great drama how absolutely stunned and angry and confused she was by Charlotte having snubbed her like that.

Rebecca peered at her. "Do you understand now?"

"I understand that Charlotte's a total bitch, but I always knew that."

Rebecca shook her head. "You know what? I think this was a bad idea. Why don't we just leave."

"Works for me. I just gotta pee."

"Okay, I'll be right here," Rebecca said.

When Annie got to a nearby bathroom, she was relieved to find the door wasn't locked and she barreled right in. And when she did, her heart stopped.

"Uh, taken!" said a woman's familiar voice.

Annie froze. Of all the rooms in this apartment, of all the freaking bathrooms, how had she managed to walk in on Charlotte making out with Hugh? "Sonofabitch..."

Hugh turned around. "Annie!"

She fled. There was nothing else she could do. She took off. As she ran from the room all she could feel was nauseated. And all she could hear was Hugh calling her name as he ran after her.

She wanted to die as she ran through the apartment, and time and space seemed to blur. She could hear his shoes as they clomped down the hall after her. But she could not stop. All she could do was run. Her whole brain seemed to seize. Her vision was gray and she couldn't see past the shield of tears that had welled up in her eyes.

A jolt back to reality came in the form of Hugh's hand on her arm. She was trapped. She turned to face him. She could see Hugh's face and knew he was talking to her, but she had no idea what he was saying. All she could feel now was that familiar coating closing over her again. That coating that had shielded her from Jason the first time he hit her. That protection she'd tried to close over herself.

"Annie, please! Wait! Please don't go like this." Hugh could get through the wall. She didn't want to hear his words but she could not shut him out. His words were finding all the little cracks and making their way in. When she couldn't make the shield protect her, when she couldn't close in her emotions, they spilled out in her own words.

"I can't believe you. Holy shit! Can't you see what you're doing? I mean... We talked about this. We talked about... You know you can't trust yourself right now—"

He laughed. He actually stood there and laughed at her. "Wait? So you're going to talk to me about trust? *You?* Considering you haven't trusted me enough to tell me one true thing about yourself the whole time I've known you. You never told me a thing about you that was real. Just a bunch of crazy stories!" His voice was shaking worse than hers. "You just don't understand what it's like with me and Charlotte."

And then the words "I know what it was like between me and you" popped out of her mouth and she was powerless to stop them.

He looked utterly confused and how could she blame him really. "Reality check here, okay? We were *not* involved. We were *just friends*—as I recall... The way *you* wanted it. And, holy cow, I mean... wasn't it you who called the 'special meeting'? The one who decided for both of us that we should go our separate ways. I mean, man. You didn't even want to know how I felt about anything. If I wanted more from whatever it was we were doing. It didn't matter to you!"

She was more confused than ever. There was too much going on. He was saying things she couldn't understand. "Wait a minute. Me? I thought it was what *you* wanted or... I don't know. I wanted... I wanted..."

He then seemed to get very angry at her. "I know. I get it. Loud and clear. To be friends. All you wanted was for us to be freaking friends. So I really don't understand where all this is coming from..."

Annie started backing away. Her vision was blurring. She couldn't feel anything except stunned. And when that wore off, all she felt was pain. A deep and horrible pain. She knew she cared about Hugh. Until this moment, she had no idea how much she cared. How deeply rejected she felt by him. How horribly betrayed to see him with Charlotte like that...

To deal with the pain of Jason's betrayal, she learned she could numb it, with anger. With wine, but with anger.

Pain turned to deep pain. Deep pain turned to anger.

Before she could think twice about it, the anger took over. "Wow. You really *are* something else, aren't you. A pathetic serial monogamist. It's sickening, actually. How you are. I mean, shit. You just swing from woman to woman. Hoping the next one will tell you what to do next. Feed you all the answers you need in life with a spoon..."

"Well at least I'm happy now."

The hurt on his face only fueled her. "Happy? Are you crazy? You must be crazy. You're a drowning victim clinging to anything to stay above water. And you choose the garbage barge..." She was finding it harder to speak without shouting.

"At least I knew I was drowning and I saved myself," he shouted back, and started wheezing. "I mean, what about you, Annie? Huh? What makes you so crazy? Do you even know? I mean, look at you. You're a mess of lies and contradictions. Nothing you say or are is true. Why is that?"

"What are you even talking about? This isn't about me."

"Isn't it? What am I talking about? Where do I begin? The stories. The lies. And, my goodness just look at you." He started coughing uncontrollably but finally caught his breath. "I mean, your necklace, for one. You say you hate Catholic people, but you're walking around wearing a diamond cross? I mean... Who does that?"

Annie's fingers found the diamond cross, and the feel of it on her skin gave her the resolve she needed. The resolve of generations.

"Fuck you!" she shouted at him. "I hope you burn in hell."

"And I suppose I'll see you there, you lying—"

"Good-bye, Hugh," she said. As Annie stormed off, she wiped the last of the tears she thought she would ever cry away from her cheek. She had now said everything she had wanted to say to him. Whether he watched her walk away or not, she didn't know or care. It was time to move on.

"Annie, wait! Please!" Rebecca called as she swooshed by her.

Annie whipped around, feeling more enraged at Rebecca than she had at Hugh or at anyone in recent memory. "You knew they were going to be here. You knew they were together! Why did you do this to me?"

"You wouldn't have accepted it otherwise." She could see Rebecca fighting back tears and it only made her more angry.

"You couldn't have just picked up the phone and said 'Guess what?'..."

"No. I'm sorry. But I know you, and I knew this was the only way you'd get it. It's the only way you ever have. I mean... how you were with Jason. How you still are. I thought maybe seeing it with your own eyes, that maybe that would shake you out of all the stories you tell yourself..." Her voice cracked. "Oh God, what a terrible idea. I am so, so sorry..."

Annie walked up to Rebecca and stared her right in the face. "You're as bad as my mother," she practically spat and started walking away before doubling back. "No, I take that back. You're worse."

"Annie, come on. Let's talk this out. Please!" Rebecca called after her. "Where are you going?"

"Far away from here!" she shouted and stormed out, slamming the front door behind her, not giving a damn about the scene she'd just caused as she raced down the sidewalk and hailed a cab to take her home.

chapter thirty-three

three years ago.

The problem with Annie, Rebecca well knew, and had always known in all their years of friendship, was that when Annie felt something, when she *strongly* felt something, there wasn't any way to convince her otherwise.

It was like the time in second grade when Annie couldn't accept getting a 97 on a spelling test and insisted to her parents that it was a perfect score anyway.

It was like the time in middle school when she didn't make the cut for the school musical, but showed up for all the rehearsals anyway.

It was like the time in high school when Annie had invited herself on a date with another friend and the friend's boyfriend, and had everyone convinced that the boy did, indeed, belong to her. Just before Jason...

Jason, whom Annie had convinced herself was a prince. A dream come true. A magical white knight.

Rebecca had always had a feeling something was off about Jason. She wasn't too keen on how Jason spoke to Annie. Not in rough tones, but in the words he used. He controlled her. When he was nice to her, it wasn't so bad. But when he wasn't...

She had tried to talk Annie out of marrying Jason, but there was no way to reason with Annie. It was like a sickness. A sickness that, unfortunately, as Rebecca had come to see in all the years her friend had been with Jason, could only be healed with a shock. In this case, the shock of what he had done to her...

But even that didn't seem to be registering for Annie.

Rebecca didn't want Annie to have to endure any more shocks, but Annie wasn't getting it. She wasn't getting that her marriage was over. That Jason didn't love her anymore. That it was time to leave. She was going through the motions of moving, while Rebecca tried so gently and carefully, but also, firmly, to guide her out of this life with Jason and into a place of peace. She wanted to accomplish this before he got back home. But if not...

No. Annie didn't need another shock. Annie needed to get out.

"We only have about an hour to go," Rebecca called out. "Can you hear me?" She stepped over stacks of books and piles of clothes and linens as she headed into the kitchen. "Annie?"

As she walked, Rebecca looked down to find an open box, almost completely packed. At the top of the box was a worn stuffed animal. A yellow chick dressed to look like a bride. She shook her head and let out a deep sigh as she plucked the chick from the box and tossed it onto the couch. She then grabbed an empty box and some newspaper and found Annie in the kitchen.

"Annie?"

Annie had the refrigerator door open and her back to Rebecca. When she called her name again, her friend turned around, and it was all she could do to look at her. She was bruised so badly and bandaged, and she had a vacant look in her eyes. Rebecca had to look away. How had this man, this horrible man, taken her vibrant friend and changed her into this empty thing? Annie turned back to the refrigerator and pulled out an open bottle of white wine.

"Come on, sweetie. We have to hurry," Rebecca said encouragingly. "They'll be back soon."

Annie stared a moment at the bottle of chardonnay in her hand and then took a huge swig. "Chardonnay is too oaky for me. Too heavy. Do you like chardonnay?" she asked, offering Rebecca the bottle.

Rebecca shook her head and Annie took another swig before Rebecca took the bottle away from her and placed it back in the refrigerator.

"*Now,* Annie. If we want to get out of here before he gets back."

Rebecca's heart broke at the sight of Annie—her blank stare. At the state of her. She knew one thing and that was that she had to keep Annie focused. She had to help her collect as much of her stuff from this apartment as possible before that asshole got back with his new girlfriend. Because despite everything that had happened, Rebecca knew that Annie would forget everything that bastard had done to her and her heart would break in half just at the sight of him with another woman, and she couldn't let that happen to her friend who had already been through too much. As Annie went to grab the bottle again, Rebecca moved her arm away, careful to be gentle but firm enough so that Annie might get the point. "Later, okay? I promise, we'll get nice and polluted later. I don't want to be here when he gets back. I don't know if I'll be able to control myself."

Annie rolled her eyes at Rebecca. "Oh, come now. Don't you think you're being a little dramatic?"

Rebecca took a breath and swallowed any harsh remark she wanted to make to such an insane question at a time like this. "Someone's got to be. Have you looked at yourself? Have you seen what he did to you?"

Annie shook her head. "It's not his fault. I keep telling you that. It's the coke—"

Rebecca knew she had to go full-on firm now and changed her tone to businesslike, without a shred of warmth or kindness. It hurt her to talk to Annie like that, but she also knew it was the only way Annie was going to be able to hear her. "And I keep telling you that it's time to go. Stop making excuses for him. It's over. Which dishes do you want to keep? Put them in this box."

"Okay. You're right. Sorry. You're right."

Rebecca then left Annie in the kitchen and headed back into the living room. She was packing up some books which she had gleaned all belonged to Annie because she couldn't imagine Jason had ever read a book in his life when she heard keys rattling at the front door.

"Dammit!" she yelled.

"What's wrong? You break something?" Annie called from the kitchen in that same vacant tone.

"It's nothing. Don't worry about it," she said, and with panic in her chest, she raced through the apartment and down the stairs to the front door, and opened it before Jason could.

"What the hell are you doing here?" she snarled at him. "I thought I told you to stay away for the afternoon so I could get her out of here!"

"My house. I can be here if I want," he said. He laughed as he pushed past her. From behind him came a tall, frizzy blonde in a tight-fitting beaded tank top and leggings. She was carrying a suitcase.

"Did you meet Tabi yet?" he asked, dead serious, then broke out laughing. Then Tabi broke out laughing too. Rebecca was disgusted.

"You're high!" she accused. "The both of you."

"What's it to you, sister?" Tabi cackled back.

Rebecca grabbed Jason by the arm as he started heading up the stairs in a last-ditch effort to appeal to his humanity. "Please, if you ever cared about her. Please come back later."

"She'll get over it," he said, and snapped his arm away. "Come on," he said, and led Tabi up the stairs.

Rebecca was stunned in place a few moments before she realized she was going to be needed upstairs and quickly.

The shock. Could Annie handle the shock? Did she need the shock?

Rebecca took the stairs two at a time but did not arrive to the kitchen quickly enough.

"Oh, and I guess you must be…" she heard Annie say. She could feel her friend's heart breaking, but she knew she had to be strong for Annie. She squared her shoulders and forced her way into the kitchen.

"Come on. Just one more box for you to grab today. I'll meet you in the truck," she said. Then turned to Jason. "I will be here without her for the rest of it."

Annie just stood there, frozen.

It wasn't working. The shock was too much.

"Annie. Come on. Let's go."

"Right. Coming…" Rebecca led Annie out of the kitchen, with Annie hesitating still. When she noticed the stuffed bride chick toy had been pulled out of this box and tossed to the couch, she picked it up, gave it a gentle squeeze and a soft kiss, and shoved it into her jacket.

Rebecca hoped her friend didn't notice her eye roll when she said, as encouragingly as possible, "Come on."

When a loud screech came from the kitchen, both Annie and Rebecca looked to the source of the noise, which, unfortunately, was Jason tickling Tabi before pulling her in to a passionate kiss.

Rebecca watched as Annie's eyes filled with tears and she mouthed a quiet goodbye. She then grabbed up a box and led her friend down the stairs and out of the apartment for the last time.

chapter thirty-four

circa 1943.

Maggie sat on the bed in her father's bedroom. This was the lonely quarters of a broken man—a man broken by love. By a love that had left him. A love that was forever lost to him.

The air was filled with the acrid stench of stale vodka. The sheets were rumpled. The once crisp-white curtains were dingy and yellowed, and the windows were never opened to let in sunlight or fresh air. Maggie had placed a small statue of the Blessed Mother on the night table to look after her father. But now it seemed like a presidio, guarding a mess of a room and a life.

In her childlike hands, Maggie held her father's revolver. She ran her small fingers across the barrel of the gun, glided them over the shaft. As she sat there, she thought of love. Of Walter. About the rush that had come from the first wave of her love for him, and his for her. About the thrill and the electric jolt that had seized her senses and filled her with a sense of utter bliss and infinite hope.

And she thought about the absolute and bottomless torment, the despair that was sure to destroy her when he went away. When he went to war. How she would never recover if Walter's love was ripped away from her.

She knew, having watched her father unravel, that there was no pain more severe than suffering the loss of a true love. Just the thought of losing Walter like she was going to lose him—whether this was just in a sense of time away, or losing him completely if he returned, as so many of the boys did, in a box. It was too much. She tried to tuck herself into a small ball, protecting herself from what she knew was soon to become her sad fate.

No. There was no way her love was going to leave her, no matter what he thought. The power to stop that desertion now lay in the cold metal pistol she weighed between her small hands.

She looked down at Walter's photo. "I won't let you leave me. I just won't," she sobbed.

Not for a minute did she think this plan of hers was a sane one. Oh no. It was the last-resort scheme of a woman teetering on the brink of her own sanity. But for some reason, that was okay. For as crazy as this act she was considering was, it gave her a feeling of peace, and that's all that mattered.

She had the power to protect herself from a pain so severe she might never recover. And she was going to use it.

So she tucked the revolver into her purse and she headed out the door.

chapter thirty-five

circa 1943.

It was a day just like any other for Walter Randalls. Maybe this one was a little better than most. He had a good round with customers he enjoyed, including Bob Jenkins who was in his chair now. The guy was older than time itself, but still had a full head of white hair that needed attention at least once a week, and sometimes more. He was a valued customer for that, but also because he had a nice disposition and he tipped well. All good things.

Despite there being so many men overseas, his boss, Stan Livingston, had still managed to run a strong business. Perhaps this was because they catered to an older crowd, but it didn't matter. Walter made plenty of money and the business thrived. He did worry how Stan would fare without him while he was serving his own tour of duty, but this hadn't been Stan's first War and his establishment had survived the first one. He was sure Stan would manage, maybe even thrive, and when he returned, hopefully Walter would not lose his job to whomever had replaced him.

He was, after all, counting on having this job. He had recently proposed to Maggie, the most amazing woman he had ever known, and he wanted to ensure he would be able to provide a good life for her when he returned from the War. Sure, she seemed annoyed about him leaving, but she had to know that it wasn't that he was leaving her—just that he had a duty to country that was bigger. Well, if not bigger, important in a different way. Other girls got it when their guys left. Before he left, he hoped she would too.

"Someone here to see you," Jenkins called up to him. Walter followed Jenkins' gaze to the front window. There she was. His Maggie. The beautiful, colorful creature who had sauntered up to his window all those months ago. Who had filled his days with such joy and his nights with excitement. Who was going to fill his life with the same for hundreds— thousands—of days more in their life together. "That's one pretty girl," Jenkins said.

Walter waved at Maggie, who waved back nervously. Poor girl. She had been so upset with him about enlisting. He felt bad that maybe she was feeling embarrassed about that now. He held up two fingers to indicate "Give me two minutes," and she held up the same to show she understood what he meant.

"How'd you get so lucky?" Jenkins asked.

"We've all been wondering the same," Stan joked.

"I have no idea," Walt said. "All I know is that I'm never letting that one go." He smiled and winked at Maggie; she gave that same nervous smile, then looked away. "Okay, Jenkins, you're good. See you next week," he said, and he placed his comb and scissors down on the counter.

Then he headed out to see his girl. His beautiful girl. Her silhouette against the afternoon sun starting to set at her back gave her a more angelic look than usual, and all he wanted to do was wrap his arms around her. And hopefully later he would be forgiven enough that he could get inside her. The place he wanted to live always.

"I'm glad you're here," he said. "I was thinking—"

"Oh Walter. Oh my God, I am so sorry…"

"What are you talking about? It's fine, sweetheart," he said, and he took a step closer to her. With the sun in his eyes like that, he could make out that she was reaching into her purse, but he couldn't make out what she had pulled out of it. Not right away at least.

"I can't… I don't…"

He squinted to the object she held in both hands. "What are you…"

Realization hit in an instant, but an instant too late. Before he knew what was happening, a loud crack sounded once, twice, and she fell backward, the recoil being too much for her small frame to steel against. In that instant, a pain like he had never known hit him in the chin and then in the groin. The pain then spread over him. Before he could process what had happened, he passed out. The pain was just too much to bear.

It was the day that everything changed.

chapter thirty-six

----

the present.

Change was good. Hugh was starting to see this now. He was starting to feel it. To believe it. Even in the short time he'd lived in this neighborhood, he could see the changes. Even in the past months. Living this close to Manhattan once meant you could enjoy the grit. The damage of years taking their toll on the landscape. The small family-owned businesses. The bodegas. The corner stores. But they seemed to be disappearing by the month—by the week really. One he liked had recently closed, along with four other small storefronts on his block. It seemed like only weeks ago that these buildings had been demolished and a giant supermarket chain with an enormous parking lot had sprung up to replace them, seemingly overnight.

But change was good. He was accepting that. He was much better dealing with that now. Change had to happen, and the best way to deal with what *wasn't* anymore was to simply accept it and move on. He'd learned that from a book Charlotte had given him. He'd opened himself to learning through the books Charlotte gave him to read, and he'd even broken down and signed up for a class. What had his resistance been? He had no idea anymore.

It was all working. Lately he was feeling that even he could move on. That he could be less damaged. That he could be better.

The one big thing that had changed over the months was his relationship with Charlotte. Perhaps it was because this was something that could change, but still be a constant for him. A constant source of support. A warm blanket of contentment that he could wrap himself in. There were no surprises. There were no extreme highs and lows like he'd known before. The wrong women. He was now with the right woman, and everything was making sense. More than it ever had for him. It was crazy, this comfort he felt. Why had he never sought this before?

And right there, as they got out of Charlotte's car and headed towards the supermarket, it hit him. He was with *her*. The one he had waited for. The one his mother had promised he would someday eventually find...

"And then I'll kiss her in the parking lot when I'm old?"

Grace giggled again. "Yes, sweetie. When you're older. Even when you're old, you'll still want to kiss her in parking lots." She kissed her son on the head. "This I promise you."

He grabbed Charlotte by the hand and spun her around. He then took her face in his hands and he kissed her deeply, right there, in the daylight, in the parking lot, for everyone to see.

She instantly pulled away from him. "Uh, there's a time and a place for these things," Charlotte said, sounding embarrassed as she tried to squirm out of his grasp. When she'd managed to escape him, she walked toward a line of red shopping carts, each neatly nestled into the others. She yanked one free. "Here, take this," she said, and pushed it in his path.

Silly.

Of course this wasn't the right time or place. Charlotte was right. So instead of arguing with her, he happily obeyed and followed her into the store, watching her form in front of him as he dutifully walked behind her. Watching her ass, he found himself momentarily angry at Annie for making fun of Charlotte's size. He was finally getting used to these moments of anger. These flashes of raw emotion that would dip into him from time to time; he was in control of them now. He had learned to let them happen and then push them away. He could control them. With Charlotte, he had learned to control these impulses. And it was good.

"We should make a paella tonight. Wouldn't that be the most fun?" she asked him, as she added a large package of rice to the cart.

"Sure," he said. "What's a pie-eh-ya? Is that a dessert?"

She rolled her eyes at him. "Honestly, you're such a cretin sometimes," she said with a giggle.

He couldn't disagree.

"I can't believe how amazing this place is," she said. "I bet they have mussels here. Fresh!"

"I bet they do," he said. "What's a mussel?"

She tossed a can into the cart and walked off a few steps without hearing him. He looked at the can. Prawns? What was a prawn? Some fancy thing that couples made. He was part of a couple now. Him and Charlotte.

As she moved through the aisles, he decided to keep himself occupied taking in labels and trying to imagine who was buying some of this stuff. Other couples. Happy couples. People who spent their evenings cooking together. People who built their lives on meal planning. People who spent their lives doing normal things together.

Only normal things for him now. He was done with cemeteries. That was the old Hugh. There were plenty of stories to find in this brave new world of the living for him. In this grocery store even.

But then it happened. Walking through the store, trying to feel normal, he started to hear the Muzak. He hardly ever noticed it anymore, but now he did. And for whatever reason, this particular song was resonating with him.

Let me drown in your laughter; let me die in your arms…

"What?" Charlotte asked.

"What?" he asked.

"You're singing."

"I am?"

"Uh, yeah. Could you please stop singing?"

Hugh hadn't realized he was singing. He didn't even know he knew the words to this song, but somehow he did and he was actually having a great time.

He laughed. "I remember this song. Do you remember this song? From when we were kids?"

She shook her head.

"Yes you do! It's John Denver!" he exclaimed gleefully. "My dad played it for my mum all the time!"

The words and the melody took him back there, back to that innocent time. Before the pain. And for that moment, he understood about the Muzak. That part of Annie, that started to make sense…

Come let me love you; come love me again…

"Can you *please* stop that? Stop singing?"

He could not. Hugh swept up Charlotte in his arms and started swinging her around.

"Hugh! Please!"

"You fill up my senses, like a night in the forest… What is this song? I need to get this song!"

She paused. She pulled herself out of his embrace again, and for the second time that afternoon. "I have no idea," she said, then positioned herself in front of the shopping cart and pushed it to the side of the aisle as she checked out more cans. "You are so embarrassing. Please stop," she chided.

Just then, a mother pushed by, her cart packed with toddlers and snack food. "Sorry," Charlotte mouthed to the woman, who smirked back at her.

The mother then smiled at Hugh and gently grabbed his arm. "It's 'Annie's Song,'" she told him, warmly.

"I'm sorry? It's what?"

She smiled. "No one ever knows that because John Denver never says that in the song at all. But that's what it's called. 'Annie's Song.'"

He could feel his chest tighten as the mother wheeled her cart away.

"Annie would have loved this," he said, more wistfully than he'd expected the words to come out. She would have loved this song, yes, but she would especially have loved this moment. Not something he could comfortably tell Charlotte. "Her passion for this crap. It was really… well… peculiar…"

"Well, then we have another excellent reason to thank God we put an end to that," Charlotte said, and gave him a playful slap to the back of the head.

"Wait. What?" Her words stopped him in his tracks. "*We* put an end to…? I don't think I understand…" It had been him who had decided to call it off with Annie. What was she talking about?

She folded her arms over her chest. "Come on, Hugh. You must now know that she was terrible for you, don't you? An awful person. Would've dragged you right down with her in all her angry insanity if I hadn't soured you on her when I did. You couldn't think straight with her. I mean, if anything, you should be thanking me."

"Thanking you? But I…"

Thanking her?

She shrugged. "Seriously, what does it matter anymore, now that we're finally together? You have to admit, everything finally worked out just as it should have."

chapter thirty-seven

_____

the present.

There was no more hope when the phone rang that Hugh was going to be calling her. Whatever it was he found with Charlotte was clearly what he needed. She could never be Charlotte. She could never be like Charlotte. Therefore, for her, as much as she hurt, she could never be what Hugh really needed or wanted.

Rebecca was right. It worked like an equation. It was logic. She had to give in to logic to survive. Logic was the enemy of madness. It was the antidote to romance. And she relied on it solely now. It was easier this way.

Yet the phone was now ringing. The landline that had seen more action in the past couple of months than it had in years.

She's never gotten the answer to why he'd called her on that line. Just another one of the mysteries that would never be solved. But logically, who cared. It didn't matter anymore.

Except that right before the machine picked up, a glimmer of hope flickered in her heart, that he did think about her like she thought about him. That it wasn't over for him. That there were still mysteries to solve...

That flicker, however, was soon doused out by the sanctimonious sound of her mother's voice, calling yet again. When was she ever going to stop calling?

"Annie, this is your mother again. Clearly, you're not going to call me back so I'm just going to have to say what I have to say into this machine and you can listen to me and let me help you, or not. It's up to you now," she said, and paused. Annie could hear the crunching of the hard shell of the M&M's her mother shoveled into her mouth, and hadn't bothered to finish swallowing when she continued speaking through the thick chocolate that swirled in her mouth and coated her words. Why couldn't her mother have a normal addiction, like other mothers had? "Do you remember that day you ran out on me in the Stop & Shop?"

Annie remembered. It was the last time she'd seen or spoken to the woman. They had a big fight over buying a bag of chips that had somehow escalated into something dark and sinister...

Annie had been minding her own business, peacefully humming along to the Muzak coming from the speakers. The melody reminding her of happier days. Of more innocent times.

She'd tossed a giant bag of chips into the cart.

"You know, the women in our family. We don't always do so well with salt." Her mother nonchalantly pulled the bag out of the cart and delicately placed it back on the shelf.

"Are you kidding me?" Annie said, and tossed the chips back into the cart.

Bridget frowned. "Well… sometimes sodium makes us a little, well, uh, nuts," she said with a gentle smile and placed the bag back on the shelf.

Annie knew the stories. She knew how things could go with the women in their family. For generations of them. She couldn't even for a minute believe that salt had anything to do with it, however. Religious fanaticism, maybe. Separation anxiety, completely. But salt? That was just nuts.

"Everything drives the women in this family nuts—including the other women in this family," Annie said, and batted the chips back into the cart.

"All I'm saying is that maybe my mother could have been helped if…"

"From what I understand, your mother could have been helped with a Prozac prescription and a vibrator."

"Annie!"

"Seriously, who cares if I'm polluting my body with sodium. It's none of your goddamned business what I do with my body!" she said, and angrily knocked in two party-size bags of chips.

"Young lady, I don't like—"

"And what about those M&M's you're so addicted to, huh? What about them and the havoc they wreak?"

Her mother took a deep breath before she spoke again. "Those… are the antidote."

Annie laughed. She couldn't believe how crazy her mother could be. Or could she… "The what? The antidote? What the hell are you even talking about?!"

"The chocolate. The chocolate evens you out. It makes you feel normal." She paused for a moment, then suggested, "Why don't we just compromise, huh?" and placed a smaller bag of chips into the cart. "For goodness sake, Annie, you just can't live your life so angry. You were never like this before. If you just went to confession…"

"What do you mean?" Annie challenged.

Her mother didn't flinch. "You know darn well what I mean."

Panic rose and turned to hurt. Hurt turned to deep hurt. Deep hurt turned to anger.

"Why can't you just mind your own business? Dammit!" she shouted, and stormed away. "I don't have to take this from you."

"I know what you did, Annie," her mother called after her. "I know darn well that it wasn't an accident."

"I can't believe this," Annie said, now frozen in place.

"You tried to play God!"

"Enough! Enough!" Annie shouted and she ran off. "Get the fuck out of my life and stay there!"

"I know how things are going with you," her mother continued. "Rebecca talks to me even if you don't. You know that. You need help, Annie. You can't live like this anymore. You can't live with this secret. I realize that. Please realize that you're not the only one with secrets. I can share with you now. Please share with me. Let's please go talk to the monsignor. Together. Let's get you help," she finished, then hung up the phone.

chapter thirty-eight

three years ago.

On a moonless night on a quiet road, a woman sat in the front seat of her car. Her heart broken from betrayal, she waited there. For him.

She had never been cheated on before, at least not that she was aware of. But her intuition burned strong. Despite the chemicals she had poured into her system to numb the pain, it throbbed. She could feel the tears starting up again. The burn in the back of her throat. The stinging in her eyes.

She had never had a man affect her the way this man had. She never had one who had controlled her like he did. For whom she felt so powerless. A man who had full command of her heart and her soul and even her mind—or at least sometimes that was how it seemed. Because why else would she be here like this, waiting in the dark? Why did she care so much?

While she sat there, she thought just for a moment that maybe it was best to just drive away. To sleep it all off and let clearer heads prevail in the morning.

She had almost convinced herself to go and had turned on her headlights when she caught sight of something in the distance. A silhouette of a man and woman pressed up against each other, pressed up against a tree. She was far enough away not to be seen, but close enough to make out the man, his bare ass grinding into the woman as she straddled her scrawny legs around his waist.

For a second she thought she could control her rage, a rage borne from hurt. A hurt so deep, she could barely understand it. She thought she could take a deep breath, put the car in reverse, and carefully drive herself home where she could dive into a bottle of wine and her pillow and cry to make it all go away.

But that was only for a second. Because a moment later, her foot was on the gas, she was in drive, and her rage was running the show. She felt both powerless to stop the car—and fully empowered to stop him once and for all. She was taking destiny into her own hands. She was playing God now. Now she was the one in control. There was a glimmer of recognition, for only a moment. Of his eyes meeting hers, of understanding, before she pummeled the car right into the tree.

chapter thirty-nine

circa 1943.

There was something about being in church that had always given Maggie a sense of peace, though it had nothing to do with a strong sense of faith or deep sense of piety. It was the grandness of the space that calmed her. The soaring ceilings. The stained-glass windows that were at least twenty feet or more high. Being in church made her feel like the world was bigger than she was, and because of that, it was somehow okay that she wasn't always in control of her world.

And she needed that sense so desperately now. Because she was clearly not in charge of her world or anything she did in it. Something else within her apparently controlled her. Something she couldn't understand. Would she get the answers here? Would Phillip... Father Phillip... Could Father Phillip give her the peace she sought? Could she feel better about what she had done by repenting for it? By asking forgiveness? Walter would not forgive her, not yet, but here she could at least feel some peace for a decision she wasn't even quite sure why she had made.

She prayed one last round of Hail Marys on her glass rosary beads and kissed the wooden crucifix with the metal Jesus at the bottom. Then she headed into the confessional, the beads firmly clutched in her fingers, and made the Sign of the Cross.

"Bless me father, for I have sinned. It's been two months since my last confession."

"What's kept you so long this time, child?" he asked, but of course he knew. Everyone knew.

Oh, what a scene she had caused. The blood. The mayhem. She remembered looking Walter in the face, his beautiful face, and all she could see was him in a soldier's uniform on a battlefield. A rifle in his hands. An army helmet on his head. A blast tearing through him…

Except the blast hadn't been on the battlefield. It had happened in the middle of the day in the middle of the sidewalk of an otherwise sleepy neighborhood. It wasn't enemy fire. It was her. All she'd wanted to do was to shoot him in the knee. Just give him something manageable, but enough so they couldn't take him away from her. She hadn't intended for it to turn out like it had.

"I'd rather not say…"

The gun was small, but it was powerful. She didn't know she wasn't going to be able to control it. To properly aim it. She didn't want to kill him. She didn't want to hurt him, not really. She just wanted to save him.

"Please Maggie. You're safe here. Tell me what you need to say."

But why would anyone believe her? How could anyone understand that kind of crazy? Maybe Father Phillip could. Maybe, just maybe, she wanted to believe he could give her the peace she sought. He could. Of course he would. If she was sorry, truly repentant, then she could be forgiven.

She took a deep breath. "I played God," she said, and then she told him everything. About the moment she first saw

247

Walter. About falling for him and sleeping with him. About the panic she'd felt when she thought he'd go to war. About her own father's pain—and about her panic.

"I know it sounds crazy, but I promise you that I just wanted to save him."

Father Phillip was silent for several minutes, and it unnerved her. Finally he spoke. "I have been thinking for weeks about what I was going to say to you at this moment. When you came to me over this."

"Tell me how I can make this better. Tell me how I can fix this. Tell me how I can fix me, and break the part in me that decided to do this."

"I don't know what to say…" he said and he paused several minutes more. All she could hear was his deep breathing as he contemplated her solution. Finally he spoke. "Maggie, what you've done is unforgivable." There was anger in his voice. It was undeniable.

She gasped. Wasn't the point of all of this that she could be forgiven? If she was sorry, deeply and truly sorry, she was supposed to be forgiven. "But…" she began, but was speechless.

"No, I can see no alternative." There wasn't even a trace of warmth in his voice. No support. Any trace of anything he'd ever felt for her had clearly been eradicated by this act.

"Your penance has to be to stay with him. You must care for him now all the days of his life. You must commit your own life now in service to him. Only after you've lived out your life in service to him might God forgive you."

"But…" Maggie couldn't stop the tears. Her mother abandoned her. Walter had tried to abandon her. And now this. Her faith. Father Phillip… just Phillip…

Now what?

"Aren't there prayers—"

"No. Just that. Prayers are not going to fix this," he said sternly and dismissively.

She quickly exited the confessional and slid into a pew in the back of the church. As she knelt there, she prayed for peace, but all she could feel was dread. Of course she would stay with Walter, in whatever condition he was in. She had already planned to do that. He was her love.

But would Walter even allow that now, after everything? And after everything that was about to be…

If there was one thing she was sure of that day, she was done with Father Phillip. He had turned his back on her, and as far as she was concerned, so had the whole blasted religion. Without granting forgiveness, without granting peace, what had it all even been for? She tossed her rosary beads into a pool of Holy Water by the front of the church as she exited, determined to never return.

Later that afternoon, Maggie wheeled Walter out in his chair and parked him in front of his shop, thinking that seeing his old friends might cheer him, while she stepped into the chemist to get the results of a very important test she had taken that morning before confession. She kissed him on the head before saying, "Be right back."

She didn't know what was more painful—seeing him all bandaged like that, his eyes ringed with black and yellow, or the deadness in those eyes when he looked at her. She was glad he wasn't speaking to her yet, although while she was afraid of what he'd say to her when he finally would again, the understanding she got from the words he never spoke was almost impossible to bear.

The only hope she had that he would some day speak to her again was that he refused to press any charges against her.

That he'd signed a form and even demanded that he be released into her care, despite the protestations from his family and friends.

He still loves me. I know he still loves me. This proves it.

Minutes later she emerged, and his expression hadn't changed. She still felt dread, but now within her she felt a glimmer of something else. She fondled her cross between her fingers. She had wanted to throw her necklace away too, but something stopped her. A sense that perhaps Father Phillip didn't speak for all Catholics. That there still might be some hope of finding forgiveness in all of this. If Walter could forgive her. That was all she'd need to be forgiven. To lift the dark black stain off her soul.

As she took the cross in her fingers, a small sense of hope entered her heart, despite the fact that he still glared at her. Because she had a secret to share with him. One she was sure was going to bring new life to them. To their love.

She ran her hand over her tummy and allowed herself a small smile as she stared into his dead eyes. "Well, it looks like you were right," she told him. "Our world did shift that night."

She then got back behind his wheelchair and took them home, planning just how she was going to tell him this wonderful miracle of news she had just received. It would have to change things between them. She was sure it would. Finally, he would be able to find it in himself to forgive her. For the sake of their baby. The miracle that their love had created.

How could he not forgive her?

chapter forty

the present.

Several days earlier, for reasons that made no sense to her, Annie stepped into Smitty's Second-Hand Shop. She made a beeline for the aisle where the glass ladybug that Hugh had wanted to buy for her had been, and felt relief wash over her when she saw it there. She stared at it a while, and while she did, the relief and peace she felt started to transform—to sadness and then to anger. She was having too much trouble getting over this. She could not get over it—she couldn't get back in control of her emotions. Impulsively, she snatched the ladybug, stuffed it into her pocket, and dashed out of the store.

Now she sat alone on the floor in her living room, absently playing with her glass ladybug. When Mr. Badass crossed in front of her, then climbed over her leg to sit in her lap, she picked him up and placed him in the palm of her hand. When she pulled him close to her face, he hissed at her. She held him in one hand, and placed the ladybug in the palm of her other hand. She sat there weighing the glass bug against the increasingly irritable turtle until there came an insistent knocking at the door.

"Come on, Annie. Open up. I just want to talk," Rebecca called from the other side of the door. There was a jingling of keys and an audible "Dammit!" Then the sound of keys being dropped into a purse with the question, "When did you change the locks?"

Annie ignored her. There was no way Rebecca was going to be forgiven for putting her in that situation like that all those weeks ago. She was furious and couldn't imagine she was going to be any other way for quite some time, perhaps forever. She hadn't talked to her own mother for years. She could shut out Rebecca.

"Look, I'm so sorry. I couldn't be more sorry. There was nothing else I could do. I couldn't sit back and let you waste any more of your life blaming yourself..."

"Great. Now I blame you," she called back without thinking. "Fuck," she muttered, realizing she'd outed herself.

"Good, you're there. Annie? Come on, Annie, please. Let me in. Actually, where the hell's the doorknob anyway? Okay, you're going to have to let me in, you know. Otherwise, how the hell are you ever going to get out?"

Rebecca had a point. Annie placed Badass and the glass bug down and headed to the bench where she kept her tools. Within seconds, she had the door opened.

"How are you still even living in this shithole?" Rebecca asked as she pushed her way inside. And just as Annie was going to close the door behind Rebecca, her mother pushed her way in.

Her heart dropped into her stomach. "Mom..."

"Sorry," Rebecca said. "I should have mentioned I wasn't alone."

"I can't believe..." *I can't believe she did it to me again!*

But when Annie looked at her mother, all she could feel was a deep sense of grief and loss. She tried to mask this under a shield of indignation, but she was finding it impossible to feel anything but longing for her mother.

"Young lady, this has gone on long enough," Bridget said in a tone that suggested she was struggling to do the same. But when she looked around Annie's apartment all she could do was shake her head. She gasped and her hand shot up to her mouth, and Annie started to see her living conditions through her mother's eyes. What had she been doing? What had she been thinking? It was clear to everyone in the room that it was all she could do to hold back her own tears.

"Mom, you don't know..."

"I *know*, Annie. I've always known." She nodded to Rebecca. "Now we both know."

Annie hugged her arms around herself. "I didn't think... I mean, Jason was such a good guy... I ruined him. I ruined his life."

"Jason was *not* a good guy," Rebecca snapped.

"No, you don't understand. You never understood him like I did. He was amazing and good to me, and then he changed. He got worn down by me. That's all. It was my fault. I just worked so much. I..."

"He was horrible and he hurt you," Bridget said, her face clenched. "And he deserved everything that happened to him. *Everything.*"

Annie didn't know what else to do. Her whole body felt weak. That coating, that shield she had wrapped around herself the first time Jason had struck her... It began to melt away. She started crying uncontrollably, and Rebecca and Bridget shared a worried glance. Rebecca nodded to Bridget, who took her daughter into her arms and Annie collapsed in her mother's embrace.

"No one blames you for what happened. No one ever did," her mother soothed, stroking her hair. "It's over now. Okay, baby? It's time to move on."

Rebecca moved in and wrapped her arms around them both as they stood in the living room and cried. "Let us help you, Annie," Rebecca said. "Please."

chapter forty-one

---

the present.

Charlotte decided it was high time she cleaned out Hugh's room and reorganized the apartment so that they existed like a couple—and not a couple of friends living together like they had been. He slept in her room every night, and had since that first night they'd come together, but it was time to take it to the next level. Maybe convert his room to an office or home gym. Maybe a crafting studio... She didn't have to figure that out now.

For the first time in years, she really felt on top of her world. Finally, everything was coming together. Finally, everything was in place. Work was going well. It looked like she was finally going to get promoted. But more important than anything else, she had finally gotten her guy.

If there was a record for how long a girl could wait before a boy realized that all he'd ever wanted in a girl was right under his nose, she would have beaten that record—hands down. From his high school dorkiness, to his parents' death. From his short weird marriage to Alicia, to his decision to move to New York. She thought for sure she was going to lose him on that one. It wasn't easy to leave Lansing like that, but if she didn't follow him, there would be no way she'd be able to hold on to him. Not with the women he'd been with since they made this move. All self-absorbed, horrible women with no values. That last one being the worst of them all.

But that didn't matter now. All that mattered now was the life they were going to build together. She would be able to give him more guidance in his career, because now he would have to let her. And soon enough, she would be able to get him to propose to her. Or maybe she'd do the proposing? It had taken so long to get to this point, how much longer could she wait to become Mrs. Hugh Jeffries?

She assembled and taped together the first box she'd brought to pack up some of the things he really didn't need anymore. She also had a large black garbage bag for the things she didn't want him to have anymore. Which reminded her... She went over to his CD collection and immediately tossed out his new copy of Peter Gabriel's *Greatest Hits*. He certainly didn't need to be reminded of that song anymore, or any of that collection.

She decided to use the box to pack up the rest of his CDs, tossing ones she didn't like or didn't think he needed to like. She only had one box for CDs—she was smart to downsize like this. Out with the old, in with the new. She'd be hitting his T-shirt drawer next, but one step at a time, she told herself. The steady horse wins the race. Because isn't that how she'd won this race?

Once she'd packed up the box, she turned toward the bed. There was something sticking out from under it, and her curiosity was piqued. She bent down to grab the edge of what turned out to be a book. Not just a book, she realized when she opened the cover, but his portfolio. The personal one. The one he never shared. She was almost shaking with excitement that she could finally see it. It bothered her a little that it wasn't him sharing it with her, but whatever. Once he found out she'd found it, and how much she loved his work, then they could share it together.

She sat down on the floor and began flipping through. It really took her breath away, how true-to-life everything was. He really did have a talent for this! All the more reason to encourage him to take some more classes and develop it.

Then she came to a photo of a small blond woman bent over a gravestone. It was so morbid and sad. She had no idea why he would have taken such a shot. She was so glad the cemetery days were behind him now.

She continued to flip through the book, really impressed by the detail he captured. The realism he saw through this lens took her breath away. She needed to encourage him to work toward getting a job that would use that talent of his. As she sat there thumbing through the book, she began to calculate a plan to send him back to school.

So engrossed was she in his work and her scheming, she didn't even hear the front door open and close when Hugh came in.

"Where'd you get that?" he asked her, and he didn't sound happy. That was okay. She could change that in two seconds.

"I found it under the bed," she said lightly. "I was just—"

"What are you doing in here?" he asked, snatching the book away.

"Oh, well, I was just getting you started to move into my room, but that's not important right now."

"You're doing what?"

Was he really raising his voice at her? *How dare he!* She sighed. "I can't believe you never shared it with me before. It's beautiful, Hugh. I have to say, I think you have a real talent!"

This seemed to take his edge off. "Really?" he asked, and joined her on the floor.

"Totally," she said, taking the book back. "Everything is perfect."

She was happy to see him smile about that. She had said the right thing. She knew how to talk to him. No one else knew how to talk to him like she did. "Sure! I mean, look at it," she said, flipping through the pages, careful to skip over the woman in the cemetery. "It's like a catalog!"

The smile vanished. "Did you say... catalog?"

What happened? How could she fix it? "Oh yes! Hang on," she said, and darted out of the room. She was sure there was a *Harry & David* catalog on the coffee table, and she could show him just how good she thought he was.

She found it and darted back into the room. "Yes, look," she said and opened the catalog, then placed it over one of his spreads. "And even better. I mean, I look at this apple in the catalog. Just an ordinary little thing. But here in your book. I look at this apple here and I just want to buy it and peel it and make it into a pie!"

chapter forty-two

circa 1945.

"Who gives this child to be baptized before the Lord on this joyous day?" The question was asked by Father Phillip, of course it had to have been him. And by the way he looked at her, it was clear he didn't think she was worthy to be offering this child in this way.

That was okay. She remained firm in her resolve. Phillip was a man of God, but he was a man all the same. A human man. She wasn't going to let one imperfect man ruin an entire religion for her.

Although the christening of the beautiful daughter she made with Walter should have been the one of the most miraculous and wonderful experiences they could have shared, it was clear that day their life together was never going to be joyful; that it was always going to be a constant misery of him punishing her for the maybe not so simple reason of loving him too much.

That Walter had agreed to show up for this at all was a miracle in and of itself, but any hope she had that this could be for her, for them, had long since died. He was here for Bridget and Bridget alone.

"I do," he quickly said, struggling through the speech impediment that had now become his reality for the remainder of his days.

Not "we," but "I."

"*We* do," she quickly corrected, grazing her hand over his, causing him to flinch away from her.

She took a deep breath and stared up at the vaulted ceiling. At the image of God and the heavenly hosts painted in trompe l'oeil there. If Walter could not forgive her, how could she ever forgive herself?

The christening was quiet. There were no godparents. There were no grandparents. Maggie's father had passed away quietly in his sleep several weeks after his only grandchild was born. Walter's parents would not tolerate being in the same room as Maggie, even if that room was a church. They had promised their son a separate celebration later. With just the four of them—meaning them, their son, and their grandchild.

Aside from baby Bridget, Maggie had no one.

For the past year or so, Walter had come to regard her with less a seething rage and more a quiet hatred. He relied on her to help him go to the bathroom. He slept in the same bed as her, but he never touched her.

When she finally told him she was pregnant that day, she thought there might be a moment's hope when his eyes seemed to glint and the corners of his mouth turned up ever so slightly. "Now I will have to marry you," he mumbled with a smirk.

There was no joy in the remark. While she had vowed to try to get him to marry her because the priest had said that was the only way the Lord would forgive her... and even then it would be a stretch... he had apparently had his own ideas about things.

"So you are forgiving me?" she asked, the last glimmer of hope she would ever feel in her sad life powering the words.

He laughed at her until he coughed. "Oh no," he said. "But at least now I will get to ruin your life worse than the way you ruined mine."

She had wished so badly that things could be fixed with Walter when she had brought the baby to him in the living room after returning from the hospital. He'd beamed with a joy it had been too long that she'd seen in him.

"She's beautiful, isn't she?" she asked, beaming back at him. He returned her warmth with the same cold, dead stare.

chapter forty-three

---

the present.

Annie entered the church with her mother. She had always hated being in this church, with the exception of her wedding day. But there was something about the church this day with her mother that was different than her childhood experience with it and since then. There was something about the grandness of the space that calmed her today. The soaring ceilings. The stained-glass windows that were at least twenty feet or more high. Being there somehow made her feel like the world was bigger than she was, and because of that, it was somehow okay that she wasn't always in control of her world.

And even as she had these thoughts, she prayed this didn't mean she was going to turn into a zealot like the others.

She and her mother headed up to the altar. She remembered walking up this same aisle with her father on her wedding day when he'd given her away. Her poor simple father. He had no idea what he had been handing her off to. At least he was finally at peace.

She thought about seeing Jason standing at the altar. Of seeing her mother and Rebecca... She wasn't going to let that memory ruin the relationship she'd been working to rebuild these past months with her mother. She swallowed it down.

She remembered seeing the old priest at the top of the aisle, standing with Jason. Father Phillip. Now Monsignor Phillip. The very same man who was standing at the top of the aisle now, waiting for them.

Annie tugged on her mother's sleeve. "Why is he here? I told you, no confession!" she said in a loud whisper. "You said we were here for your mother."

Bridget Collins nodded at the old priest, then leaned in to reply. "Not confession," she assured. "That's not what this is about. It's about my mother, I promise you. Don't worry."

When they approached the altar, the monsignor gave her mother a quick kiss on the cheek and nodded to Annie as Bridget dropped a few coins in the metal box in front of the rows of prayer candles. Her mother handed Annie a long match she'd lit from one of the burning votives, and Annie lit one of the candles.

The monsignor then took the match from Annie and lit one on his own, saying a soft prayer under his breath as the wick caught the flame.

They all stood there quietly for several minutes, reflecting as the candles flickered. Then the old priest cocked an eyebrow at them, and when Bridget nodded back, he walked off.

When he was out of earshot, her mother spoke. "I loved him, once."

Annie wasn't sure she'd heard correctly. "What?"

"I did. He always loved my mother, and somehow loving him made me feel closer to her. After she left us."

Annie wasn't sure she understood what her mother was telling her. "I'm sorry?"

Bridget laughed. "It's true. My mother was very special to him. He told me all about it when I was older. He was so devoted to God when he knew her. So fixed on his calling. He could have had her, but he never strayed. Not then. And then she met my father. Walter. And she gave up on Phillip. He never really got over it."

Annie thumbed her cross. She tried to imagine her mother's mother adoring this old fossil of a man. She tried to imagine him young and desirable enough that two generations of women would have loved him like they had.

"And when I was twenty, well..."

Annie was aghast. "Oh dear Lord... What?"

"It's not as torrid as you're making it sound." Her mother shook her head. "You think you know everything about your mother. You think I never lived before you and your father. That I never loved. But—surprise, surprise. I did. And hard."

"Mom! A priest?"

"Well, technically he's now a monsignor. But yes, he was a priest then. A priest who had never fully gotten over my mother. Who had never forgiven himself for what he believed to have been his hand in her undoing."

"But she... You told me she..."

"She did. But only after there was nowhere else for her to turn." Bridget Collins let out a long sigh. "We look like her, you know? You and I. Especially you, though. I should show you a picture."

"I didn't know there were any."

"I have them. Anyway, I think Phillip believed that in being with me, he could somehow undo what he had done to her. At least that's what he told me. He never loved me, though—as much as I loved him. It was never about me. He loved Maggie. Always."

Annie was having considerable trouble absorbing what her mother had just told her. "I can't believe you slept with a priest. That doesn't make any sense."

"Wait—no. I didn't sleep with him," she said, reaching into her purse to grab a few M&M's and sneak them into her mouth. "We just kissed. Just once."

"Mom, you kissed a priest."

Bridget sucked on the chocolate. "Please don't cheapen it like that."

"I'm sorry. But, come on. That's a little crazy, no? I mean, does the crazy ever end with the women in our family?"

Her mother shook her head again. "It was just the one time, and it was done. After that, he devoted himself completely to his calling, and then I met your father. Even during the time your father was in Vietnam, Phillip... *Father* Phillip... nothing ever happened between us again. Instead, we just became friends, just as we've been nearly these past forty years now. I still loved him, though. In many ways, I loved him more than your father." She pressed her lips together in thought. "Religion, I don't know, I guess it gave me the solace to get over him. Inasmuch as I could."

Now it was Annie's turn to shake her head. How could the one thing that would be a constant reminder of someone she loved be the thing that freed her from loving him? It made no sense. She couldn't tell her mother that, though, she well knew. "I can't believe I never knew any of this."

Bridget let out a small laugh. "Oh my dear... why would I have told you? Look, you know as well as I do that we all have our secrets. No one gets to go through this life without pain and secrets."

Annie reflected on her mother's words. If only her mother had trusted her sooner. If only her mother hadn't held back. If only her mother had been honest about her piety. So many things would have been different.

"Sometimes we have to let our secrets go, though. We have to set them free so we can forgive ourselves and move on. One day you'll share yours. If not with me, you'll share with someone. And you'll feel better. I promise, you will."

Annie found that hard to believe, but found it even harder to reply. What was she supposed to say now? She wasn't ready to tell her mother the truth. She wasn't sure she'd ever be ready to tell her mother or anyone else the terrifying truth about that night. The night she'd lost control by believing she had control.

They sat together in a companionable silence, watching the prayer candles flicker in the dim church lighting. The candles they had lit for Maggie burned strong. Annie thumbed her cross and almost felt like Maggie was there with them. In the quiet of the church. In their thoughts and in their hearts.

Bridget soon broke the silence. "Thank you for being here with me today," she said. "Some may think it's strange that I still commemorate this day, that Phillip and I still commemorate the day my mother gave up on us. But October 19... I can't seem to fix any other association to it, even after all these years."

The date triggered something in Annie. "Wait, what's the date again?"

"October 19," her mother said.

"Holy shit, I gotta go," she said.

"Annie, please!"

She looked around; the trompe l'oeil figures painted on the church ceiling sneering their judgment at her. "Sorry. I'm sorry," she said, and she kissed her mother on the forehead. Her mother's skin was shiny and felt sleek on her lips, and she smelled of Ponds cold cream. She'd missed that smell. She had no idea how much she had until that moment.

"Where are you going?" her mother asked.

"I have something I need to do," she said, and she wasn't sure why she was feeling so deeply compelled to do it. "Let's call it a leap of faith." She then grabbed her purse and she darted out.

chapter forty-four

---

the present.

Annie Collins sat quietly on the ground next to the grave of The Brothers Novotny in Calvary Cemetery in Queens, New York. She contemplated her mother's story and the decisions women in her family had made, decisions that had forever altered the course of their lives. She wondered about her own decisions; the course of her own life. And, above all, she wondered if she was a bigger fool than all of them had been, waiting, like an idiot, for this lost boy to find himself and her here.

Why she was here? Why she had raced away from her mother in the church to get here? Did she really believe things would turn out?

Yes, yes she did. Despite everything, a little flicker of faith, of hope, still crackled within her. Although it was starting to flicker out.

On top of the in-ground stone was a large rock, and under that rock was Annie's stolen glass ladybug. She had been carrying it around for weeks for reasons that made no sense. And then, just minutes ago, she smashed it with the rock. Apropos, because even while she had been healing these past months, she still felt shattered. And now, thanks to therapy, all the pain she had fought so long to swallow down, to enclose in a part of her she'd never let anyone touch, that Pandora's Box was wide open.

She had to admit that it had been rough at first, but she was finally starting to make peace with herself and with her past. At least with her distant past. At least about the parts of it she told. Because there were parts of it she would never tell. Maybe she would have told Hugh. Even today. But clearly that was part of her past now, too.

After almost two hours of waiting, she was starting to feel ridiculous. He wasn't going to come. Of course he had forgotten—about the Brothers Novotny and about her by now. Maybe he never cared for her the way she'd cared for him. At least now she'd have closure on it.

Except just as she was about to give up and get up, a voice interrupted her thoughts. "What happened to the Stop-n-Shop?"

Her heart beat wildly. She looked up. "Hugh?"

"This isn't supposed to be your madness, you know," he said, waving to indicate the cemetery.

She felt instantly stupid. "I guess it was time to try something new?"

He nodded to the gravestone. "You made it."

"You remembered."

"Someone had to remember poor Stan on his birthday," he said, then squinted at the broken glass, looking like he was trying to make sense of it.

She didn't feel like explaining. "Where's Charlotte?" she quickly asked, then immediately regretted the question. "Oh God, she's not here…"

He gave a weak laugh. "No. That's over."

Her heart jumped. "What happened?"

"Long story."

"Short version?"

"The harbor was too, uh… safe?"

"Oh…"

"And she looked at my portfolio. The old one. And she loved it."

"And you?"

He shrugged his shoulders. "Sometimes you learn the hard way."

"I guess we all do."

He looked back again at the black and red shards of glass. "What was that?"

"Oh. Ladybug. Well… at least it used to be."

He pursed his lips. "You sure do get angry a lot."

"Compared to the other women in my family… I'm a lamb," she said, and she shivered. He sat down beside her and took off his jacket. He draped it over her shoulders. She smirked at the message on his T-shirt: *The Truth Will Set You Free.*

"Jesus? Really?" She joked with him but felt a chill run through her, remembering the words her mother had just spoken to her:

Sometimes we have to let our secrets go, though. We have to set them free so we can forgive ourselves and move on. One day you'll share yours. If not with me, you'll share with someone. And you'll feel better. I promise, you will.

"Jesus? Is that who said that? I always thought it was Socrates," Hugh said, bringing her back to the present. "Maybe Jesus stole it from him?" He cocked an eyebrow.

She squeezed her eyes shut, then opened them again. She wished she could tell him how much she loved when he did that thing with his eyebrow. The oddest little quirk, yet it set her heart on fire. Maybe someday she could share at least that truth with him.

For now, she opted for being flip. "Yeah, maybe. Can you sit over there though, so when the lightning bolt strikes, it only gets you?"

"I'm sure Jesus wouldn't give a crap about that. But to be honest, I don't really care. I'm not here for Jesus. I'm here for the truth," he explained, pointing to his shirt apparently for emphasis.

She let out a soft laugh, then got serious again. "You really want to know?"

He nodded. "Tell me. Please?"

She shook her head. "I don't think…"

He shocked her then by taking her hand in his. "It's okay. Really. I really want to know." His face instantly calmed her. She believed him. She wanted to believe him at least, to trust him. To share that last piece she had never shared with anyone else. She took a deep breath before being able to speak. Something she'd learned in therapy.

"Well…" she began, "as you may already have figured out… my family's such a mess. I can't even believe it." She paused for a minute, not really knowing how she was going to tell him what she was sure he was not going to want to know once he learned it. But she soldiered on. Therapy had taught her that, too. To keep going. To not judge herself—just to release. "My grandmother. My *real* grandmother," she said, now holding up her necklace. "This was hers."

He nodded, encouraging her to continue.

"She, um... She kind of went nuts. She sort of, uh, shot my grandfather."

"Wow. That's not something you hear every day."

She shook her head. "No, it's not. Oddly enough, she wasn't trying to kill him. She was, uh, trying to *save* him." He cocked his eyebrow at her again. That thing he did. It made her soul come alive. He immediately changed his face back, though, to the way he used to look at her. Like he wanted to know everything there was to know about her. She didn't feel afraid anymore.

"It had to do with the war," she explained. "Some cockamamie scheme to keep him off the front lines. Anyway, he was never the same after that."

"And her?"

She grimaced. "You don't want to know."

"You're right. I don't. At least not now. Now I want to know about *you*. I'm ready to hear it—about Jason. Something happened there. Something you're hiding. I can *feel* it. I know it's dark, but please trust me when I tell you, I'm ready to hear it."

She hesitated. Now she was starting to feel panicked. How was she ever going to be able to tell that story without scaring him away for good? She tried to deflect the question, "Did I ever tell you about—"

He held his finger to her lips. "No, please. Not another story. The truth this time. Whatever you did to him, I can take it. I promise. I can handle it. I'm done with the 'safe' thing, remember?" He leaned in and stroked her face with the back of his thumb. "The truth, Annie. Please."

"I don't even know where to begin," she said. She took a deep breath and looked away from him. She pulled his jacket around her and she breathed in his wonderful scent. And at

272

that, she felt her resolve release. Finally, she could talk. To him. Whatever he was or was going to be to her.

"As you know, I was married once. He was older and he wasn't always very nice..."

chapter forty-five

three years ago.

Jason Scott hadn't meant to look at the clock. "Shit," he said. He took one last long thrust into Tabi and came explosively. Man, how he hated to leave her bed. But he had to make nice with wifey because he wasn't ready to shack up with Tabi yet, and where else would he go if Annie threw him out?

"I gotta go," he said, and lifted himself off and out of Tabi.

Her arms clenched around his neck. "No, stay. Just this time."

"Not possible yet, sweetheart. Someday," he lied.

"You need to leave her. If you really loved me, you'd leave her."

"Not that simple and you know it. Just give me some time. I'll figure it out."

Not that he was going to figure it out. Somehow his piece on the side was trying to wriggle her way to the center, and he didn't want anyone there. Not Annie, not this woman, and not Marie, the hot twenty-something he'd just met at his NA meeting. As much as he loved kneading that tight little ass with his hands as he pushed himself into her. He wished he had time to stop over there, but he'd be in deep shit if he didn't scramble home soon.

She leaned over and the sheet slipped off her, revealing her perfect ass. He wanted to mount that so bad, it nearly killed him to pull his pants up and not off. "Take another hit," she said, now leaning over the night table.

That he had time for. He breathed in the white powder and got that familiar shot of intoxicating invincibility. Nothing ever made him feel like blow did.

He did another line with her. Then another. Now he felt like a man. Not the crippled emasculated piece of faggot shit his little wife made him feel like. He tore off his pants again and with a roar, he entered Tabi again. So hot and wet and alive. He came even harder than he had the first time. He wanted her again and again, but he knew he had to go. "I'll call you," he said, and got dressed and left.

It was late when he got back to the apartment, but there Annie was, still awake, sitting on the couch, hugging a pillow to herself and scowling. If only that little bitch could greet him with a smile once in a while. Get up and give him a kiss. A blow job, like it was so much to ask. He never had to ask Tabi or Marie for BJs. They got down on their fucking knees for him and sucked him off like pretty little vacuums.

But not his wife. No, not her. She was always so angry at how much work she had—and at him for how little he worked. Well, fuck her. It wasn't like it was up to him when the work came. She knew what she was getting when she got into this with him. Not his problem.

"You make dinner?" he asked her.

"Dinner? Are you kidding? Where have you been? Do you know what time it is?"

"None of your goddamned business!" he yelled back.

She jumped off the couch and leaned toward him, sniffing. "Oh God, I can smell her on you. You were with her, weren't you? With that Tabi person?"

If she had not said the name with such sarcasm and venom, he probably could have dropped it and just gone to bed, but her tone enraged him. "At least someone knows how to treat a man right!" he shouted.

"Maybe you should get the fuck out!" she screamed back at him.

"Maybe you should shut your fucking stupid mouth," he roared back and pushed her out of his way.

And then she did something she never did. In his estimation, the craziest thing she ever did.

She pushed him back.

chapter forty-six

---

the present.

"I knew where he'd come from. I could smell her on him, even across the room. But that wasn't the issue that night. Not the big one. The big one was that earlier that week I found out I was pregnant and I had yet to tell him."

"Oh man…." Hugh said.

Annie trembled and shook in Hugh's arms, but he held her tight. He wanted to squeeze the shakes right out of her. He wanted to calm her, but he didn't know what he could do except to let her talk. So that's what he did. He held her and encouraged her to continue. "Okay. It's okay. Keep talking. It's okay…"

He knew she was struggling to get the words out, but he didn't know how to help her. He didn't know how to assure her that with him, she was safe. No matter what.

He knew Jason had abused her. He'd sensed that all along. He'd seen that before with other women. There were women you could just never make feel safe. He didn't want Annie to be one of those women.

She looked up at him. "I needed to terminate the pregnancy. Except I *couldn't* do it. The way I was raised. All the crazy Catholic ideas... I mean, I tried. I made an appointment to have an abortion. I never made it there. I was so scared."

The pieces of this puzzle were starting to click together in Hugh's brain and he was terrified of all the conclusions he couldn't prevent himself from drawing. What kind of a person was he? He was mad at himself for thinking such things about her. This wasn't who she was, he was sure of it. "I don't understand..."

"It gets worse," she choked through her tears. "I promise. Stick with me and I promise it will always, *always* get worse."

"I don't believe that and neither do you," he said, but feeling uneasy that maybe what she was saying, that it will always get worse, was true.

"You will. Just wait," she said, and let out a long breath. "Anyway, I finally knew what I had to do, and that was the night I was going to do it.

"As I told you, he came home late, as expected, high on coke, as expected, and smelling of that horrible woman... I knew before that night that I needed to free myself from him. It was only that night I figured out how."

"Okay, I'm listening," he encouraged.

"When he came in, I picked a fight with him. I had had some wine and I was feeling sort of numb, but I had already made up my mind about things, so I shouted horrible, nasty things at him. I told him he had a tiny prick. I asked him how his new girlfriend could possibly have gotten off on it, gaping whore hole that she was. I said every horrible thing I could imagine and things that were so awful I couldn't even imagine what dark place in me they'd come from.

"And he just got angrier and angrier. I could see it. I could feel it. He screamed at me that night and he pushed me out of the way. And then I pushed him back. I never fought back, but this was different. This night I had a plan.

"I edged my way to the stairs, still shouting anything I could think to say. And I didn't feel scared, not even a little bit. I felt... empowered. I felt strong.

"Anyway, when I was at the top of the landing, he was on me then. His hands clamping down so hard on my shoulders.

"'You take that back!'" he'd yelled in my face. "'You take that all back, or I swear to God I will...'"

She stopped. Annie's beautiful eyes were filled with pain and tears, and he almost started to regret what he was putting her through. Except that he knew, deep down, she had to go through it. This was a horror lodged inside of her that she couldn't live with anymore. He could feel it. He could feel her again. He already knew the truth, and in his head, he was terrified to hear it. But in his heart, he knew he had to let her speak it.

She killed him. The husband. In self-defense maybe, but she killed him all the same. He understood. He could deal with that. He knew he could deal with that. "I'm here. It's okay. Please, tell me."

She took another deep breath. "Then I closed my eyes and said a prayer. And then I spit at him. I saw my own death in his eyes when he wiped my spit off his face. I knew then we were well past the point of no return."

"'You stupid little bitch!' he'd screamed so close to me I could feel his sour breath. Then he backhanded me and knocked me down. So I got up again, and he hit me again.

"I made sure to have my back to the stairs when I got up again and I spit in his face again. That time he hit me so hard, I landed at the bottom of the stairs."

Hugh gasped. "That's just horrible. That's just so... So..."

She held up her hand to make him stop talking. "It isn't," she said in a hoarse whisper. "It's not even close to the worst of it."

He was doing it again. *Idiot! Stop talking!* He forced himself to try to keep his big mouth shut.

"And I lay there for a while, wondering what would come next, but then not wondering at all. I didn't feel anything in those moments. No pain. No distress. I only felt, well..." She looked up at him then, seeming calmer than he could ever remember her. "Free."

He tried to reassure her with his eyes but inside all he could feel was deep panic. If she was aware of that panic, he couldn't tell.

"The last thing I remember from that night was him stepping over me and calling me a stupid bitch before heading out and slamming the door behind him. That's when I could feel the bleeding start."

"Wait—he left? He just left." Hugh was confused. "But then how...?"

"Honestly, I prayed that he would kill me that night. That all of the problems would go away, and me with them. But I lived. The baby didn't, but I did." At that, she burst into tears. "I would be lying to you if I told you that *wasn't* the plan. The great and horrible crazy plan. Fuck," she said.

"Fuck," he echoed. This was not what he was expecting.

"I buried the guilt of that in the 'fact' that it wasn't my sin. I mean... how could it be? My husband abused me. He threw me down the stairs. He tried to *kill* me. How could any of that be my fault...?"

The calm had given way to fresh tears as she started to tremble again. "All these years I tried to make myself believe that I wasn't at fault in any of this. I simply made myself believe that if there was a sin here, the sin was his. All this time...."

Hugh felt overwhelmed. This was almost too much. No, this *was* too much. He didn't know what to say. Even in all his wildest imaginings, he could not have imagined anything like this. "Talk about a comfortable madness..." he tried.

"Oh God. Crazy, yes. But I would say it's made me anything but comfortable all these years."

Hugh sat back against a neighboring grave stone, trying to get a sense of calm, in the heat of this mad confession, from the coldness and hardness of the granite. "I don't know what to say," he said, then reflexively jumped up.

"I told you it was crazy," she sobbed after him as he darted away. "I told you it was too much. Yeah the truth will set you free. Free from me!"

chapter forty-seven

---

circa 1950.

When Bridget was born, Maggie and Walter Randalls hired a nurse to help take care of the baby, and she ultimately ended up staying on with them to help take care of Walter as well. Anne's presence in their life was an unexpected relief—for both of them—and Bridget took to the nurse like a second mother.

And as the years went on, more as a first.

It wasn't only Bridget who showed an obvious affection for Anne. The nurse had also managed to bring the smile back to Walter's face. The only time Walter ever smiled was when he was with Bridget and Anne.

By the time Bridget was five or six years old, Maggie had fully began to feel like an intruder in her own house. A stranger lurking around what would have been an otherwise happy family. She continued to try to seek comfort in church, despite Father Phillip completely shutting her off.

She could find solace nowhere.

So on an unseasonably warm October day in 1950, after her daughter had run right past her, and not for the first time, for a snuggle with Anne, Maggie made a decision. She straightened some pillows on the living room couch and organized some papers on the coffee table, all the while humming to herself.

When she was content that the living room was in order, she took her cross off her neck and left in on the table she passed in the hall on her way to the basement. Still humming, she took another sad look at the family that was not her family and headed down the stairs into the cold, moldy abyss.

And still humming, Maggie removed a panel from the back wall and pulled out the revolver she had used to shoot Walter. That she had hidden away from that day, as if hiding it could make her forget. Could make any of them forget.

She then sat down on the cold basement floor, and, still humming, she placed the gun in her mouth and pulled the trigger.

chapter forty-eight

the present.

It was much too warm for October—especially considering that October was nearly over. This is what Annie Collins thought to herself as she made her way through the cemetery, trying to remember where she had parked her car. Comfortable for a change in a pair of jeans and a light sweater, she tried not to think of anything else but the weather. But the frustration wouldn't let go of her. It seemed it never could.

Why couldn't she just keep her big stupid mouth shut? Hugh didn't need to know any of that. Of course he'd fled. What sane person could hear that and stay?

"Crazy woman crossing," she joked to herself, out loud. "You can print that on a T-shirt."

"I might just do that," came a voice from behind her.

She froze. "What are you doing back here?"

"I had to get something," he said. He was holding a single yellow rose.

She was confused. She couldn't take her eyes off the rose. "I don't understand…"

"I really don't understand either. To be honest, you really scared me. I tried to leave, believe me. Was almost all the way out of here. But then I couldn't. I couldn't bring myself to leave you."

"Why...?"

"I don't know. There's just something about you."

"Something batshit."

"Maybe. But more than that. Something that just gets *me*, you know? I mean, I'm not that together myself. And maybe crazy just needs crazy?" He grabbed her hand. "Annie, I really haven't been able to stop thinking about you. Even when I was with Charlotte. You've always been there. In my brain. In my soul."

"But you *ran* from me. I told you everything. I told you that I made my husband make me miscarry my baby. I never told anyone everything like that. And you took off on me."

"I did, I know, and I'm sorry. That was a really dick move. I just needed some time. You have to believe me. I haven't been able to reconcile what really went wrong between us. I know I had crap and I always knew that you did too. I didn't know how much, but I always felt something with you. Something..."

"Dark? Sinister? Ugly?"

He smiled. "Never ugly. Look, I've missed you so much. When I came here today, I made a decision. A decision that if you, by some miracle, made it here today, that I would make you talk to me. That I would make you tell me what really happened. And that I would accept whatever you told me. That I would forgive you, no matter what."

"Oh, that's very generous," she said, hoping the sarcasm she felt wasn't lost in her tone.

"I know you have this issue with the whole Catholic thing, but isn't one of the main points there that you can do a lot of crazy bad shit and still be forgiven?"

"I don't see..."

"Look, I'm not going to lie and tell you what you did was right. But from what I understand, it was a horrible situation and a scary time. You caught me off guard because on some level, I always knew he'd abused you. This will sound weird, but I just sort of felt that about you, you know?"

She didn't understand how deeply he saw into her. "Sort of...?" What else could she say?

"Anyway... I thought that well, maybe you had something to do with his death. You know, self-defense."

"Uh, no. That was all Tabi. And not self-defense either. Not really. She ran him over with her car when she caught him cheating on her. Killed him, herself, and the other girl. Pretty grim. Surprised you didn't know about it. Made all the local papers. But I guess you were still in Michigan or something. I'm sorry you thought I killed him."

"I don't really know what to think. All I know is that whatever happened, and all that happened, it's in your past now. You need to leave it in your past. You can't change it. You can only move forward. You told me that."

She smiled. "And I guess you never put it on a T-shirt?"

"Neither did you," he said. "But look, all joking aside, you have to forgive yourself now and move forward. There's no other way." At that, he handed her the rose.

"For me?" she asked, her heart beating fast.

"For friendship, right?"

She looked down. He didn't want her. How could he possibly want her after what he now knew? "Oh... right..."

"For a start," he said, gently stroking her hair. "Let's see where it leads."

Her heart sank.

Friends. Just friends.

She was so frustrated now by her own stupid rules. At the wall that she had built around herself to guard herself from him. At the wall she had built around him to protect him from her. She could have just let things happen. If she could do it all again, she would let things happen naturally. Organically. Because now she felt it was never going to happen for them.

Except...

There was something about the way he looked at her when he said those words to her, "Let's see where it leads." Something that was pure and real and magical that made her feel, that made her *know*, that this was indeed going to lead to something great, as crazy as that seemed.

And when he stopped short as they got to the parking lot of the cemetery and he looked around. And when he cocked an eyebrow and got that goofy grin on his face. And when he grabbed her hand and pulled her close to him. And when he wrapped his arms around her and held her tight. And when he pushed away from her ever so slightly and cupped her face in his hands and swept his lips over hers...

Then, it was *then*, that she was sure.

Acknowledgments

There are many people to thank when a book is completed. For a book like this, though, born out of heartache, and, ultimately, if you can still strive for it, hope, it's difficult to quite know how to thank people... But pain is the mother of art. No pain, no art. So I'll just take a sweeping broad stroke from my earliest days through all the times my heart has been broken. Thank you to any of you who threw me into the pit because it was only by clawing out that I have earned the strength and grace that are the benchmarks of who I have become. And have given me so much great material. :-)

Thank you Peter Gabriel, Olivia Newton-John, and John Denver for the music that runs through this piece—and for graciously giving permission to lend your art to enhance mine.

Thank you, Tom Kaspercyzk, for helping create such a powerful cover. I freaking love it! A big thank you to Jackie Bouchard and Carolyn Dembeck, who helped find the last-minute typos. Thank you to Stacey Price for another fantastic formatting job for both the paperback and ebook editions.

An amazing and huge thank you goes to those who have read this story over the years in its many incarnations, encouraging me to make the most of the "mess," especially Shawna Mullen, Greg Goldstein, Diana Gliedman, and Stephanie Garcia. And Pete, especially, thanks for your story insights, input on the cover art and copy, and incomparable fashion sense.

Thank you to those who have infused my life with the incredible moments that inspired so much of the magic in these characters. Notably, Carl Arnheiter. I have never forgotten the time spent at Calvary or Knowles, or how geese could be herded. Thank you for that. Christine Mayer, although our lives have taken us on separate journeys, I will never forget how your small frame once managed to carry an air-conditioner larger than you down all those stairs and into the car decades ago. Your incomparable strength is always with me.

A special thank you goes to my Beach Babes: Eileen Goudge, Meredith Schorr, Josie Brown, and especially to Julie Valerie and Jen Tucker. Julie, your comments led to the development of a crucial plot layer, and Jen, your jokes are like a twelve-year-old boy's—which is why we get each other. (You also gave good notes.) You guys feed my writer's soul and keep me well-nourished. I cherish all of you. Your input, friendship, and unwavering support.

And lest you think I forgot about Samantha Stroh Bailey... No, never. You are my editing partner. My best friend. My sister. Not only do you make my words make sense, you make my *world* make sense. I'd be lost without you. I think you read this story more than anyone. Thank you for all your amazing suggestions.

Much love and gratitude goes to my family, most especially to my auntie, RoseMarie McHugh. I hope you know and understand how much of that familial love and gratitude belongs to you.

A special thank you goes to you, Christopher, for putting up with me for so long, and for hearing about this story for all of these years. I know you don't always believe that I love you, but I truly do. You are, and will always be, my family.

Finally, a big, mushy thank you to Madeleine and Juliana, my two greatest gifts. Each of you inspires me daily, and if it hadn't been for both of you, I may not have ever finished this project. Mad, it was you who insisted I give myself a publishing date, which lit a fire underneath me. And Jules, I promise I will try to get back into bookstores so you can attend a signing of mine some day. May you both never lose sight of your center and may you always feel your power. You are both beautiful beyond words, inside and out. (And you, too, Elsa.)

I'm truly amazed that a book that has taken me fifteen years to complete is finally done. I couldn't be more grateful that this story is now in your hands, dear reader. Thank you for taking a chance on it and thank you, again, for taking a chance on me.